I0831167

THE STARLIT SUN

ERIN HALLI

The Starlit Sun

By Erin Halli

Erin Halli
Publishing

For permission requests, contact author.erinhalli@gmail.com.

Book Cover Design by Lara Klein @ 2025 (@laraaklein)

Character Art by Michela Fiori (@michi_illustrations)

Proof Read by Noemie Mayer

First Edition Published December 2025

Published by Erin Halli Publishing

Hardcover: 979-8-9937964-4-4

Paperback: 979-8-9937964-3-7

E-Book (ASIN): B0FW5LZJK6

Content Warning

Please read with care. While not core themes, this book includes sensitive subject matter as follows: Loss of a loved one, depression, anxiety, a slightly graphic death, explicit sex scenes, trauma-related guilt, drinking, strong language, and grief. The various types of angels and realms in this story are fictional and aren't intended to represent or reflect any real-world religion.

To soulful readers who struggle with goodbyes and long for their most cherished loved ones to live forever.

How We Got Here

How about a quick refresher on what happened in *The Masked Flower* before you embark on Kai's journey? Feel free to skip this if you have recently read it or intend to read it one day.

In *The Masked Flower*, an events director named Iris loses her brother, Kai, in a horrific accident. Because of the depth of their bond, this loss profoundly impacts her.

In a strange turn of events, rather than leaving her side forever, he transitions into her guardian angel unbeknownst to her. His mission is to help her embrace her grief and move on which is no small task, given how she can't see him. When Jasper, a broody antique shop owner, stumbles across Iris and spots Kai without realizing that he's her Guardian Angel and *deceased* brother, things take another unexpected turn.

Then, in an effort to save Jasper's shop, Aged Emporium, Iris offers to host a fundraiser ball, promising to donate all proceeds to his shop. As they grow closer, Kai becomes increasingly invested in their relationship, meddling in more ways than one.

Eventually, Kai ventures to the angelic Middle Realm's library to gain clarity on *why* Jasper has the ability to see him, bumping into Cleo during his visit. At the end of *The Masked Flower*, Kai knows Iris is in good hands, so he says his goodbyes in a surprising way which leads to the events of *The Starlit Sun*.

Prologue

When the girl begged him to unveil himself, he saw it in her olive eyes. For the first time in quite some time, a trace of it lingered in her unflinching gaze.

He'd waited a long while to see it again.

He often wondered if it would ever return.

Against all odds, it did.

"Can I please see you one more time? Just once? *Please?*"

At that moment, he knew—he'd do whatever she asked. He never could say no to her. Instead of revealing himself instantaneously, he had to concentrate though. This would be his first time breaking a divine law of this magnitude. He didn't know where to begin.

"The truth is, seeing me won't make the pain go away, Irie," he said lightly as a gentle breeze engulfed them—he had to tell her that. For all his jokes and schemes, Kai Greene could never truly lie to his sister.

He needed her to understand this wouldn't fix everything.

But it would help. He knew it would.

As her eyelids fluttered shut, he blinked and focused harder. Although one living being had been able to see him up until this point, he hadn't ever actually crossed the veil to *reveal* himself to someone. He wasn't even sure how to do this, but for her, he'd try.

Following his instincts, he kept his eyes shut, drawing from his aura within. He reached deeper and deeper inside himself to tap into a well of untouched divine energy gifted from the Golden Realm's divine rulers. Once he discovered it, he grabbed hold of it fiercely within his own mind, channeling it through himself to collide with the thin veil blocking him from her gaze. He hadn't ever used such strong divine energy. Most angels who haven't ascended don't know where to access this energy, but as if it were predestined, he somehow found the threads of this magic.

Divine law or not, he had to cross the veil.

Focus, focus, focus, he repeated inwardly as he pushed through the veil, holding on to his sister even tighter. During Guardian training, mentors specifically avoided teaching pupils how to cross the veil to prevent this act of rebellion.

Fortunately, Kai had never been a fan of rules.

Using all his inner energy, he continued to push his way through, hoping—*pleading*—this would work. If this worked, he knew without any trace of doubt that she would get the final piece of closure she desperately yearned for. Sure, maybe that piece wasn't a necessity, but it would make her happy. That was enough for him.

Suddenly, his world seemingly cracked, and he crashed his way through the invisible barrier. He felt her, and not in the way he usually felt her when funneling his healing aura into her. He felt her soft breath on his chest, the warm wetness of her tears seeping into his shirt, her head resting directly under his chin. She thought his form felt more defined, but she assumed it was a figment of her imagination.

With her eyes closed, she sobbed into his chest while he rejoiced.

It *worked.*

Kai crossed the veil. It shouldn't have worked without proper training, but it did.

"I know it's cliché as hell, but it's not goodbye," Kai whispered into her hair. "As much as it kills me to say it, you're in good hands—I know *Truman* will keep you very safe."

She opened her eyes, and to her utter shock, hazel eyes peered back into her own. Her jaw dropped in disbelief, but he simply grinned in the way he always did.

"I want you to promise me to live every minute," he said in reverence as he gazed into his sister's eyes.

Then, he pulled away, fading into the sky where he'd always belonged.

You may wonder, *What did he see in her gaze that caused him to compromise the integrity of his mission?*

It was *hope*. Pure, undiluted hope.

In one moment, three monumental acts simultaneously occurred, tangoing together in a dangerous dance that altered the threads of his fate as we knew it.

First, Iris Greene saw her Guardian Angel in the flesh.

Second, Kai Greene broke the afterlife's most divine law.

And finally, *she* watched it happen.

One

Kai

Saying goodbye is hard for her. I knew it would be. However, I couldn't have predicted how downright impossible it'd be for me to let go of them.

For a single moment, everything feels perfect. Holding Iris and her boyfriend in my arms feels *right*. As much as I want to sit in this moment forever, my stomach is twisting, and a sense of dizziness is taking over. The Middle Realm has hooked me—roughly, I might add—and is reeling me back in, similar to the way a parent might yank their child's arm after they've gone astray.

Now that I've tasted the life I once had, I don't want to kiss this world goodbye. In fact, if I could, I'd press my lips against its edges and kiss it for the rest of time.

...I may have taken that a bit far, but you get the point.

I let out a long, somewhat obnoxious sigh in defeat, knowing it's best to give in to the forceful tug. This is actually my first time feeling the tugging sensation. Considering angels don't ever cross the veil to reveal themselves to humans, I imagine my afterlife body isn't built to sustain this realm anymore. I try to fight the tug a bit longer, but I don't want to piss off the Archangels even more than I probably already have, so I give up.

Choking back tears, I say goodbye and close my eyes, traveling through space and time to end up back where this chapter of my afterlife started.

The Middle Realm.

Once I land on my own two feet, the tugging sensation ends. When angels travel between realms, they depart and arrive at the start of a glistening selenite bridge that leads upward to this realm's headquarters. It's an opulent palace of sorts and exactly what you'd imagine an angelic castle to look like, but, dare I say, it's even more pristine.

While the rest of this realm is built on the land, the realm's headquarters float high above the land on a layer of fluffy clouds at the end of the selenite bridge.

The Middle Realm's air is crisp and soothing like the gentle patter of rain on a cloudy day. Thankfully, we still experience day and night here. It's cool—we can see more colors in the sky as angels than we did as mortals.

A majority of the angels here a spend their days at the headquarters, fulfilling their assigned roles while opting to spend evenings in their homes, usually located just outside the main palace in the living quarters. Some angels choose to live in simple homes, others choose apartments, and the lucky ones who have high statuses or have stayed here a long time live in mansions of their own. We call our homes 'havens.'

Despite all the buildings in this realm being located outside the headquarters, a thick barrier of glass separates this realm from the Golden Realm. The glass serves as a veil, revealing the colors and clouds of the world beyond while concealing the finer details.

Visiting that realm is impossible until ascension, but you can still see it vaguely from down here. In fact, there's a chamber located at the top of one of the many staircases in the headquarters encased by a miniature dome of glass, magnifying the Golden Realm's sky. The Golden Realm is vast in comparison to the Middle Realm—it has to be less stuffy.

I was tempted to ascend right after my death, but I knew my sister needed me more than I needed that extra level of peace.

Now that I've experienced a taste of Earth in the afterlife, I'm not as inclined to rush my ascension anymore. If I'm still even worthy to ascend, that is.

Once an angel accomplishes their assignment in grace—whether that be guarding, watching, or serving—they're rewarded with a set of shiny new wings and permitted to ascend to the Golden Realm. It's rad because angel wings aren't all the same color. We don't even get to choose the color.

Most angels immediately ascend after they complete their mission, but some do opt to stay in the Middle Realm until they feel truly ready to ascend. Angels that remain in the Middle Realm work as Guardians, Watchers, Hunters, Officers, and Educators.

Different positions have different responsibilities. Honestly, I don't know much about the other positions, because my sole focus over the past couple of years has been guardianship. My mentor, Matt, only taught me and the other pupils what we needed to know.

I learned how to use the divine abilities given to all Guardians, such as soulsight, teleportation, and healing.

I gathered the basics of divine gifts in the Middle Realm by practicing with my cohorts. It took some time to get used to the new light energy within me, but after some time, teleportation and healing felt as easy as breathing.

Soulsight, on the other hand, has been a different story. Essentially, soulsight is similar to mind reading, but not as clear—it's like an off-brand, generic version of mind reading. To use the gift, Guardians simply have to gaze into the eyes of others and choose to tap into the power. Then, they will see various images and sometimes words highlighting the soul they're assessing.

Instead of receiving clear thoughts when looking into minds, though, I often see an assortment of juicy images I usually have no idea how to decipher. Sometimes, I understand the pictures I see. Other times, I see odd items—like lemons, for example. *Lemons*. I mean, how could lemons possibly make that much of an impact on someone's life?

I've gotten more used to exercising soulsight over time, but it's never been quite as easy for me as it is for other Guardians to use. Call me crazy, but I don't know if I like intruding on people's minds—it's almost like showing up in sweats to a pool party you weren't invited to.

The easiest gift, and most dynamic, has been teleportation. I *love* that gift. I can't help but crack a smile just thinking about all the places I've teleported to over the past few years. It's what young Kai always dreamed it would be.

To teleport, you simply set your mind on a designated place, whether it be in the land of the living or the Middle Realm, close your eyes, and bam. You're there. It takes zero muscle or brain power, and it only takes a little divine energy. It's the best. Period. And unlike mortal air travel, other angels can't track exactly where you teleported to.

The only limitation for Guardians is that they can't travel too far away from their assignment. So, I had to stay near my sister throughout my mission. Considering I love Chrysocolla Cove as much as she does, it wasn't half bad. Now that my mission is over, I could potentially travel wherever I'd like to go... in theory.

Healing was fairly simple to learn, too. During my mortal life, I watched tons of movies about characters who had healing abilities. Interestingly, the primary focus of healing in those films was healing physical ailments and injuries. However, here in the afterlife, we're gifted healing powers to heal less noticeable wounds—the emotional ones. The wounds other living beings don't often see.

Matt assured us that this particular act would take up a majority of our time in the Guardian field, and man, was he right. I did it hundreds of times for my sister after the accident—my death.

You gathered that, right? The fact that I'm dead and have returned to the realm for others like me who have transitioned into angels?

Of course you caught on. Smart cookie.

Anyway, after my death, she needed all the warmth she could get.

Ah, Iris, also and better known as Irie. My little sister.

My early departure from life over two years ago nearly broke her. And although her grief fought hard to consume every fragment of her being, she fought even harder. Every step she's taken since my death has been a battle, and hell, she's fought beautifully.

Looking at her in the eyes today filled a hole in my heart I didn't even realize existed. I needed that moment as much as she did.

Revealing myself to her was my choice. Was it the right one, objectively speaking? Maybe not.

But did it feel right? Absolutely.

I take a deep breath—probably the deepest breath I've ever taken—and walk across the bridge to the golden front entrance of the headquarters. Noticing the pale yellow clouds floating on either side of the path, I pass through the gate and ascend a marble staircase that leads to the bridge ahead. The clouds give off an illusion of privacy along the route—I can't see beyond them on either side, but I'm well aware that if I step off the path, I won't land on solid ground.

Once I reach the double-doored entrance, I gulp another breath of air and stride through the opulent, tall doors with my head held high, walking through the grand hall to the main foyer.

The foyer, located centrally in the headquarters, is surrounded by several grand birchwood staircases, leading to training rooms, classrooms, the library, and more on upper levels. While staying here, I spent most of my time in the training rooms, classrooms, and my quaint living haven back across the bridge in the living quarters.

I'd rather be caught dead—*the irony*—than spend time at the library willingly.

No offense. You do your thing.

A sea of winged angels flows through the palace around me as I reach the center staircase leading to the throne room, a few floors up. Just as I'm about to take my first step onto the stairs, I'm pulled sharply from behind. I grimace. *What now?*

You know, Matt always liked yanking me around during my training sessions with him. Maybe he's here to watch my ascension. Well, he'll be sorely disappointed when he learns what I've done.

I spin around with a smirk plastered on my face, glancing up to greet my mentor, only to see... no one. I mean, no one near me, that is. I see a lot of angels, both winged and not, passing through, but my perpetrator is nowhere in sight. It's as if they evaporated into thin air. I lift my eyes to the upper floors surrounding me in case Matt took flight and I somehow missed him when, in an instant, someone yanks me *again*, and okay, yeah, I have to say, this is getting old. This time, they pull me downward by the collar of my shirt.

Oh. That's why I missed her. I expected to see Matt, who's roughly the same height as I am, but instead, my assailant is at least a foot shorter than I am.

She whispers sternly, "Follow me."

The first thing I notice is her deep navy blue wings tucked tightly against her back, detailed with a handful of black and silver feathers.

Deciding it's best not to question her, I follow her down a wide hallway to the left of the foyer I haven't ventured in before.

Shortly after my kidnapping, we reach a tiny room at the end of the hall. Upon entering, she doesn't bother to turn on the lights, and then hastily locks the door behind her and walks past me, keeping her back toward me. She's breathing hard.

Logically speaking, a woman just locked me inside a dark room.

I should be unnerved. But I'm not.

"It's good seeing you again." I toss her a crooked smile in the dark, hoping she can still see my expression. "Mind telling me why we're here? Should I be whispering right now?"

She scoffs, and although I can barely see her, I know she's shaking her head.

Oh, she's *not* happy with me.

"You're going to be the death of me," she mutters, stepping farther away into the dark, nearing a small desk.

I take a step toward her. She doesn't step away—I like that. I like that she isn't backing away.

"I hate to be *that* guy, but you're already technically dead, so..." She lets out an exasperated groan. "I mean, we both are. The only difference is one of us has flashy wings and the other was about to get a wicked set of his own before he was so *rudely* interrupted."

She whips around and stalks close to me, our faces mere inches away from each other now. "Would you please be serious for once in your damn afterlife?" she hisses. "Do you have any idea what you've done?"

Oh, now *this* is interesting. She knows.

She pins me with a look of concern.

I might be reading the situation wrong, but she looks... restless. Damn, I'm more screwed than I thought, aren't I?

"I know exactly what I did," I breathe, keeping my cool. "The real question is, how do *you* know?"

Two

Cleo

Idiot. He's a hopelessly optimistic idiot. And it's going to get him locked away. Or worse.

This isn't our first encounter. Recently, he needed help accessing the library—more specifically, the archives chamber within the library—and I assisted him. We exchanged small talk, I shared my name, and that was that. The moment hasn't crossed my mind since.

Yes, I've been watching him, but he doesn't know that.

Ugh. I know what it sounds like, but there's more to it than meets the eye.

"So, you're an Archangel, huh? Thought so. You give off the vibe." He stares straight ahead, nodding. "It makes sense. I wondered how you already knew my name the other day when I visited the library. Do Archangels know the names of all angels?"

My lips press together so tight they burn.

"I'm not an Archangel, Kai." My eyes bore into his. "I'm a Watcher."

His eyes widen as he peers back into mine. "Whoa... I don't think I've met any Watchers yet. In fact, Matt specifically told us we didn't need to learn about Watchers, so he taught us the bare minimum... You watch the Guardians, don't you? How does that work?"

"We don't have the time for a full lesson on how watching works—"

"I'd beg to differ," he cuts me off and crosses his arms. I can't stand being interrupted, but I let it slide. "We have all the time in the world. Honestly, I really want to hear about what your nine-to-five looks like."

He spots the small sofa just behind me and lazily walks toward it, patting it down.

"What are you doing?" I turn toward him and narrow my eyes.

"Obviously making myself comfortable. You should try it—you seem tense." He plops down, leaning back in the seat, then runs his hands through his hair nonchalantly. My lips part in temporary shock at his lack of regard, then I straighten, folding my arms tightly while continuing to lean against the desk.

"Fine. Yes, Watchers watch Guardians, but we're not always *watching* you all—that would be a major invasion of privacy, and quite frankly, I have much better things to do than watch angels do frivolous things." I've definitely seen some things I didn't want to see while doing my job before. I let out a sigh. "I digress. Watchers are retired Guardians who choose to stay in this realm—Eloras, in case you needed a reminder—rather than ascend to the golden lands above. We're tethered to our Guardians, similar to the way Guardians are tethered to their assignment, except we feel a physical thread inwardly connecting us to our assignments. Most Watchers are assigned to dozens of angels at any given time.

"When our assignment is close to breaking a divine law, we feel a tugging sensation, and then we draw from our magic within to pinpoint which angel is the culprit. Once we identify the angel, we can tug on our connected thread to reel them back in. If desired, we can instantly teleport to their side to prevent them from wreaking havoc further."

He furrows his brows and then nods slowly. "So, I was being watched this entire time?"

"No. You weren't watched the entire time. As I just stated, we only monitor angels for rule breaking, really," I say plainly.

"How long have you been watching me?" he asks with a tone of suspicion in his voice.

"I was assigned to you a couple of months ago," I answer honestly. I've got nothing left to lose at this point.

If he's a sinking ship, I'm the anchor pulling him under even deeper.

"So, this means you knew that Jasper had the ability to see me when I ran into you recently?"

I nod.

"Did you know *why* he could see me this entire time?" His jaw tenses, his patience wearing thin.

"I had my guesses."

"And you didn't care to fill me in on those guesses when I visited the library, *desperately* seeking answers?" he accuses.

Ah, he's growing irritated. *Good.* Maybe he's finally comprehending the gravity of this situation.

"Why would I?" I gasp in surprise, then smile coyly. "You appeared to have it all under control."

"Well, I did have it under control, but the outside counsel would've been real nice." He schools his features, no longer carelessly slouching. No, his knee is shaking rhythmically, and he's rubbing his thigh, seeming uneasy now. "I crossed the veil and revealed myself to my sister. I also kept Jasper's ability to see me a secret."

"Yes."

"I'm doomed, aren't I?"

"Yes. Unequivocally doomed, Kai Greene." He nods, then shuts his eyes tightly. *Finally.* He gets it. "Do you need a refresher on the five Guardian laws?"

"Why would you ask that?"

I lean in close to him. "Rule number one: do not harm your living being. Rule number two: do not alter fate—"

"C'mon, I know—"

"Rule number three: remain focused on your guarded's journey throughout your mission. Rule number four: stay in proximity to your assignee. Rule number five—"

"You've made your point. I get it. I broke some rules, like the most sacred rule. I *know*—"

I lift his chin and whisper, "Do not cross the veil to reveal yourself."

"Wow, okay. You are one for drama, aren't you?" He holds my gaze, unyielding. "For the one hundredth time, I know I screwed up. If the only reason you dragged me into this room—against my will, I might add—was to drill shame into me even further, congrats. You did it." He stands up, brushing his shoulder against me as he walks toward the door. "But guess what? I'd do it again in a heartbeat for her."

He turns his back on me and reaches for the knob.

"Kai, wait—" And only for a split second, my voice breaks against my will. I clear my throat. "Don't tell them."

He pauses, resting his hand on the doorknob. "Why shouldn't I? My destiny seems to be set in stone. What difference does it make?"

"Do you truly not care if they imprison or banish you from the realm? Do you not care to get your wings?"

"It's not that I don't care. I just care more about staying true to who I am. I've had to hide a lot of information recently, and it's getting old. I'm ready to set the truth free."

Does he truly have no regard for the consequences of his actions? I've been in this realm for decades, and during all that time, I have never come across an angel who broke this particular rule.

Not only will he be punished—I will be, too. I should've stopped him. As soon as I felt the thread tugging, I could've teleported to his side and forced him to submit. I also probably should've alerted the Archangels that Jasper could see him.

But for reasons I can't logically explain, I didn't.

Now we're both doomed.

This might have been romantic in another story.

"I'm not afraid." He turns around nonchalantly to face me, but upon glancing at me, he cocks an eyebrow. "Are you?"

I press my lips into a firm line. "Fine. If you won't withhold the truth for yourself, consider doing it for me. You're not the only one your heinous action affects. I'll be punished, too."

As if a layer of fog has lifted from his gaze, realization crosses his features. "I see. You could've stopped me from crossing the veil to reveal myself, but you didn't. I broke the most sacred law under your authority."

I nod, tucking a strand of black hair that fell into my face behind my ear and fidgeting with my light blue blouse to do something with my hands.

It's ridiculous. During all my years of watching, I intervened in the simplest of rule breaks. Once I scolded a Guardian who teleported to Singapore for a quick getaway while his assignee slept one night. I've stepped in when Guardians pull small ghostly pranks on the living.

But I didn't step in when Kai broke the biggest damn rule in the book.

"Just trust me. We'll be fine." He tosses me a reassuring grin as his hazel eyes soften. My cheeks grow warm under his gaze.

Basking in his warmth for even a millisecond feels dangerous. He may appear harmless to the world, but I know danger when I see it, and he has danger written all over him. Knowing my fate rests in his hands brings me no comfort.

"Your judgment will take place this evening just after the sun sets. There's no need to head to the throne room until then; they won't let you in until it's your turn. Believe it or not, it's actually customary for Watchers to greet their Guardians like this upon their mission completion."

"You're telling me that yanking me into a dark closet with zero context is *customary*? Angels are so unhinged, holy hell." He pushes his hand through his waves and fixes his gaze on our surroundings again.

I suppress a smile at that and flick on the lamp.

"Ah, well, this *closet* is actually my office. It's not much, but I'm quite fond of it." I gaze around at the small room, taking account of my white desk, cream-colored sofa, lamps, and bookshelf. Tonight, he may very well ruin everything I've worked for in one single meeting with the Archangels.

"Why do you have bedding in your office?" His voice disrupts my thoughts as he quirks his head toward the pillow and folded woven blanket resting beneath the sofa.

"And why is that any of your business?" I raise a brow, to which he groans. I don't hide my smile this time. He notices.

"Whatever. Okay. Well, thanks for the rundown. You were very... *efficient*," he says. "I guess I'll see you at my judgment tonight?"

"That, you will. Enjoy your last couple of hours of freedom," I mumble, reaching down to grasp the knob and turning it slowly. "If you choose not to tell, just know—your secret is safe with me."

"And *your* secret is safe with me." He wiggles his eyebrows, stepping into the hallway and heading back toward the foyer.

We are indeed undoubtedly doomed.

THREE

CLEO

I turn and stroll back to the soft cream-toned sofa—more of a love seat, really, but it's deep—sinking into it and slouching to rest my elbows on my knees, cradling my jaw in my palms. I part my lips, close my eyes, and focus on breathing.

Is it warm in here? I lift my eyes to the temperature reader resting on the wall opposite of me. The temperature is perfectly ordinary, which is odd considering everything inside me is screaming that nothing is *actually* ordinary at the moment. Now, I wouldn't go as far as to describe my present situation as extraordinary, because that would imply that all is well—better than well, even—when in fact, all is undeniably *not* well.

I'll admit, it's been some time since I felt this level of stress in the afterlife. Eloras is a paradise of sorts, abundant in pastel clouds with platinum beams of starlight throughout, complete with a sheer layer of refreshing angel mist.

Many of the angels who live here have bright countenances and even brighter smiles, which I'd credit to our leaders. The Archangels in charge have made this realm a home for countless angels over the last several thousand years. The angels who reside here have completed their mortal lives, most of which served guardianships of their own at one point.

I unexpectedly awoke in Eloras after meeting an early end to my life nearly half a century ago, when I was only twenty-three years old. Choosing between ascending immediately or serving a guardianship was simple. I chose the latter.

A majority of Guardians who serve guardianship missions immediately opt to ascend after completion. I didn't. That choice was also relatively simple for me, but that's not relevant.

Four lead Archangels—Luke, Annalise, Nial, and Jessenia—serve as judges of sorts over the hundreds who reside in this realm. The Seraphim who rule the Golden Realm chose each of them. Three of the four Archangels have been here since the beginning, sent directly from Aurathine, otherwise coined as the Golden Realm. In contrast, the final Archangel, Jessenia, is a newer recruit who's only been in Eloras for a few centuries. She's still learning, so she shadows the elders in their judgments and counsels, then occasionally greets new angels who awake after death alongside other stationed greeters.

The Archangels were gifted their light magic from the Golden Realm's wells of divine light energy. All angels in Eloras are given divine energy, but unlike the Archangels, we aren't given the power to access all our sacred energy. This is why Kai crossing the veil shocked me—he had to dig extremely deep within himself to conjure enough light energy to cross the veil.

The Archangels hold additional gifts that lower-tiered angels, like Kai and me, do not. They were granted the ability to warp time as we know it, create illusions, alter memories, and more. We aren't given the privilege to know all the gifts Archangels hold in this realm, as we cannot exercise such divine light power ourselves anyway. I've always been rather curious about the unknown gifts myself.

Although, I am thankful to hold the gifts I have. For instance, angels in this realm are given the power to heal. To cultivate the gift of healing, we practice healing one another in training. Healing can drain angels, but as long as it's done in moderation, it isn't harmful. It's essential to choose when it's necessary to exercise this gift wisely. Drawing that energy from within and transferring it to someone else is soothing, but receiving it is even better.

Typically, Guardians' judgments go well. Only souls with good intent get offered the chance to be Guardian Angels—adults who made thousands of objectively good decisions throughout their mortal lives. Consequently, they tend to behave exceptionally well while watching over their assignment. Sure, occasionally, some Guardians break minor rules, but rarely do Watchers have to intervene and prevent Guardians from committing severe crimes against divine law.

Guardianship timelines also vary. Some serve a guardianship for years, whereas others only serve for a handful of months—it all depends on the state of mind of the assigned living being. Kai served as his sister's Guardian Angel for about two years, give or take. He seemed to enjoy the mission. When watching him in his final moments in the land of the living with his sister and her boyfriend, the genuine smile that stretched across his face was nearly contagious.

During those last few seconds, it failed to meet his eyes, though. I doubt he even realized it. I found it odd that his smile didn't reach his eyes.

In contrast, my Guardian experience was quite different. I served a stranger—Meredith—for about a year. She struggled heavily with PTSD after serving as a nurse in the military and witnessing ungodly things unfold right before her eyes. A petite woman with a bold presence, she and I were close to the same age at the time. She may have only served in the war for a handful of months, but its terrors crept their way into her and altered how she processed fear. She struggled like this for over four years before I joined her side.

She frequently took cover when doors slammed too loudly, intensely observed her surroundings with the keen eyes of a hawk, and wept into the late hours of the night all while living alone. Unlike Kai's assignee, Meredith never found a partner to lean on.

During our time together, I funneled all the healing light I could muster straight into her. We got into a comfortable routine. I've never been much of a hugger, but on tough days, I'd wrap my arms around her and transmit my divine healing aura. After only a couple of minutes of transmitting that light into her, she'd finally exhale, allowing her shoulders to slump and her chest to stop heaving. Sometimes, people just need a minute to decompress.

Eventually, she grew strong enough to soothe herself without my aid. At the beginning of my guardianship, she was alone, and by the end, she remained alone. Oh, but how she had *grown.*

I found the conclusion to her healing journey inspiring. Rather than relying on other living beings to aid her in her endeavor for peace, she had to depend entirely on herself.

Upon my guardianship's completion, I teleported back to Eloras and met a Watcher who greeted me at the bridge to the headquarters. She briefed me on what to expect during the judgment. I found her role fascinating, though our interaction was far less climactic than the encounter I just shared with Kai in my office.

The Watcher's job looked like my cup of tea. I'd been seeking a solid reason to stay, so the timing worked out well.

During my judgment, I asked for a chance to stay in Eloras as a Watcher.

"Why would you choose to stay here when you're eligible for immediate ascension to the Golden Realm beyond?" Luke's piercing electric blue gaze bore into mine from his throne's starlit golden dais; the golden glow in his gaze hinted that he was attempting to exercise soulsight, but my mental shields remained steadfast.

Most Guardians focus heavily on learning how to use soulsight during their Guardian training. I, however, primarily focused on mastering the ability to keep colleagues out of my mind during practice. I had no desire to share scraps of my mind, nor do I now.

To block others from seeing into your mind, you focus on the energy waves the angel is exuding to enter your mind and ward them off using your waves of divine energy. This act creates a shield to block the waves from invading your mind. It takes a strenuous amount of self-discipline to keep shields in place, but it's worth it.

"Why shouldn't I?" I retorted, keeping my chin held high. Apparently, not many Guardians chose to become Watchers at the time. "I'd get to spend more time with my friends here."

"What friends?" Jessenia chimed in from Luke's left side in a starlit seat of her own, tilting her head and blinking her silver eyes innocently. Had it been anyone else who said that, I'd have been offended. But Jessenia is the purest. She genuinely had no idea what friends I was referring to. To her point, I didn't, either.

"Oh, Jessenia, how we cherish your pure heart." Annalise stifled a chuckle, sitting to Luke's right who suppressed a grin of his own. Nial maintained a smug look, crossing his arms, sitting in the golden throne next to Annalise. "In all sincerity, we find it peculiar you'd choose to stay. If you ascend, you'll almost immediately get to reunite with your—"

My head pounded as she neared the end of that sentence, and I spoke without thinking, interrupting Annalise, the graceful one. "I want to continue helping angels in Eloras. I love helping people. I believe my sole purpose is to help others."

I rested my hand over my heart for dramatic effect. At first, Annalise appeared caught off guard by my interruption, parting her lips and widening her ebony eyes. Jessenia smiled curtly in response as a look of confusion crossed Luke's face.

Then I heard a deep rumbling laugh from their right. I whipped my head toward the sound, seeing Nial clap his hands in amusement. I narrowed my eyes at him, not missing how unruly his black hair was. He appeared as though he had just rolled out of bed.

Wow, I knew I wasn't known for being friendly, but I was quite perturbed by their response.

"Could've fooled me, Miss Graves," Nial drawled as his amber eyes peered into mine, a spark of curiosity caught in his gaze. "But considering we're always looking for more Watchers, I don't see the problem here."

He glanced at his cohorts, and they all locked eyes. Jessenia raised her eyebrows in surprise, Luke pushed his hand through his golden waves, and Annalise pressed her lips into a firm line. Mind speaking among a group—how intriguing.

Kai got a lot of mind-speaking practice with his sister's partner due to the bond. In fact, the first time his thread ever tugged me had to do with his interaction with Jasper in the forest.

Unfortunately, I didn't get that luxury. During my guardianship, I mind spoke with a few stray animals, but I never got the chance to mind speak with living beings like Kai did. That's when Kai's journey of rule breaking began to unravel.

Shortly after the Archangels' internal discussion, they permitted me to stay as a Watcher indefinitely. Thankfully.

It took me several weeks to learn the ropes of watching, but my watching mentor, Stephen, taught me everything I needed to know.

I learned how to unlock a different component of divine energy—thread bonding. I found this aspect to be relatively intuitive. Essentially, to connect with Guardians, Watchers reach inwardly to pull out a thread of divine energy to connect with each of their assigned souls. It's a bit trippy at first, but after years of practice, I've grown to enjoy fabricating these types of bonds with my Guardians.

I've been assigned hundreds of Guardians over the past few decades. Anytime they get remotely close to breaking a larger divine law, I feel a tug on the thread and frequently teleport to their side to intervene. Seeing as there aren't many afterlife laws, we take offenses quite seriously. Our Guardians also have a 99 percent success rate at healing their assignment.

That said, I have witnessed a handful of angels who guarded their assignee for years without success. Even in instances in which the living beings didn't fully heal, the Archangels still classified the guardianships as successful due to the care the Guardians put into their missions. Most of those angels immediately ascended. Many angels who stay in the Middle Realm after their mission visit the land below from time to time. I haven't visited the land of the living for leisure since completing my guardianship.

Settling back into my sofa, I curl up, loosely draping a light blanket around my shoulders. I glance at the wooden bookshelf next to me, shelves overflowing with fictional books consisting of fantasy, classic romance, and royal politics. I consider reaching out my hand and grabbing a book to escape in for just a little while, but I know better.

Not even my favorite romance novel could push aside my current state of dread.

Instead, I practice a grounding exercise, closing my eyes and running my fingers along the seat's plush surface, focusing on the way it feels. I run my fingers in circles over it, counting down from one hundred, taking note of my office's current scent—rain. I've always enjoyed rainy weather. Here in Eloras, we're gifted shimmery angel mist every morning, but it's been a long time since I felt the sensation of rain on a cloudy day…

Kai's predicament—*our* predicament—is unprecedented in every possible way. What a mess we've made.

Four

Kai

Getting into trouble makes some people queasy. My sister is one of those people. Anytime she screws up, her stomach ties into knots, and she stumbles over her usually well-composed sentences. She tries to cover up her tracks, but she's a pitiful liar. Always has been. You know the kind—the ones who lie with rosy cheeks and smiling eyes. Growing up, she tried to hide stuff from me, but it never worked. One look at those cheeks, and I'd know. Eventually, she gave up on keeping secrets from me.

That's one of the many ways in which we're different.

I've never had as much trouble keeping secrets as she has.

Getting into trouble didn't scare me during my mortal life, either. I remember breaking all kinds of rules throughout my adolescence just for the hell of it.

Even breaking the law during my mortal life didn't faze me.

About a decade ago, I was twenty, home for the summer after my second year of college, feeling untouchable. Katherine—my girlfriend at the time—was out of town all summer, and I missed her. So, one night, my buddies and I stayed up late, partying our asses off. I just wanted to get my mind off everything.

After one too many shots of Fireball—I know Fireball is disgusting, but consuming it is a rite of passage, an adult ritual if you will—a daring side of myself unleashed itself. Yes, even more daring than my usual self if you can believe it.

It's not that serious, and quite frankly, I don't even know why stealing a street sign is illegal, but it is. Lots of teenagers do it.

However, stealing a street sign naked is *even more* illegal.

Going into it, I knew stealing the sign was illegal, but my naive, drunk self had no self-preservation instincts. I didn't realize that doing so naked would end up being twice as illegal. If only I had a Guardian Angel guiding me that night, maybe I wouldn't have been such a dumbass...

But Kai, that's what parents are for. Yeah, I know. However, my parents didn't care what I did with my spare time as long as I maintained straight A's and stayed on the varsity baseball team. An entirely different experience than a lot of people, I'm aware.

Sometimes, people forget that just because your parents let you do whatever doesn't always make them good parents.

Cool parents from the outside looking in? Sure. But good parents? Debatable.

I digress. I'm sure you can guess what happened next anyway.

As I ran butt-ass naked back to my boy's truck, I tripped while holding the sign and tumbled to the ground. Everyone got a good laugh out of that, myself included, until beaming red-and-blue lights entered my peripheral vision. I tried to get up, but being as inebriated as I was, I stumbled and plummeted again, laughing my ass off.

As the world spun around me, lying naked on the road under the night sky didn't matter. Katherine traveling for the summer without me didn't matter. My parents not caring didn't matter. As I gazed up at the stars—unsure of whether the stars were there or figments of my imagination—nothing mattered at all.

That night, the police shoved me into the back of a cop car in nothing but a pair of handcuffs and a towel. Within a matter of seconds, they stole my dignity *and* street sign. I had nothing.

Yet, I *still* wasn't afraid of getting in trouble. It's like I always knew that whatever trouble I'd get into during my mortal life wouldn't matter in the long run.

They fined me over a thousand dollars for the incident. My parents paid for it all—and I was very thankful—but to teach me a lesson, they required me to pay them back every cent. Fair enough. I spent the rest of my summer working as a valet driver for a nearby resort. Iris and Katherine wondered why I had zero free time, and I played it off. I pretended to be saving up for an upcoming trip to Costa Rica. Only a partial lie—I *was* saving up for that trip, too... just on the side. Semantics.

Costa Rica ended up being a blast, too. I miss traveling. Thank goodness I traveled to seven countries before literally dying. Except for the drunken, sad-boy summer without my girl, I spent nearly every adult summer traveling abroad. I visited Japan, Italy, Greece, England, Brazil, Costa Rica, and Canada. I took every chance I got to escape.

Getting into trouble with the law shook me, but tonight, something much worse could happen. And for the first time in an extremely long time, I'm feeling uneasy. I pride myself on thinking one step ahead of others, but for once, I can't predict what'll happen next.

I glance outside from the window of my quarters and lean on it for support, seeking guidance only the stars can offer me.

The sun is setting, meaning it's nearly time for my judgment based on what Cleo said earlier. Keeping my arms crossed, I stare outside at the blue-pink sky, contemplating how I'll approach the evening.

If I'm being honest, I'm *a little* excited to see the throne room—I've never had the chance to see the Archangels in action like this, and I've heard a lot about them. During my training, we touched on their hierarchy a bit. The Archangels reign over the Middle Realm, whereas the Golden Realm is run by Seraphim—higher angelic beings. If this weren't my own judgment, I'd be way more stoked. If only I could meet them under more casual circumstances. That would've been nice, I think.

My haven is cramped but equipped with everything I need. Behind me, a queen-size bed rests on a white wooden bedframe and headboard, and then there is a nightstand to the left near the window. A narrow hallway extends from my bedroom to the living area, which includes a charming living room, and a minimalist kitchen. The kitchen is the smallest part of the haven, with only an opal counter space, white wooden cabinets, and a porcelain sink.

Angels don't eat in the afterlife. Mildly disappointing, I know, but I don't experience cravings of any kind, which is a perk. I learned firsthand during my guardianship that angels *can* eat, but food doesn't sustain us. Instead, we find sustenance in an occasional good night's rest and breathing in this realm's air. I visited the Middle Realm every now and then during my guardianship to replenish my magic when I didn't have the desire to rest.

I drift away from the window and walk down the hall toward the living area. I've had the same quarters since my passing. Most angels ascend shortly after their guardianship, and seeing as many missions only take a couple of years, we have a pretty steady rotation of angels moving in and out of the quarters.

If I hadn't crossed the veil to reveal myself to Iris, this would have been my last day here.

My throat thickens as I imagine what lies ahead.

I could lie tonight. I know I could. But something tells me the Archangels wouldn't buy it. Ancient beings who rule the Middle Realm? Yeah, they'd see through my bullshit faster than a cheetah racing a rabbit for gold in a 5K run.

But if I don't lie, what comes next? Could I be imprisoned for breaking the most divine law? Will I be banished? Will they *vaporize* me? Will I ever even be allowed to ascend?

I've heard rumors that if an angel offends the Archangels by breaking a divine law, they vaporize them right on the spot without a second thought. I've also heard that the Archangels are seven feet tall and utterly impossible to fight off. Guardians don't often see the Archangels, so their appearance is a complete mystery to me.

I gulp and loosen the collar of my button-down cream shirt, re-tucking it into my brown slacks and tightening my black belt just to give my hands something to do. I don't regret what I did, but the suspense of not knowing if I'll make it might eat me alive.

As the sun begins to set, I realize procrastinating the inevitable won't save me. It's time to greet my fate.

I refuse to face certain darkness with anything less than a smile.

Venturing outside my quarters, a breath of fresh angel mist immediately covers me from head to toe. The crisp mist fills me with light, giving me the extra push I need on my short walk to the headquarters. I follow the selenite crystal path leading to the palace's bridge, passing by several other living havens similar to mine.

A green square courtyard lies just ahead. The selenite path is lined with a multitude of flower beds featuring white peonies and hydrangeas—among several other flowers I can't quite name. A pristine opalite fountain spewing sparkling water lies at the square's center, serving as the perfect focal point, while four other selenite paths fan out from the fountain to various other parts of this realm.

The path to my right leads to other living quarters for Watchers and Educators. To my left, another leads directly to the town's marketplace, full of little shops, booths, and the atrium. The walkway straight ahead leads to a grand stone staircase connecting to the palace's bridge.

I drag my feet down the path with my hands in my pockets, fixating on how to manage tonight. Before running into my Watcher, I had every intention of confessing my wrongs, accepting I didn't have anything else to lose.

Cleo's words alone didn't scare me. No, the flash of emotion is what got me—the trace of fear etched in her gaze. It appeared to be a momentary lapse; she doesn't seem like the type to wear her emotions on her sleeve. But for the briefest of seconds, her apprehension was so *potent*, it leaked out against her will.

Wouldn't it be wiser to be truthful tonight? Shouldn't Archangels value that? Maybe if I walk in there and put myself on blast, I'll get to prance out with a fancy new set of wings and ascend to the realm above amid a choir of angels singing.

But maybe not.

Lost in thought, I don't even realize I've made it inside the building. I'm standing directly outside the throne room. I look up at the skylight above, registering the sun setting. I give the middle-aged angel with warm green eyes guarding the room a friendly nod, to which he shakes my hand.

"Kai Greene, I presume?" He smiles, looking me up and down.

"In the flesh." I smirk. "Well, not quite in the *flesh*, but you get it."

He grabs his stomach and chuckles loudly. Damn, it's good to be back in the Middle Realm around people who get me. Jasper clearly didn't.

"The Archangels are thrilled to make your acquaintance. Your Watcher and mentor are already inside. Go on in, son." He pats my back and then opens the grand golden doors for me.

I stride past him, tossing him the widest grin I can, then turn toward the room, keeping the grin plastered on my face. A wave of calm energy washes over me as I stroll deeper into the vast room.

The throne room is even more serene than I imagined. Several large marble columns grace the room, giving it a timeless allure. Its walls are made of beaming selenite, similar to the walking paths throughout the realm. A glow radiates from within the room, and my lips part in shock.

The arched ceiling is adorned with angelic mosaics. My eyes veer toward the angels, cherubs, and pegasi illustrated throughout the piece. I desperately want to understand the story behind the art—how did it get here? Did Michelangelo pass through here and finish this project on his way up to the Golden Realm? Did the Archangels wave their fingers to weave this into existence?

At the other end of the room stand four separate thrones, one for each of the Archangels. It's a relief that they aren't all seven feet tall—that would've been slightly more intimidating. Although, a couple of them look a lot taller than me. All of them have enormous iridescent—almost transparent—golden wings that glisten as if covered in droplets of starlit water, too. I've heard they have the largest sets of wings in the realm.

In gazing at each angel, I realize I do not recognize them at all, except one. The one with silver eyes and icy-white hair sitting on the far-right throne looks vaguely familiar, though I can't quite place my finger on how I know her...

Focus. I snap out of it, turning my attention to the other three thrones. Each Archangel reacts differently to my gawking and gaping.

The blond golden-skinned male in the center—yes, I know using the term male feels formal coming from me, but these angels seem too refined to be referred to as anything else—has his eyebrows slightly raised. I notice his cerulean eyes and chiseled cheekbones before glancing at the bronzed female Archangel on his right. Her ebony eyes hold a knowing look, as if she already knows all my secrets. The raven-haired, porcelain-skinned male to her right, on the other hand, appears bored. I'm borderline offended by his entire lack of interest. I peer into his amber eyes, attempting to gauge his character, but alas, his face remains entirely unreadable.

Again, my eyes wander to the platinum-haired, fair-skinned Archangel on the far-left throne. She smiles coyly before averting her gaze.

They're all glowing.

Predictable.

Just behind the Archangels, a spiraled staircase of nearly blinding light stretches upward beyond the ceiling and into the sky. It's rumored that the light serves as a path ascending directly to the Golden Realm above, cutting through the Middle Realm's dome.

"Welcome, Kai Greene," a velvet voice breaks my concentration as the throne room door closes, locking me in here with these ultrapowerful beings. "We're so pleased to see you. To get the formalities over with, we'll start with introductions. I'm Annalise."

She nods to the man on her left.

"I'm Luke," he calls, his deep voice echoing throughout the massive room. He quirks his head to his left.

"I'm Jessenia," the female says in a chipper tone. A beat of silence passes between them. Luke pierces the other male to his far right with a lethal gaze, clearing his throat.

"Oh, right. I'm Nial. I've been working here for the last several thousand years. My greatest strength is that I know how to detect lies, my greatest weakness is—"

"That's quite alright, Nial. No need to bore the Guardian to death." Annalise presses her lips together in a tight smile. She raises her hand and waves her fingers in an interesting pattern, conjuring a glass goblet filled with an icy liquid that materializes in mid-air. She holds the glass up to her lips to take a sip and releases a breath, tossing the glass behind her. This time, it disappears in mid-air.

Now *that*'s a cool trick.

"What? Just sharing my elevator pitch. I'm getting rusty in my old age." Nial smirks, tossing a quick wink—so fast I nearly missed it myself, and I always catch a good old-fashioned wink—just beyond me. I turn my head, following the line of his sight and landing on a face whose eyes are already on me.

Cleo. Her features, petite and soft, contrast heavily with her intense brown eyes and grimace.

"Let's begin, shall we?" Luke interrupts.

"Let's," I say in complete confidence.

I've got this.

Five

Cleo

A current of chills spreads across my body. The air is different right now—it's thicker, less predictable. I glance to my right at Matt, Kai's mentor, to see if he can sense the change or if it's just me. His brown eyes remain fixed on the Archangels, his brown hair perfectly styled, and tan arms resting at his sides.

Unlike me, goosebumps aren't covering his arms.

Heavens, what on earth is going on with me?

I school my features, folding my arms and standing straight, awaiting the Archangels to speak.

Luke gazes over at us and says, "You may be seated."

Finally. If I kept my knees locked any longer, I would've collapsed. I sit down on the intricate hand-carved bench perpendicular to the thrones and scan the Archangels. Nial's eyes linger on me—he is one of the few beings who knows how to get under my skin, and tonight, he's doing it well.

In the corner of my eye, I spot Kai glancing at me, too.

Pull it together, I whisper, attempting to enter his mind for the first time. I know he mind spoke with Iris's partner multiple times, so I figure it's worth a shot to see if we can communicate similarly. *Stop staring.*

A moment of silence passes between us, leading me to believe my attempt to enter his mind was feeble.

And if I don't want to stop? his voice interrupts.

So, it worked. Interesting. To be fair, I haven't attempted to mind speak with another angel before this, so I wasn't sure what to expect.

I turn my attention to the Archangels. They're currently sorting through their documents, following basic judgment protocol by making sure they follow the proceedings in the divine order. *Now isn't the time for jokes.*

Who says I'm joking?

My stomach drops, but I continue watching the Archangels as if unaffected.

You're always playing, *Kai.*

Nial clears his throat, pinning me once again with his amber eyes, attempting soulsight. After his failed attempt, he rolls his eyes. "We keep our judgments simple—"

"And efficient," Luke adds. "Only the purest souls are offered the chance to be Guardians—"

"Therefore, we exert a *tremendous* amount of trust in our Guardians and those who watch them. During your judgment, your word is as valuable to us as all the riches in the realm," Annalise chimes in. "We trust you will share your experience in its raw, purest form—"

"By being entirely truthful," Luke states, plainly. "You may share whatever details you find necessary; whether your guardianship takes five minutes or five hours to share, it matters not. What matters is—"

"The story you tell and its main character," Jessenia joins. "We may have all the time in the realm, but—"

"Our time is precious, so waste it not," Nial finishes. "Kai Greene, tell us about your sister and her journey to peace."

Kai scans the Archangels and chuckles. "That's it? You don't rewind the tapes and watch the journey yourselves? You just... trust Guardians to be truthful because of their nature? You don't even use soulsight for this?"

All four Archangels nod in harmony. I'll never get tired of watching the way they finish each other's thoughts. I've attended hundreds of judgments for my Guardians, and although the order in which they speak changes, they never fail to work in perfect synchronization.

"If that's the case, you're in for a wild ride. I've got a good one for you." Kai winks at Jessenia nonchalantly, and for the first time in my afterlife, I catch her cheeks reddening. *Is she blushing?*

Looks like it. Kai's voice enters my mind unexpectedly. I didn't realize he could still hear my inner dialogue... *Sit back and relax. I've got this.*

Often, when an angel recounts their guardianship to the Archangels, they stutter, barely capable of forming coherent sentences. Odd, too, because most of the time, they haven't even broken any major rules during their guardianship.

Kai, however, maintains the calmness of a candle's flame despite breaking our most divine law.

He recalls his journey with his sister, starting with the very moment he died.

Kai took several days to wake up in Eloras after his passing. As unusual as it may sound, it usually takes time for the dead to awake in the afterlife. An angel greeted him as he came to his senses. Then, he skipped ahead to the moment he decided to guard Iris. He mentions how hard he worked to help her find peace after his early departure.

She means a lot to him. Enough that he was willing to risk his entire salvation. I can understand why. My family and I were extremely close in my mortal life. I'm not sure if I would've done anything differently in his shoes. Perhaps that may be part of the reason why I didn't intervene the way I've been trained to.

Several minutes later, he reaches the part of the story I enter in, though he doesn't realize that. My head grows heavy as I brace myself for impact.

He could ruin me entirely. I'm certain he will.

"...That's when I realized Jasper could see me," he deadpans as all the Archangels express looks of shock.

Heavens, *no*. He just told them Jasper could see him.

"He could *what*?" Nial asks in a sharp tone, boring his gaze into Kai's. The other Archangels look equally disgruntled.

"Yeah, he could see me. Plot twist, am I right?" He shoots them a playful gaze. I wonder if he knows who he's playing with and what they're truly capable of.

I gulp, swallowing as my throat tightens.

"Oh, c'mon, don't look at me like that. Don't worry, I solemnly swear it was for a good reason." He tilts his head at them, recognizing they aren't reacting. I'm willing to bet they're all having a combined mental council as we speak. "You know, I was going to save that reason till the end of the story, but seeing as you're all so invested now, I'll spoil it. He and Iris share a very rare and sacred bond, if you're catching my drift."

Jessenia begins clapping her hands as Luke reaches over to stop her, shaking his head. She shrugs. "Well, I quite like this part of the story."

"Me too," Kai sighs.

"Cleo, did you know about this?" Nial tears his gaze away from Kai to me, motioning for me to stand.

Pull yourself together, Kai's voice taunts me. For once, he's right. I need to calm the hell down.

"Yes." I nod, rising, then pushing my shoulders back and firming my stance. Matt's jaw drops beside me.

"How long have you known?" Annalise questions me, eyeing me up and down.

"I had suspicions early on, Your Grace, but—"

"She put the pieces together long before I did and didn't tell me nor anyone else. Pretty rude if you ask me, but I get it. Once she realized they were brought together by fate—"

"Forgive me, but I believe the question was for Cleo," Luke states. I gulp again and nod slowly.

"It's true. I determined the reason why they could see each other prior," I affirm, attempting to appear disinterested.

"It all makes sense now..." Nial scratches the scruff on his chin and then gazes at Kai. "When we were recently notified of your question about how living beings can see Guardians at times, we were confused by your need to understand this theory. In reality, you asked because the boy could see you."

Kai nods slowly, crossing his arms. "Yep. I submitted my question in the drop box earnestly, hoping one of you'd be able to *shed some light*." He wiggles his brows, and Annalise surprisingly suppresses a small laugh, covering her mouth.

Heavens, how old are these Archangels? Why are they so enamored by him? For once, I agree with Nial's discernment.

The Archangels all gaze at one another for a moment.

"Cleo, why didn't you tell anyone?" Matt whispers as he nudges me, boring his gaze into mine.

"I didn't believe his ability to communicate with Jasper hindered his mission," I share nonchalantly, just loud enough so the Archangels could hear me. "I think their shared connection ultimately sped up Iris's recovery."

Matt nods in understanding, letting out a sigh. Finally, Luke breaks the silence. "Considering you didn't necessarily break any Guardian rules by developing this relationship with your living being's soulmate, you've been cleared. You may proceed with your story. You've caught our attention."

Kai nods at them in thanks and continues, oozing with confidence, when I finally connect the dots and understand his plan. No *way*.

By taking a risk and confessing a risky truth like that, he gained their trust and respect. I've seen enough of these trials to know this one is almost over. They likely won't have any other questions, and then they will award him his wings and send him on his merry way to the realm above. In the meantime, I'll get to continue working as a Watcher, maintaining an entirely calm existence.

This might *actually* work. He isn't as thoughtless as I suspected.

Just as I begin to embrace the calm, an intrusive thought creeps up in the back of my mind: He could still do it—share our little secret and ruin everything. Accepting the amount of power he has over the trajectory of my afterlife makes me dizzy.

"...and they lived happily ever after. The end." Kai flashes a crooked smile at them, and again, Jessenia claps. Being younger than the other Archangels, she holds a certain youthfulness about her that they don't have. Odd, considering she's still hundreds of years older than me.

None of that matters at the moment, though, because he got through his story and didn't expose us.

I'm free from this nightmare at last. We both are. Relaxing my shoulders, I stifle a shy smile of relief.

Suddenly, the grand doors burst open, revealing someone I would've never expected to see.

"Stephen, what an unexpected delight," Annalise calls out to him. Stephen has a frantic look in his eyes as the angels guarding the door hold him back. The look in his eyes is one I haven't ever seen. "Guards, you may release him. Is everything quite alright? The realm isn't falling through the sky in rapid succession as we speak, is it?"

Luke and Nial chuckle, and then Stephen looks directly at me gravely. My face pales. Something is wrong. Something is very, very wrong.

"I do apologize for my interruption, but I'm here to deliver information of the utmost importance," he says, out of breath, locking eyes with me. "I know about a Guardian breaking the most divine law."

Some of the Archangels gasp as they rise from their thrones. The sudden commotion is so loud that I can barely register anything happening around me.

Kai remains cool, unfazed by the outburst. I, on the other hand, have stopped breathing.

"That is a grave accusation to make. Which Guardian was it? Where are they now?" Luke presses for more information. Stephen moves his gaze from me to our main subject. Luke's eyes widen in realization as Annalise begins shaking her head in denial. Nial presses his lips into a firm line, his jaw clenching. Jessenia sits down, looking paler than she did only mere seconds ago. I can't breathe.

"The culprit is standing in this room," Stephen drawls, approaching Kai to stand eye-to-eye with him. He looks above Kai's shoulders to meet my gaze again before hissing, "But you already knew that. Didn't you, Cleo?"

Six

Kai

Damn, are the Oscars a thing in the Middle Realm? I need to know immediately because this guy just put on the performance of a lifetime. His ragged breathing, his crazy eyes, and that *hiss*? Get out of town. Watch out, Middle Realm, someone has a flair for the drama.

My eyes drift over to Cleo. Her lips are pressed into a flat line as she stares him down with a serious expression. I can also see a sense of something else in her gaze, something deeper I can't place.

While standing, she maintains a perfect posture, showing no ounce of fear, but I catch her knee twitching. I act without thinking, running to her side just in time to catch her as her knees give out. I scoop her into my arms and kneel, analyzing her features. As a coach in my previous life and a pitcher before that, I learned what to watch out for on the field—pale skin, imbalanced steps, knee twitches, and more. I'll admit, I find it odd that her knees gave out, considering our bodies don't work the way they used to. Perhaps I still have more to learn about the afterlife.

As I hold her in my arms, I take note of the stiffness of her limbs—even her feathered wings feel strained.

How much tension has she been holding in? I didn't know bodies could be this tense in the afterlife.

"I'm fine," Cleo says, her eyes darting off to take a look at our audience. For the first time since our archives adventure, I'm close enough to see golden flecks dancing in her eyes again, even as she avoids my eyes. "I just stumbled."

"You sure, angel?" I ask gently, failing to mask the concern in my voice and not particularly giving a damn about who hears it. Her fall was freaky, and *not* in a good way. Didn't like it one bit.

"Certainly." She wiggles her way out of my grasp to stand upright, and I oblige. She pats her dress down, then lifts her chin to the Archangels. I'm not enjoying the anxious look she's sporting at the moment. She's been so well composed up until this trial. This has rocked her.

And it's my fault.

Scanning the room, I notice everyone else's stares for the first time since Mr. Drama's outcry.

Look, I know it may not make much sense, but I broke a huge law of the afterlife. Sure, my reveal didn't harm Iris, but the fact that I did it at all and hid it from them doesn't make me look so great. I'd assume this probably hasn't happened in a very, very long time.

I get why everyone is frazzled, that's all.

"I heard them discussing it today. Instead of greeting him and introducing herself to him in the foyer, she pulled him into her office. I found that strange—especially because Cleo doesn't let many people into her office.

"So, I followed them just in case something was wrong. I waited outside her office and overheard him say, '*I crossed the veil and revealed myself to my sister. I also kept Jasper's ability to see me a secret.*' That was all I needed to hear. I bolted away and processed what I heard. As you all may know, Cleo and I were once close, so sharing this isn't easy. After thinking about it, I decided it must be done."

I sneak a peek at her, noticing she's scowling deeply at Stephen. In turn, he's smirking at her coolly.

Luke pins us with his golden gaze and asks skeptically, "Kai. Cleo. Do you have anything you'd like to share? Do Stephen's accusations hold merit, or would you speak against them?"

Cleo's gaze remains stoic.

"We can do this the easy way or the difficult way. The easy way comprises of you both telling us the truth. If that doesn't work, we can enter your minds to watch the interaction in *full.*"

My mouth opens to speak before I can think better of it.

"You caught me." I smile sheepishly before clearing my throat and schooling my expression. "I crossed the veil to reveal myself to my sister."

"Why would you do such a thing?" Annalise whispers.

"At the time, it seemed like the right thing to do. Cleo had nothing to do with this, though. I'm the one who broke the law."

"By not intervening or reporting your indiscretion, she's guilty by association," Jessenia says softly.

"Please, be seated. We need to process this and determine a suitable verdict," Nial interrupts, staring at us. "For both of you."

And that's where I draw the line. Away with the calm, collected Kai—he's left the realm. "Punishing her won't be necessary."

"Says who?" Stephen sneers.

"While your intentions are noble, it would be best for you to refrain from speaking until the sentence has been determined," Jessenia says plainly. "Stephen, I'd advise you to sit down on the bench and do the same."

She's definitely the group's nice angel—I think the others are too disgruntled to speak at the moment.

"But seriously, just punish me twice as hard to make up for her violation. I can take it," I urge them harder. Jessenia winces, a look of pity crossing her petite features.

I sneak a timid glance at Cleo, fixating on her unreadable eyes as she sinks into the bench—her mental shields are too good. It's damn impressive. She parts her lips, as if to say something, then closes her mouth, pressing her lips together tightly.

"We do not take commands from Guardians, Kai Greene," Luke states boldly. "Now, if you'll be so kind as to allow us time to deliberate."

Guess who can cross *giving a group of almighty Archangels a direct command* off their bucket list?

Me. It's me.

My jaw ticks, and I reluctantly bite my tongue, walking to the bench and taking a seat next to Cleo. The more I speak, the more I could negatively affect our outcome—a bad habit of mine.

The Archangels are all conversing privately within their heads, careful not to convey any emotions outwardly. I watch each of them, hoping to catch a fragment of emotion to no avail. My knee brushes against hers, and she quickly scoots closer to Matt, who hasn't looked me in the eye once since the news broke. He and I are close—well, we were close. Given his crossed arms and emotionless expression, he doesn't seem to be a big fan of me at the moment, and I can't blame him. As my mentor, this doesn't make him look so hot, either.

It's wild. While guarding Iris, I had zero intention of ever revealing myself to her. I knew the rules, and for once, I *wanted* to follow them. I wanted to ascend more than anything—the Golden Realm sounds like a dream come true. Then, Jasper showed up, looking at me in the eyes and shit, and everything went to hell. I had to cross the veil and reveal myself to Iris. The second she hummed the word *please*, I had no other choice.

I don't regret it, I don't regret it, I don't regret it. I repeat this in my mind, convincing myself that my decision was just. I shut my eyes and roll my head back to rest on my shoulders for a moment. I'll be the first to admit that I didn't fully understand how my choice affected other angels. And while I testified to the Archangels, for a second, I *truly* believed that the violation wouldn't come to light. I thought wrong—nothing new.

I open my eyes and catch a glimpse of her through my peripheral vision. Her regal demeanor rivals the Archangels'. Her eyes, open and alert, remain on the Archangels as they deliberate. I see a calmness in her expression I didn't see before... As though she's given up and accepted whatever fate lies ahead of us.

Stephen sits on the stone bench across the room from us, pinning her with his malignant dark eyes. Instead of shying away, she turns to look at him, piercing him with her own gaze. I don't know their history, but I find his glare foolish and petty. He appears to be around my age, if not a little older. Obviously, he died before me—otherwise, he wouldn't be strutting around the headquarters this arrogantly—but his physical appearance doesn't surpass the age of thirty.

His beady eyes—so brown they're nearly black—continue to bore into Cleo's. Finally, she looks away, glancing back at the Archangels with an unimpressed sigh. He narrows his eyes further before turning his attention toward me. Damn, where's the movie popcorn when you need it? I point my hand to my chest and mouth, "*You mad at me, bro?*" tossing him a shit-eating grin and raising a brow.

This is entertaining. Not as fun as messing with Jasper, but still fun.

Suddenly, someone clears their throat—Luke. The Archangels settle back into their thrones, except Annalise, who remains on her feet.

"Wouldn't want to interrupt your staring contest," Nial drawls, leaning back in his throne and flashing a quick look at Cleo before looking down. "We've deliberated and come to a decision. Please rise."

He motions for us to stand. Annalise takes center stage now—it almost seems as though she's been leading this procession. I wonder if they take turns leading Guardian rulings.

"Kai Greene, believe what you may, but you're not the first Guardian who has crossed the veil to reveal himself. You certainly won't be the last. Dozens of angels have revealed themselves intentionally to living beings on Earth. Some have revealed themselves with intentions to impress living beings, seeking glory. Others revealed themselves as a show of power, exerting dominance over the living."

I hear a soft gasp from beside me. Good, I'm not the only one who's shocked.

"As Archangels, we do not reveal the identities of those who break this divine law. Instead, we tend to wipe them from afterlife existence, banishing them for taking advantage of their divine power in selfish ways. These banished beings become fallen angels—stripped of their divine light and forced to remain in the shadows of the land below for all eternity."

I gulp, readying myself for impact. I've never been a fan of the dark.

"However, it *is* rare for an angel to cross over the veil to reveal themselves for the purpose in which you did. Therefore, we do not find it necessary to banish you from the realm permanently," Jessenia affirms with a soft smile. A sigh of relief escapes me, while Stephen's jaw drops in disbelief.

"You got me good. I thought I was about to be forced into a never-ending emo phase." I push my hand through my hair nervously. They don't laugh this time. Maybe they're too old to understand that one.

"Despite your pure intentions, we must maintain order in the afterlife," Jessenia replies, losing her smile. "We must punish you—and Cleo—for this act." *Damnit.*

"We've determined the suitable punishments, which read as follows..." Luke holds out his hand, and a talisman flies into it from the pillar of light behind him. He begins to read.

"First, Mr. Greene will remain in the Middle Realm indefinitely.

"Secondly, Mr. Greene will work in the Library of the Sky indefinitely.

"Thirdly, Mr. Greene will not be awarded his wings indefinitely.

"And finally, Mr. Greene will be prohibited from visiting Earth indefinitely."

The temperature in the room drops as my entire body tenses—the same way it did during the car accident right before I died and joined the stars.

Indefinitely.

Being forced to stay in the Middle Realm to work in a dusty-ass library for an indefinite amount of time sounds like my own personal hell. The Archangels know exactly what they're doing.

I can think of no worse way to spend my afterlife. Hell, being a dark fallen angel would've probably been more fulfilling than this.

"If I may, Your Grace," Matt speaks up for the first time since the ruling started. Luke nods at him, permitting him to continue. "Not receiving his wings and being forced to stay in the Middle Realm seems a little harsh, given his pure intentions."

"We must maintain order." Luke tightens his jaw. "The fact of the matter is, Kai broke our most sacred divine law by crossing the veil and revealing himself to his sister. This cannot be undone. To avoid punishment, we'd need to revise the sacred rules, and we cannot do so without convening with the Seraphim in the realm above. As such, we cannot simply ignore this. He must be punished."

"Quite frankly, he should be grateful we aren't resorting to banishment," Nial adds, narrowing his eyes. I press my lips together and nod my chin at Matt. *Thanks, buddy, I know you tried, but I'm doomed either way.*

"Moving on." Luke clears his throat, turning his attention to Cleo. "Cleo, your punishment reads as follows:

"*Cleo Graves will be suspended from her Watcher position from this day forward until we see fit. Instead, Ms. Graves will be tasked with watching the Guardian she failed to watch properly—Kai Greene.*

"*She will aid him in the Library of the Sky.*

"*She will ensure he does not travel between realms.*"

Oh, no. She is going to hate this. Working in the library is the most mundane job possible in the Middle Realm... I'd rather be sentenced to shining floors every single day of my existence here than sit and sulk in the library. I bet she echoes my sentiments.

I glance at her briefly, seeing flames erupt in her golden-brown eyes.

Oh, hell yeah, we're on the same page. This might work in my favor.

"Should either of you have any questions regarding this verdict, speak now." The Archangels strike us with their gaze.

"What will happen to my current Guardians?" Cleo asks with an edge to her voice. Interesting that the first question she asks is about others.

"We will have Stephen reassign them as he sees fit," Annalise answers.

"Whoa, whoa, whoa," I interrupt. "Why *Stephen*?"

"Kai, Stephen is one of the lead Watchers in the division. He oversees Cleo and has worked with her for decades. Apart from his theatrics today, he is one of our division leaders, and we trust his judgment," she reassures us. I clench my jaw, while Cleo simply nods in response, slumping her perfectly straight shoulders in defeat for the first time since I've known her.

"Any other questions?" Nial asks.

"How will you ensure I don't leave the realm?"

"That's not a suspicious question at all." He rolls his eyes. "We'll share those details with Cleo alone. If you don't have any other questions, you're dismissed, Kai Greene. You may depart to your quarters and ready yourself for a day of *lively* work in the library tomorrow." He smirks. Nial may be my least favorite.

With that, I look at Cleo one last time, apologizing as sincerely as I can with only my eyes at first, before remembering I can mind speak to her. *I'm so sorry I dragged you into this, angel. I'll make it up to you. I swear it.*

Her brown eyes gaze into mine, void of all emotion. *Good night, Kai. Please stay out of my head.*

SEVEN

CLEO

"Matthew and Stephen, you're free to depart as well," Annalise says, barely audible over the ringing in my ears. I haven't been able to retain much at all over the past five minutes since Luke announced the consequences to our actions. Listening has always been my strong suit. I developed my speaking skills over time, but my ability to listen and retain information is a gift. It's something I've never taken lightly.

Ironic given how I currently can't comprehend a single word coming out of anyone's mouth.

Thoroughly rattled and ruined. Just as I suspected I would be.

He's blaming himself—anyone in his shoes would. I fell into a state of shock when he offered to take on my own punishment as well as his. I'll admit that was considerate, but it was also foolish. He clearly doesn't fully understand the weight I carry in this. But I do.

I should've stopped him.

Iris had already found peace by the time he revealed himself to her.

She would've been fine without seeing him.

Mere moments ago, we would've applauded him and cheered for him as he ascended the spiral staircase to the golden stars.

If I had simply done what I was trained to do—what I've already done *countless times*—he may have been entirely blameless.

Instead, for some godforsaken reason, I went against my natural instinct and didn't intervene. He couldn't see me as I stood behind him beyond the veil on that mountainside. No one could. I was simply the breeze that encircled them, for all they knew.

I observed the entire moment, taking in the tears lining his eyes, the undying love they shared, and how he held her tight against his chest while she sobbed tears of relief in knowing with absolute certainty that he was okay.

Much to her displeasure, he will no longer be okay.

I haven't known Kai for long, but I've known him long enough to know this particular punishment will be insufferable for him. The way he teleports from place to place without a care in the world as often as possible is testament enough to how much he seems to dread being stagnant.

Don't even get me started on my demotion to the library. I clench my teeth. I'm not angry—I am enraged. After decades of serving as one of the most devout Watchers in the division, I absolutely cannot imagine a lower position in the realm to fall to.

Just my damn luck.

How *dare* Stephen intervene? I tried to exercise soulsight on him to understand why he betrayed me like this, but I'm admittedly out of practice. I've grown far too used to blocking others out of my soul as opposed to tuning into theirs.

I lift my eyes from the ground to the Archangels again, noticing all their eyes resting on me. I refuse to display even a shred of weakness in front of them. I'll own up to my mistakes and prove myself worthy of maintaining my position again. I'll do whatever it takes, even to his detriment. I can't afford to make more mistakes in the Middle Realm—I don't belong anywhere else.

"Well?" I ask, boredom lacing my tone. Jessenia widens her eyes in surprise.

"Are you okay?" she asks kindly.

"*Am I okay*?" I grit my teeth, attempting but failing miserably at hiding my displeasure. I know she's the purest one. Logically, she doesn't deserve this backlash. But it's not personal—I *detest* that question. Always have. Willing to bet I always will. "You just stripped me of my title, demoted me to the—pardon my French—fucking library *indefinitely* to watch over a wingless Guardian, and you're inquiring about my current emotional state? If you have to ask, you're not as all-knowing as they say you lot are."

"*Enough*, Cleo," Nial barks, gravel in his voice. "We didn't ask you to stay behind for you to berate the youngest among us. If you experience any further emotional outbursts, you will regret it. Mark my words."

Chills spread across my arms, no doubt the physical reaction to the force of his divine power rumbling throughout the throne room.

I simply nod in response, taking a quick breath to steady myself, and look at Jessenia.

"I'm not offended, Cleo. It was naive of me to ask, but I feel like it's important you know I was coming from a place of compassion. We have known you longer than you can comprehend. We care, despite how it may seem. It's not like you to break rules like this. We simply want to know why you didn't prevent this from occurring in the first place." She tilts her head. "It's most curious. We would like to learn."

Can't they see that I don't even understand what possessed me to make this decision? I cross my arms in response, quirking an eyebrow. "You'll be disappointed to know I have no rhyme nor reason behind this poor decision."

Annalise interrupts, "As soon as you determine what led you to make this choice, do let us know. Additionally, this sentence will not prevent you from ultimately ascending, should you choose to do so. You'll still be qualified to ascend once the consequences run their course."

"Onto the important part—your duties in overseeing Mr. Greene," Luke's voice chimes in, clearing his throat. "Tonight, we'll craft a ring to prevent him from using his teleportation abilities between realms. We haven't had to craft one out of golden starlight in quite some time, so we need to channel our combined golden light energy into it. It will be delivered to your room by morning. Once he slips the ring on, he will not be able to remove or alter it himself. The only way to remove it will require your signature. With your touch alone will he be granted his ability again."

"How will the ring recognize me?" I ask, puzzled as to how this will work. Fascinating. If I weren't still fuming, I'd be honored to be trusted with such knowledge.

"It's nothing to fixate on—the ring will be delivered in a pure golden ring box infused with our divine energy. Simply rest your finger on the box and channel your healing aura into its edges until it opens on its own. Once it opens, slip the ring on one of your fingers and hold it over your chest. In doing so, you'll fuse your magical signature with the ring and become its keeper, similar to how you'll be Kai's keeper for the time being," Nial finishes explaining. "Once he puts the ring on, only you will have the power to take it off. You can choose whether you'd like to disclose its purpose to him or not."

"I see... While Kai is living out his sentence, are there any other restrictions I should be aware of? Does he have a curfew or anything?" I nod my chin at them, awaiting an answer. The group bursts into laughter.

"No, he won't have a curfew. We promise we aren't asking you to babysit the man." Annalise suppresses a smile and lifts her chin. "You don't need to watch him twenty-four-seven. Although he broke the divine law, we didn't find reasons to fear him when exercising soulsight. He doesn't seem inherently dangerous."

Well, that's debatable.

I'm surprised they had the capacity to perform soulsight so subtly; at no point do I ever remember seeing their eyes melt into bright gold. Archangel perks, I suppose.

"But again, we take the divine laws seriously, and as such, we have chosen to implement these consequences for both of you until further notice. We cannot allow him, under *any* circumstances, to travel back to the land below. Now that he has crossed the veil once, reaching within himself to cross it again to reveal himself to others—say, his former lover, for instance—would be almost too easy. We can't risk it." Annalise shakes her head, while the others nod in unison.

"Understood. At what point will I be able to rejoin the Watchers division? May I keep my office?"

"We aren't enforcing an expiration on this sentencing. You were an accomplice. We debated the matter of your office and ultimately decided that you may keep it for now. However, you *will* face the consequences set before you, or other more dire consequences, for you in particular, will follow," Annalise affirms. My throat involuntarily squeezes as I gulp. The only more severe consequence for me would involve the staircase just beyond them.

"I won't let you down." I nod, bowing my head before them. "Thank you for not resorting to other worse punishments. May I please be excused?"

They all nod. I turn around and hastily vacate their vicinity, tucking my wings in as much as possible and retreating to my haven.

"Starlight be with you till we meet again, Cleo," Jessenia calls out as I walk away.

I gaze in the mirror and hardly recognize the woman who stands before me.

Her midnight blue wings appear limp on her backside. Her dimples hide within her deep tan cheeks. Her shoulder-length black hair, usually voluminous, is flatter than ever. Her restless eyes appear more ebony than honeyed, not a ray of light in sight.

I poke and prod at her face, tugging at different parts until the jabs redden her skin. She stares back at me from beyond the glass, haunting me. I've never fully loved the look of my dark wings, either. I guess my soul must be extra gloomy.

A soft knock interrupts my fixations. I pat my face, then walk out of my bathroom toward the front door, knowing exactly what awaits me—the enchanted ring. Opening the door, a familiar face greets me—not one I expected to see at my haven's door at midnight.

"Hello, Cleo," he purrs, his amber eyes locking on mine in a predatory way as he tucks his wings in and steps into my quarters nonchalantly. Archangel perks—they *do* own the place. "I figured I'd hand-deliver this. Wouldn't want it ending up in the wrong hands."

"Nial." I nod, reaching out my hand for the box. "Thank you. I've got this."

"Not so fast." He pulls the ring box back, farther away from my grasp. "Aren't you at all curious why you were able to retain your office?"

"Nope." He scoffs at that. "What? Do I have *you* to thank for that?"

"Yes, in fact, you do. I require your thanks at once," he drawls. I roll my eyes in response. "They didn't realize how much time you spent there, so they thought removing it from your possession would be an easy call. I persuaded them otherwise."

"Thank you." I bow sarcastically, snatching the ring box from his grasp. "Now, if you'll excuse me, I have a date with an enchanted ring."

"Cleo. It's no secret I've come to enjoy our friendship over the years. Well, I mean, the other Archangels don't realize we're friends, so I suppose it's a secret in a way." He runs his hand through his black wavy hair and shrugs nonchalantly. "As your *friend*, I came to warn you that what's coming is bigger than you can comprehend. I implore you to have an open mind. And tonight, when you transfuse your magic into that ring, you'll lose your tether to your Guardians below until further notice."

"*That's not suspicious at all.*" I use his own words against him, shoving him and sighing. I'll miss keeping an eye on my Guardians. It makes my stomach churn to think of Stephen reassigning them to other Watchers tomorrow. He nudges my foot playfully with his, bringing me back to this moment. Truthfully, Nial is one of my only friends in the Middle Realm, and we aren't even very close. "If you came here to speak in riddles, I'd consider it a job well done."

He raises his brows and walks toward my front door to leave. "Don't say I didn't warn you. I fear I cannot say more than that. It will be a while before we meet again. You know where to find me should you need anything."

I bow, smiling softly. "Of course, *Your Grace*."

"Glad to see you remember who you're talking to." He smirks, nodding his chin at me, then runs his hand through his black locks as he exits, tucking his massive set of wings inward to fit through the doorframe. He rarely visits me, let alone at night.

The first time we crossed paths after my guardianship ruling was years later, after he had a particularly bad day—riddled with bad rulings, disagreeable council meetings, and exhaustion. We ran into each other on the selenite bridge to the headquarters. We quite literally bumped into each other. At first, I scowled and released a groan as I bore my gaze into his and reprimanded him for not knowing how to observe his surroundings properly.

He pulled the *Do you know who I am?* bit, to which I responded, *Yes, of course I know who you are, Your Grace.*

He looked at me with a keen fascination I hadn't seen him fashion before. He walked me to my quarters, telling me all about his horrid day while I listened—remember, I've always been a good listener. Since then, we've kept in touch; we have always only been friends, nothing more. It's been nice to occasionally chat about our bad days.

However, despite the nature of our relationship, I knew he wouldn't exercise any bias when voting on the ruling for us earlier. Ultimately, his Archangel duties outweigh any fleeting moments of friendship in his ancient existence, within reason. I respect it and wouldn't have held any negative outcome against him personally.

Well, *most likely* not.

Sue me. At least I'm being truthful.

As I watch him stroll down the breezeway, I admire his colossal sparkling wings while he fades into the air, no doubt teleporting back to his manor.

While watching him walk away, I catch myself wishing he could stay longer.

Although I enjoy alone time, sometimes I miss spending time with loved ones. In my mortal life, I was the oldest of three, and throughout my childhood, every waking moment outside of school was spent with my siblings. I helped teach them how to read and write. I even packed their lunches with my mom sometimes. I loved them fiercely—so fiercely, they teased me for being overprotective often.

My mom appreciated the extra support in caring for my brother and sister. She had a lot on her plate. Between raising three kids while my dad worked full-time and running a tailoring business from our home, she was often scattered. She thanked me frequently—so frequently, I found myself wondering if I may have been doing too much. I'll admit, I didn't sleep well and stressed a lot about their well-being.

My dad didn't quite share the same outlook as my mom. He appreciated my help. That much was clear. But there was more to it.

I remember, one night, shortly after my thirteenth birthday, my dad invited me to sit on our front porch together for a hot-chocolate chat. Hot-chocolate chats were our thing. Anytime one of us had a particularly rough day, we'd resort to a hot-chocolate chat. Sitting on two old wooden rocking chairs, I swayed mine in peaceful bliss, savoring the warmth of the cocoa on such a chilly winter day, when my dad broke the silence.

"You do too much for your age, Clo." I cut a glance at my dad, tilting my head.

"What do you mean? I'm thirteen now. I think... I could probably do even more."

He shook his head fast and took a sip of his cocoa upon hearing my response. "Not on my watch, kiddo."

"Why not?" I asked, using my spoon to swirl the marshmallows around my light blue mug.

"As you all get older, your brother and sister need to be able to stand on their own two feet. You'll always be their guiding light, being their big sister and all, but at the end of the day, you've got to focus on you and your needs." I stared into his big brown eyes, not quite understanding. Up until then, I thought taking care of them was my responsibility as their big sister. I didn't have time to think about my own needs. "Just promise me to take care of yourself the way you take care of them, okay? With grace and love."

Not fully understanding the deeper meaning behind his words at the time, I nodded slowly. "I promise."

Then, I took another large sip of my hot chocolate, coating my upper lip in a thick chocolate stache and grinned widely at my dad.

"Nice, Clo. But you'll never beat mine." He smiled mischievously, then dipped his *real* mustache in his hot cocoa, coating it in chocolate and marshmallows. I giggled and rocked excitedly in my rocking chair. I closed my eyes and leaned back, finding delight in this quiet moment with my dad.

Snapping out of the memory, I squeeze my eyes shut and shake my head. I walk back into my haven and shut the front door behind me, heading back into the bathroom to gaze at my reflection one more time before resting.

"I can't say I've been good at keeping my promise lately, Dad." My voice comes out in a soft, broken whisper as I peer into my own eyes. "I'm sorry for that, too."

EIGHT

KAI

Pacing in a dark hallway filled with shadows, I pause. Closed doors of varying shapes and sizes surround me. Some wooden, some metal. Some tall, some miniature. They all have one thing in common: each door is locked. As I run from door to door, jimmying the doorknobs, a wave of anxiety overtakes me, knocking the breath out of me.

I'm stuck. Again.

There is no escape.

I won't ever escape.

I slip from sleep, immediately jolting and gasping for air, the faint glow of moonlight beaming through my bedroom window bringing me back to my senses. *What the hell?* I haven't had that particular dream since before my death. It's as if the ruling stole the temporary sense of peace I've felt the past two years... This must be a joke. A cruel, sick joke.

I run my hand through my hair and take a deep breath, lying back down. Judging by the sky's current state, the sun won't rise for another hour or so. I don't have to head to the ancient library until then. I squeeze my eyes shut, forcing myself to forget the details of the dream I just had.

I could go back to sleep—heaven knows I need it after the roller coaster I've been stuck on over the past twenty-four hours. Or I could get a head start on the day with a good walk. Maybe it's time I smell the roses or something like that. I'm sure that could be considered therapeutic.

Regardless of where I go from here, there's no way I'll fall back asleep after that one... So it's time to wakey-wakey.

I meander into my bathroom casually, slipping out of my pants and turning on the shower's valve to the warm side. The Middle Realm wouldn't be nearly as opulent without showers.

In good ole angel-afterlife-fashion, the shower isn't like the ones in the land below, though. No, instead of plumbing, the water disperses from a small rain cloud resting inches below the bathroom's marble ceiling. The realm's divine light powers the cloud, gifted to us by the Archangels. I guess this is one thing I can thank them for.

As I step into the shower, I close my eyes, stand under the piping hot water, and focus on what lies ahead. It's funny, but I envisioned my afterlife almost entirely differently from my experience so far. Before dying, I thought there could be something else, something bigger in store. I had no clue what that something really was.

But becoming a Guardian Angel for my grieving sister and breaking a divine law so big that it ruined my chances of ascending anytime soon? Yeah, *that* sure as hell wasn't on my bingo card.

Where do I go from here, though? How long will I have to serve in the library? Will I *ever* be permitted to ascend, or will I be stuck here forever? What about my wings? Nearly everyone who stays in the Middle Realm has wings. I was looking forward to seeing the color of mine, but knowing it could take a million years to ever earn them takes the fun out of it.

Look, I know, I know—I broke the law. The honorable thing to do is to accept the consequences and let it be. I had fully intended to do that last night, but as soon as they declared the verdict, my optimism depleted.

The way they punished Cleo struck me, too. It doesn't take a genius to gather that she finds purpose in her role in the Middle Realm. Being suspended indefinitely over something so seemingly minor irks me.

I roll my head back and release an exasperated sigh. After spending a sufficient amount of time wallowing in self-pity, I decide it's useless and step out of the shower, wrapping a fluffy cream-colored towel around my hips.

Stepping out of the bathroom into my bedroom, I notice a beam of light shining in through the window onto my bed. The sun breaks across the sky, casting it into shades of lavender and pale pink. It reminds me of the sunrises I used to watch on Earth. While this sunrise is objectively more vivid, I can't stop images of the Cove's sunrises from flooding my mind. My old home.

Visiting my old hometown would probably give me the reset I need. A quick visit to the Cove wouldn't hurt anyone. Hell, no one would even miss me here... If only it were that easy. I turn away from the window and decide to get dressed.

It's like it's the first day of school. Only, instead of making new friends, I'll be cozying up with dusty old books and scrolls, my only companion being an angel who would set me on fire if she could.

I press the library's sensor with my pointer finger and await for it to unlock. Hearing the latch click, I open the golden doors and take in the vast space.

I have always called this the "ancient library" because, well, it *is* ancient, but I guess it's technically known as the "Library of the Sky" here. Striding leisurely, my eyes drift up to the arched ceiling covered in oil paintings of clouds. Yet again, I can't help but wonder who we hired to paint all the murals in this realm. The style of these paintings reminds me of the famous *Starry Night* painting, with its swirling blue sky. Maybe that same artist took the liberty of painting these clouds after his death.

Unlike other parts of the realm, we can't have authentic clouds in here, not with all the books and scrolls. Several tall mahogany bookcases surround me, containing thousands of books varying in color, shape, and size, complete with timeless ladders to reach the highest shelves.

It's settled. Jasper would enjoy this space. I think.

A circular marble information desk with golden accents takes up the middle portion of the room—I presume that's where they'll station me. Damn, do I feel inadequate; I haven't checked out a library book in over a decade, and I never even set foot into the library of the high school I coached at.

Venturing around the desk, I catch a subtle waft of eucalyptus. I follow the scent through the bookcases on either side of me, which leads me to an occupied book nook with a window view.

Am I surprised she got here early? Not in the slightest.

"Eager, are we?" I call out, approaching the cozy spot she's claimed as her own.

I'd estimate she arrived at least an hour before me based on how comfortable she's made herself here, covered in blankets and all. Her head turns toward me, her dark eyes lifting from the book she's holding to me.

"Must you always speak so loudly?" she whispers coolly, turning her gaze back to the book.

"*Must you always speak so properly*?" I whisper mockingly. She rolls her eyes, unamused. Again. "Whatcha reading?"

She continues reading, ignoring my question. I step closer.

"Would it kill you to try?" I smirk, scratching my chin. Talking to her is like talking to a wall. I draw a breath, turning around and walking back to the information desk to await further instructions from the library's overseer. They haven't arrived yet—I can't blame them, I'd sleep in, too, if I could—but I'm sure they will soon.

Can't kill someone already dead inside, a voice whispers so faintly from several feet behind me I almost miss it. I toss her a glance, noticing she's still reading—almost as if she didn't utter a word.

My mind must be playing tricks on me. Wouldn't be the first time.

I approach the desk and step into the center behind the counter, noting two comfortable beige chairs for the first time. I lean back into one, resting my arm on the rest, and then glance at the staircase leading to the archives, recalling my last encounter with Cleo there.

Despite not sharing her theories about the nature of my relationship with Jasper, Cleo really has come through for me. Without her, I would've never been able to learn why Jasper could see me. Hell, I wouldn't have even been able to visit the library.

And what have I done in return for her? Nothing. Zilch.

In fact, I hurt her.

And that doesn't sit right with me.

I can't blame her for giving me the cold shoulder, but damnit, my stomach is in *knots* over it.

"Kai Greene, I presume?" A different voice interrupts my spiraling thoughts. I glance up to see a woman with short, curly black hair and blue eyes standing over me. I rise out of my seat smoothly and reach out to shake her hand. "I'm Hadley, the library's overseer. Welcome! Have you seen Cleo yet?"

"Oh—"

"I'm here, Hadley." I turn to face Cleo as she slips her novel back on the bookshelf behind the desk.

"Splendid, you both arrived earlier than I anticipated." Hadley claps her hands together. "What a good way to start your divine services here! Come along, eager beavers. The sooner I show you the ropes, the better." She waves her hands for us to follow her. I take the lead, following right behind her as Cleo trails me. Wait a minute... I don't think I've gotten a single word in since meeting this angel—

"The library is organized into three different sections. The first is a collection of novels for entertainment purposes, located on the left side. The second is a collection of nonfiction books, situated on the right side. The third is the archives chamber, located on the upper level near additional lounging areas. You two have visited the archives before, so I don't anticipate needing to emphasize the importance of keeping track of those. Those scrolls and tomes may not be taken outside the library, unlike our entertainment and nonfiction books," she explains while walking, brushing all the book spines we pass with her fingertips.

We reach the staircase and ascend, arriving just outside the doors to the locked archives. This level's walls are lined with tall windows, flooding the space with soft, natural light. To enter the archives chamber, we have to use a separate sensor from the one outside the library. Hadley presses her finger against the sensor, unlocking the door.

The massive, circular room has one small window—unlike how the rest of the library is full of windows. Instead, it primarily glows with soft, warm beacons of candlelight. In the center of the room sits an oversized, round, purple amethyst table, with several candles placed on marble candlesticks resting atop it, their flames never-ending and lighting the room. The walls feature built-in shelves that extend from the floor to the high ceiling. Rolled-up scrolls, ancient books, various knick-knacks, and *dust* flood the shelves.

The room is overfilled with so many items that some scrolls, letters, and books sprawl across the porcelain floor itself. It's nearly impossible to find specific information in the archives, considering how dusty and chaotic it is. Finding records here during my guardianship was challenging, to say the least.

"You will work on several projects for the library during your sentence, including organizing books, auditing scrolls and tomes, renovations, and more. On a day-to-day basis, you can expect to assist several angels with finding and checking out books." She nods her chin toward the chaos engulfing the shelves. "Tidying up and reorganizing the archives will be your main initiative and highest priority. This space has been the least nurtured as of late, so it needs lots of love."

"How long do you expect this project to take?" Cleo stands next to the amethyst table, her arms crossed, brows low.

Hadley chuckles. "Well, there are roughly a thousand articles that need to be organized and audited here, so I'd estimate it will take several weeks. The better you two work together, the sooner you'll finish the job!"

Weeks. We'll be spending *weeks* in this dusty-ass chamber, sorting through old stuff I couldn't care less about.

"*Great,*" I mutter under my breath, my tone laced with sarcasm.

"Should you need anything at all, please come find me. I'm around most of the time."

"That's it? No further instructions?" I ask, confused.

"That's it. You two can decide amongst yourselves how to go about this first project," she affirms, turning to leave.

This might be the most laissez-faire work environment I've ever had. That's one perk, at least.

Hadley's footsteps echo down the staircase, leaving Cleo and me alone together. Wasting no time, she joins my side and reaches into the pocket of her loose black linen pants, pulling out a small object.

"Here." She holds up a box, opening it so I can see a solid gold ring. "Put this on."

"Damn, we're moving too fast. At least take me to dinner first, Cleo." I scoff while gazing down at her and stare at the ring. Something about it seems... off. She pinches her nose with her opposite hand and lets out an exasperated huff.

"I suppose I'll have to put it on for you." She grabs my right hand—her touch gentler than I expected, considering her hostile tone today—and slips the ring on my pointer finger. As she does, a burning sensation spreads across my hand, funneling through the rest of my body. The ring melds with my skin, causing panic to rise in my chest.

What the hell is this thing?

She doesn't let go of my hand, though. Her touch remains soft, reassuring, even—reminding me of a blanket's embrace on a winter day.

The feel of her hand over mine comforts me in a way words can't adequately describe.

Nine

Cleo

Well, the Archangels certainly didn't prepare me for *this.*

I prefer to be fully aware of all possible outcomes for any given scenario well in advance. I had no idea the ring would practically sear his skin, for heaven's sake. This magic feels big—bigger than us. Far older, too.

Last night, when I intertwined my own light magic with the ring, a tingling sensation spread across my body, making my head feel light. A wave of exhaustion overcame me, prompting me to fall asleep shortly after the ordeal had ended. *Ordeal.* Frankly, it was more ritualistic than anything else.

However, I didn't anticipate the ring to impact him so intensely. His skin is reddening, taking on a fiery sheen. My lips part as I stare at his contorted expression in utter confusion, gripping his hand. His warm hand squeezes mine so tightly my bones crack.

"Is this cursed ring from Hell itself?" He grits his teeth, clenching his jaw and gazing into my eyes with desperation. A bead of sweat rolls down his cheek. Sweating in the afterlife is *extremely* uncommon. "How much longer will this take?"

He must be in so much pain. My face remains indifferent while my chest tightens. "Don't fret. It should be over soon enough, okay?"

He closes his eyes and nods swiftly, giving my hand another squeeze. My hand tightens around his against my will.

I have no idea how long this will last. The last thing he needs is uncertainty, though.

I tug him toward the amethyst table at the center of the room and pull out a wooden chair for him, prompting him to sit. He sluggishly follows my lead, slumping into the seat and releasing my hand. I walk around the circular table to sit across from him, crossing my arms and watching him closely. He leans forward with a wince and rests his elbow on the table, supporting his jaw. He glances up at me and peers into my eyes. "Take my mind off this, angel."

There he goes, calling me *angel* again. Involuntarily, a hint of heat rises to my cheeks. I'd rather do anything other than small talk, but given his current sorry state, I have no choice but to comply.

"What's your favorite part of the afterlife?" I ask, leaning back in my seat and crossing my legs, still watching him. I run my hands across my thighs, smoothing out my black linen pants, then fidget with the collar of my cream-toned blouse.

He shakes his head, fixating on the table's purple surface.

"It's arguably the worst possible time to ask what I enjoy about the afterlife." He half smiles as I narrow my eyes at him. "*Fine.* I'll humor you. I like teleporting."

"Fair enough," I say.

"What's your favorite part?" he asks quietly.

"I don't know if I have one."

"You're kidding." He quirks an eyebrow.

"Sadly, no." I shrug.

"Nah, I'm not buying it," he prods.

I sigh, pressing my tongue into my bottom lip. Knowing he needs a distraction right now, I begrudgingly come up with something on the fly. "Fine. I suppose I like flying."

"Now we're talking." A wide grin stretches across his glistening face, and his eyes flicker to my feathered wings resting behind me. "What's it like?"

"Oh, it's what you'd expect—breezy, quiet, and a smidge terrifying... but also mildly invigorating." I nod my chin at him, eyeing the space where his wings should be. I wonder what color his wings would be. "Maybe you'll understand what it's like one day."

"Centuries from now, I'm sure." He scoffs. "So, you must have been a Guardian before being a Watcher, right? Did you enjoy being a Guardian?"

I tilt my head in response, unsure of how much I should share. "I did. My assignee was close to my age, which made it simpler to connect with her."

"Did you know her before you passed away?"

"No, I didn't."

"I wonder how different the experience would've been if you had chosen someone you knew," he says, taking in a deep breath. Little does he know, I often wonder the same myself.

He huffs a puff of air and holds out his right hand, staring at the ring. His skin, no longer swollen and red, glows as brightly as it did before. "Mind telling me what dark, cursed magic my body consumed just now?"

I suppress a smile. "It wasn't dark magic. In fact, it was light magic—the magic of our Archangels."

He nods, biting his lip. He inspects the ring again, grabbing it with his opposite pointer finger and thumb. He fiddles with it, twisting it. When he attempts to slide it off his finger, though, it doesn't budge. For a split second—so quick I nearly miss it—sheer panic crosses his features before he masks his fear with a convincing amount of calmness. "So, I can't take it off, meaning it has to have some sort of divine purpose. Let me guess: this ring is like a magical probation bracelet."

"Exactly," I say. "This ring will prevent you from being able to teleport to the land below."

"Predictable. I've seen enough movies to know a magical probation bracelet when I see one." He drums his fingertips on the tabletop and lets out a long sigh. Then, he rises from his seat and strolls over to the wall, eyeing all the books and artifacts. "Well, now that we've taken care of that, I guess it's time to get to work. This place is a mess."

Yet another piece of his freedom was stripped away only moments ago, but rather than sulking, he presses forward effortlessly. He asks over his shoulder, "How about we start by taking all the books off the shelves and placing them in the center of the room until we can determine how we'll organize them?"

"I'd rather decide how to organize them now before we begin moving them," I say, still seated, pulling out my leather journal from my woven knapsack and a—you guessed it—feather quill pen. I flip the journal open to a blank spread to plan this out.

"*Well*, if we're concerned about time management, it makes more sense to take them off the shelves first and execute a battle plan after." He spins to face me.

"We have all the time in the realm, Kai. I'm not concerned about how long it will take. The top priority here is efficiency."

He raises his hands in defeat and shrugs. "Fine, *you* can start thinking of a master plan to organize all this junk. In the meantime, *I'll* begin removing the knick-knacks and old scrolls. I'll wait to deal with the books. Let me know when you come up with a plan."

I scoff, and he salutes me mockingly. I gaze down at the empty page before me and begin to formulate a plan. He turns back toward the shelves, grabbing *artifacts* as if they're nothing more than toys. *Knick-knacks*, in his words.

Hours pass, and although I've settled on a plan of action for the records and artifacts contained here, we've accomplished *nothing* today. The archives chamber is in more disarray than it was before we entered this morning, which is no small feat, I might add.

Books and artifacts are sprawled across the floor, making it challenging to navigate through the chamber without nearly tripping.

I grew exhausted of dealing with my wings bumping into various objects, so I tucked them inward. Tucking wings is more straightforward than it sounds—angels with wings can tuck them in at any time by concentrating hard enough and forcing the wings to bend at their will. Unlike most people, wings are good listeners.

When I mentally ask my wings to flutter away, they comply and contort like magic, appearing smaller in size, nearly entirely hidden by my frame. I often tuck them away before bed—I've always enjoyed sleeping on my back, and tucking them away is the only way I can do that comfortably.

Kai's jaw practically hit the floor as he watched me tuck them earlier, exclaiming he had no idea wings could be manipulated in such a way with a mere thought.

Nearing the end of only my first day, I already dearly miss being a Watcher. As a Watcher, I never finished a workday feeling unfulfilled. Monitoring so many Guardians kept me busy. When I wasn't busy, I could simply slip away to read a book and return home to my favorite fictional worlds and characters.

Now, despite being surrounded by books, I've never felt farther away from home.

Focusing on the upper level, Kai is using a library ladder to de-shelve items on the opposite side of the round chamber near the entrance.

I hate to admit it, but removing the items first wasn't a bad idea. I've been working on assembling the artifacts and scrolls he's removed so far into sections on the stone floor, based on chronological order, and taking note in my journal of the year each item was created. He discovered some fascinating artifacts relating to mythological creatures. I make a mental note to revisit those records later—I've always found Greek mythology riveting.

Hearing heavy footsteps ascend the staircase to the archives, my eyes drift to the entry.

"What's up, Matt?" Kai calls from atop the ladder, sliding down carelessly to greet his mentor. He pats his shoulder, tilting his head. "What are you doing here?"

"I just wanted to check on you. Yesterday was a shit show. I can't imagine how you're feeling." He shakes his head and runs his hands through his brown hair. He glances at me apprehensively, then nods his chin and tosses me a sorry smile. "Hey, sorry to see you here, too."

"No one is sorrier than I," I call back. Matt and I have known each other for a long time. He's always been friendly to me. I don't know if I'd go as far as to call him a friend, but we're certainly not on bad terms at all.

"Anyway, there's a party this Friday. We have parties often in this realm, but we don't often welcome active Guardians. Wouldn't want to distract them from their mission, you know? The party is in the main courtyard's atrium. You should come. It'll take your mind off things."

"Dude, you already know I'll be there." Kai claps Matt's back again. "Thanks for inviting me. I've been needing a release. This will be awesome."

"Sounds good. Just let me know if you need anything else before then. I've gotta get back to the new recruits downstairs, but I'll see you then," he says, stepping toward the entrance, then meeting my eyes. "Hope to see you there, too. It's been a while."

I shake my head, flashing him a half-hearted smile. "I'm good."

He shrugs and grins, leaving the chamber and shouting over his shoulder, "Worth a shot."

I get back to work, keeping my head down.

"Why not go to the party?" His voice interrupts my rhythm from atop the ladder on the far side of the room.

"I have other plans," I say nonchalantly, tucking a strand of dark hair behind my ear and glancing back at the sparkling artifacts before me.

"It's a shame—you're like my only friend here. It'd be fun to see you out of your element for a change," he says, sighing.

"We both know I'm not your only friend here. Everyone loves you."

He presses his tongue against his cheek, then mumbles, "Well, you're the only friend I want to see at the party."

I drag my gaze back up to meet his from across the room and arch an eyebrow.

"Fine, partying definitely doesn't seem like your thing."

"Because it's not."

He gives me a knowing grin I don't particularly like. I suppose I don't hate it either, though. Why does his smile have to be so infectious?

He extends his arm upward to reach for more books. Without meaning to, I catch myself staring at the definition of his arms and taking in how fit he is.

"So, do angels drink at these parties?" he asks, interrupting my train of thought again. I nearly physically shake my head to snap out of it. This time, I'm glad he interrupted. The last thing I want to do is ogle his strong arms.

"Um. Yes. Angels drink at the parties. The drinks aren't quite drinks, though—they're lighter and taste crisper. More airy. They do, however, alter the brain in the same way alcohol does," I answer as I walk very carefully back to the main table, cautious not to step on any of the items decorating the ground, and add another note in my journal regarding the transparent crystal I just held—a reading sphere from the fourteenth century. *Utterly fascinating.*

Kai claps his hands, nearly stumbling off the ladder and dropping the book in his hand before grabbing hold of it again.

I stifle a laugh at the sight of his clumsiness. It's almost... endearing.

He lets out a sigh of relief. "You have no idea how happy I am to hear that. I've never been much of a drinker, but damn, I could use a drink right now."

I'd say he's probably earned that much.

We continue sorting through items in silence for the remaining hours of the workday. It's funny, he strikes me as the type who would prefer to fill silence with the sound of his own voice, but instead, he seems fine with the silence—comfortable, even. I guess I haven't fully figured him out quite yet. Throughout the day, angels enter the archives and attempt to browse the collection, only to realize it's currently a lost cause.

I step just beyond the entrance point to the balcony at the top of the staircase, glancing through the large windows at the sunset beyond the library's walls. Beams of soft light filter into the room, speckling the bookshelves on the level below us. The vast room's golden sheen is cathartic, really.

"Golden hour at its finest," a hoarse voice whispers over my shoulder. I elbow him in the ribs instinctively, spinning toward him. He bends over, clutching his rib cage and exhaling with a laugh.

I lift my chin at him, beaming. He quirks a brow, still gripping his stomach.

"Well, shit. That's the first real smile you've worn today," he says, shaking his head and smiling with his eyes. "You're a demonic little angel, aren't you?"

I wave my hand dismissively. "Workday's over. You're dismissed."

He tilts his head. "Dismissed? I'm your *coworker*, not your *employee*. We're practically equals now in the eyes of the Archangels."

I roll my eyes, descending the stairs and summoning my wings back to spread them as wide as possible to serve as a barrier between us. He ensures the entrance to the archives is closed before trailing behind me.

He's *infuriating*.

And I don't know what frustrates me more—him or the fact that he is actually right.

As of yesterday, I'm no more than a simple angel, doomed to work in the library for the rest of my mundane existence.

Ten

Kai

Days tend to meld together when you're doing something you don't particularly care for. Cleo and I have sorted through all the artifacts, and it's only been a few days since we started.

She's come up with a classification system based on chronological order. If you flip an artifact upside down, you'll see a symbol indicating the century it was created—she taught me that. Consequently, we've been focusing on batching the artifacts together in different groups, sorted by century. We've even assessed artifacts dating back to the first century. I can't wait to rub this project in Jasper's face after we meet again one day.

Friday arrives quicker than expected. Thankfully. I sigh in relief as I enter my haven and eagerly change out of my jeans and sweater into black pants and a collared short-sleeved black button-down shirt. I'm giving the monochrome fit a whirl. Sure, it's been years since I've been to a party, but I remember the ins and outs of partying like it was yesterday. I want to appear approachable—just not *too* approachable. Hence, the black ensemble.

The sun went down hours ago, yet I still can't stop thinking about work. More particularly, my coworker.

Watching her take in the sunset at the library earlier this week caught me off guard.

She likes to act like she doesn't care, but the look in her eyes as she got lost in that golden sheen held something I couldn't decipher. Something more potent than sadness, stronger than frustration.

In that moment, I wanted nothing more than to exercise soulsight to see if I could discern the darkest corners of her mind and help her... But I resisted.

I'd prefer to get to know her the good old-fashioned way.

I wander over to my mirror, checking myself out. I push my fingers through my hair and splash some water on my face. Tonight's going to be *lit*, as my old students would say. I exit my haven and make my way over to the atrium in the marketplace downtown, to the left of our living quarters.

Firefly-lit lanterns light the path from the square to the marketplace, composed of several shops constructed around the atrium in a rectangular manner. The atrium is an open courtyard filled with artsy, angelic statues, four-tiered garden-style fountains, and a variety of flowers, all set against a striking view of the night sky. From this realm, the sky isn't only black—it's a mixture of black, blue, pink, and purple. During daylight hours, the atrium is a sight to behold, but it's otherworldly at night—fitting, considering this realm is far from worldly.

Immediately upon entering the courtyard, I'm offered a foggy substance in a tall champagne flute by an angel with golden-blonde hair and bright yellow wings. "Drinking tonight?"

"Is that even a question?" I throw her an easy smile, glancing at the mysterious drink in her hands. "What is it?"

"Alcomist. Instead of drinking it like orthodox alcohol on the land below, you can simply breathe it in. A pleasant buzz is guaranteed after only one glass."

"Say no more." I grasp the glass and take a deep whiff, inhaling it like air. Refreshing. Cleo was right. It has a crisp taste to it—like how I'd imagine candied icicles would taste.

"Delicious, right?" the angel asks, beaming—evidently a bit tipsy herself.

"Right." I grin politely, then wander away from the entrance, venturing deeper into the party and scanning the crowd of dancing angels. The music is ethereal—it sounds indie. Props to the live band of angels. I'm sure Iris or Jasper would know this type of music well.

Angels all around me seem to lose themselves to the music, their bodies flowing freely in line with the melodic notes. I'll admit, I'm surprised by the closeness the angels are all exhibiting—during the day, most of these angels maintain chipper countenances and relatively professional demeanors. At night, a different side of them seems to unmask itself.

As my eyes search the crowd, they drift over to the stone seating placed throughout the atrium and catch someone I wasn't expecting to see. Before I can think better of it, I breathe in more alcomist and stride toward the seating area, landing directly in front of my target.

"Can I help you?" Stephen asks, his tone drenched in dismissiveness. I tick my jaw. His arm remains wrapped around a blue-eyed angel with long straight red hair. "I'm in the middle of something."

My eyes drift back to the redheaded angel, and I plaster a charming smile on my face. "Mind giving us a moment to catch up, red?"

She twists her hair around her finger, eyeing me and smiling softly. She rises, but before walking away, she whispers in my ear, "Come find me later."

I gulp in response.

I plop down on the stony seat to his left—thank gosh it has cushions—entering his personal space with zero regard. Stephen clenches his jaw, pinning me with a glare. "What do *you* want?"

"Why'd you do it?"

"Do what?" His glare turns into a cocky smolder.

"Don't bullshit me. Why *the fuck* did you do it?" My irritation is growing stronger by the minute. This isn't normal for me. I don't lose my cool.

"You broke our most divine law. You didn't really expect to get away with that, did you?" His jaw drops, and a look of performative shock crosses his features.

"Not that," I drawl, cracking my knuckles. He's a big guy, but I could take him. Easily. I didn't like the way he sneered at Cleo throughout our sentencing one bit. I pierce his eyes with my gaze. "I couldn't care less about you exposing me; I made my choice. I accept the consequences. Why did you bring *her* into it?"

His lips part, and a flicker of confusion crosses his eyes before he deadpans, "Stay out of it."

"Not my style." I toss him a lopsided grin, taking another deep inhale of the mist, realizing for the first time how light my head feels. *Whoa.* Deciding I've wasted too much time on his sorry ass and I have a party to get to, I whisper, "You've done enough damage as is, and she deserves a hell of a lot better. *Leave. Her. Alone.*"

Then, I give him my *best* predatory smile, reveling in the way his throat subtly bobs upon hearing my words.

I saunter back into the crowd, giving way to the music and dancing with the angels, continually scanning the crowd and taking note of the wings I see.

Green, red, blue, black, white, silver, and yellow wings surround me, all of which are magnificently unique, but none as breathtaking as midnight blue.

I must really get under my new best friend's skin. And no, she doesn't know we're best friends yet, but she'll figure it out soon enough. Sadly, I haven't seen her tonight.

It feels like forever since I last saw her. It's been a whole, what? Six hours? That's six hours too many tonight if you ask me.

I thought she'd be here. I have no clue why I thought she'd join me tonight. I mean, she made it very clear she had other plans. But what other plans could she possibly have that would take precedence over the most amazing angelic party ever with her new best friend?

I've danced with so many people—women and men—I've lost count. I've also lost count of the number of alcomisty breaths I've taken.

...You caught me. I've had a lot to drink... or breathe, is it? Frankly, I'm surprised *you're* surprised. I'm an angel, not a saint. Drinking my sorrows away was the plan for tonight all along. Keep up, buttercup.

The only thing that would make tonight even more spectacular would be a certain short, feisty brunette with golden-brown eyes.

I mean, seriously. What could she possibly be doing right now? I'll bet she found a way to work after hours and is taking pleasure in working overtime. She's probably in her office right now, sitting at that little desk of hers, twiddling her thumbs and *wishing* she had attended the party tonight.

Good. She should know she's missing out.

...I have the best idea.

My feet start walking before I can fully register where they're going.

Up, up, up they go. Up the stairs and across the rainbow bridge, into the palace, my greatest foe. One step in front of the other: left, right, left, right, right, left, left, right.

The building's bright lighting nearly blind me as I make my way through its grand hall, staying on the first level because, although I can't entirely remember why I'm here, I'm certain this is where I'm meant to be.

Oh, *fuck*. I'm wasted.

I chuckle, laughing at the sheer ridiculousness of it all, as I stumble through the hall for what feels like forever. Then, I lean on a door for extra support during this difficult time.

Feeling adventurous, I turn the doorknob to this dark mysterious little room on the first floor. I sniff the air, catching the scent of eucalyptus. Oddly enough, it's comforting.

I venture deeper into this dark abyss, leaving the door cracked open and embracing the dark with a warm smile. The light from the hall barely shines into the little room. I glance to my right, my eyes catching on something moving. The light from the doorway casts only a shred of light on the being.

I squint my eyes and realize it's her—the angel I've been looking for all night.

But why is she sleeping on this couch here in this little room?

Her head rests gently on a beaten, worn-out pillow, her thick, dark hair splaying across the pillow in all sorts of directions, and her wings are nowhere to be seen. She must have magically tucked them away again.

A knitted blanket is loosely draped around her waist, nearly falling off.

Oh no, we can't have that.

I approach her as quietly as I can given my sorry state and gently wrap the blanket around her, tucking her in.

Upon closer inspection, I notice a hardcover book in her grasp, still open. I smirk softly, admiring her obvious passion for reading. I may be an idiot sometimes, but it'd take an even bigger idiot to miss the way she stares in longing at all the books in the library daily.

Deciding I've overstayed my welcome, I step backward, meaning to leave, but stumble and nearly take down a chair with me.

She immediately jolts awake, rising and staring at me in horror.

"Kai... What are you doing here?"

If I continue to back away slowly while maintaining eye contact, the predator may leave me be.

I continue backing away, not breaking our gaze.

She fully sits up and rubs her drowsy eyes while letting out a yawn and stretching.

Uh-oh. I must be *really* wasted because I'm convinced that was the cutest fucking thing I've ever seen.

"And I repeat, for emphasis: *what the hell are you doing here?*" she asks again, irritably.

I stop backing away and lean against her doorframe to steady myself, crossing my arms in an attempt to look as *not drunk* as possible.

Sober—the word I'm looking for is sober. Duh.

Wait, am I standing right? Do I usually stand with my legs crossed? Maybe I should cross my legs... I slowly begin to cross my legs and lose my footing, nearly stumbling again and covering my mouth to hide my grin.

Note taken—no need to cross my legs.

"You know, I liked you better when you were sleeping." I nod, wearing a lopsided grin, my eyes flickering to her ensemble peeking out from under the blanket—a silky long-sleeved black blouse with matching silk shorts. I swallow a smile at how nicely our clothes mesh together on this fine evening. Suddenly, the temperature seems higher, so I unbutton another button of my shirt. Her eyes lock on my chest, then dart away.

"You know, that's a pretty problematic statement," she quips.

Sharp as a nail, this one.

I hold up my arms in defeat, nearly toppling over and letting out a laugh against my will. It's like my mind knows this is the last place I should be in this inebriated state, but my feet brought me here, and they've remained planted despite my better judgment. "I just had to see what plans you blew me off for."

I may be wrong, but I swear, I just saw her cheeks go a little pink. "I didn't blow you off. I blew the party off. You said it yourself, I'm not a partier. Are you really that surprised?"

"That was reverse psychology, sweetheart. I thought you caught my drift, but alas, I was sorely mistaken," I sigh exasperatedly. "Don't worry. Now that I've seen what you blew me off for, I'm good to go. I'll get out of your air."

Hair. I meant hair. But it's better to leave it; I wouldn't want to draw attention to my mistake.

She breathes out a puff of air and pats the seat next to her. "Sit."

"Ever the flatterer, aren't you, angel?" I chuckle, shutting my eyes and feeling a little dizzy. I walk over to her side, plopping down and sinking into her couch. At least it's comfortable. I lean my head back, resting it against the wall, then look at her. She's already turned on the lamp next to her and picked up her book to resume reading, leaning on the armrest away from me beside her lamp and wooden bookshelf. "What are you reading?"

"Just a silly love story about a princess and a masked bandit," she answers quickly, turning the page, her eyes skimming the new one already.

"I love those." I smile, closing my eyes. "Is it your first time reading it?"

"It's my first reread," she says nonchalantly. "Do you like to read?"

"I'm not a reader. I think I could be, though. I just haven't found the right book. Maybe you could help me find it."

I crack my eyes open and gaze into hers, the gold in her eyes more pronounced than usual. Those golden flecks remind me of shooting stars.

"I'd like that," she whispers, continuing to avoid my gaze.

It's interesting. During all our exchanges up until now, she's never shied away from meeting my eyes. Tonight, her boldness appears softer.

Suddenly, my eyes feel heavier than cinder blocks. My head feels like a weighted blanket, too. I find myself tipping over like the Leaning Tower of Pisa until my head lands on something soft and warm. I cuddle into the soft spot, reaching my arm over to hold on to it tighter.

I hear a soft gasp followed by the faintest chuckle, so quiet I'm convinced I imagined it. I latch on to that magical sound, committing it to memory before darkness consumes me.

Eleven

Cleo

He snores.

See, I shouldn't know that he snores. I shouldn't know that he mutters in his sleep. I shouldn't know what his touch feels like.

But now I know.

And I have no idea how to feel about it.

Naturally, rather than actively dealing with this, I continue reading my book as if nothing has changed. I was once told I have an avoidant attachment style. I'm starting to think that may be true.

I turn the page, attempting to focus on the story, ignoring his quiet breathing and warm, soft skin entirely.

Sure, I'm no stranger to physical contact, but that doesn't mean I'm keen on it. A touch is a touch, nothing more. I'm practically numb to it. Although this is arguably more innocent than the sensual interactions I've had before, it's *torturous.*

I should've kicked him out of my office when he was still upright.

What was I thinking? Inviting him to sit with me? Has my sanity gotten that far away from me now? *Why* do I continue to compromise my standards for this man?

Suddenly, he buries his head deeper into my waist and wraps his arm—somehow even more sculpted than I expected—around me tighter, pulling me against him. My body jerks away instinctually at first, but then involuntarily leans into his. It's more comfortable leaning into him than the armrest at the moment, that's all.

I continue reading, absorbing the story as much as possible, when my eyes grow heavy. I rub them and press on. I've grown used to the weariness.

No matter what I do or where I go, I never seem to get a solid night's sleep. Sleeping in my haven is a pain; the afterlife is supposed to be peaceful, but at night, it's anything but. When I can't fall asleep there, I often walk to my office. The loveseat isn't nearly as comfortable as my bed, and the pillow is worn out, but it's better suited for someone like me.

I'm exhausted. So damn exhausted.

I thought angels weren't supposed to tire this easily, but I'm an anomaly, I guess. I'm sure that watching all my troublesome Guardians has worn me out over the years. I smile to myself before remembering.

They aren't your Guardians anymore.

You have no one.

It's what you deserve.

I abruptly close the book and rub my temples in response to the voice taunting me from within.

It's true, though—this *is* what I deserve.

Being a Watcher was fulfilling for a while, but that fulfillment was never meant to last. I was the catalyst for my own demise.

A nose nuzzles into my side, and I allow myself to sneak a glimpse down at him. His full lips are parted, breath hot and steady on my waist. His long, dark eyelashes nearly touch his cheeks, and up this close, I can see a faded mole near his nose. A thick lock of tousled light brown—almost blond—hair falls on his forehead, just above his full eyebrows. His face, completed with a sharp jawline and high cheekbones, appears calm.

Fine. I'll admit it. He is objectively a striking man.

He's even sort of… beautiful, in a way.

But he's maddening.

My eyes linger on his resting face a tad longer than necessary before my lids lightly flutter shut, giving into the siren-like call of sleep.

Then, and only then, do I let my body fold into his fully, choosing to ignore the way my arm drapes around his back and how my body molds into his so well.

Something jagged pushes into my side, abruptly waking me. I drowsily blink open my eyes, slowly noting a bright beam of sunlight pouring in through my window, which shines on my desk and books.

Great. I overslept.

However, I did manage to sleep through the rest of the night—a miracle in itself.

My hand inches over to my side to identify the culprit stabbing me, gasping sharply upon detecting its edges.

Kai jolts awake after I gasp, placing his arm over me defensively, quickly glancing in all directions.

"What is it?" he asks, maintaining a protective stance. Goodness, he must have grown too used to guarding his sister. I push his arm off me.

"*My book.*" I yank it out from underneath my side, holding it up and inspecting it, sitting entirely upright.

The hardcover book is undoubtedly unsalvageable.

Spine, cracked. Pages, torn. Cover, bent.

This might be my breaking point.

I keep my book collection in immaculate shape, meticulously inspecting it every month for any signs of wear and tear—hoping they'll never reach the same state as those in the archives.

I've collected novels from the library for years. Anytime Guardians bring back new books, I scour the stock, selecting only a handful of romance and fantasy novels for my own collection.

I'd been saving this particular reread for a bad time, and this week was, well, you know, arguably one of the worst I've had since setting foot into Eloras.

How could I be so careless?

"Here, let me take a look at it." He reaches for it, eyeing me.

"It's no use. It's ruined," I mutter, staring off. "You know, maybe it's symbolic. It's a metaphor for my afterlife."

He looks at the book closely, handling it gently in his large hands. "Yep, it's ruined. Guess you won't be needing it anymore, huh?"

He says this like it's no big deal, and to someone like him, losing a book means nothing. For me, though, it's yet another thing to let go of. My dad is the person who introduced me to this book. My shoulders slump just a bit. "Guess not."

"Here, I can take it off your hands," he says, tucking it into his side and rising from the couch. "Time for work."

His tone is far too chipper for my liking, especially considering we're gearing up to work together on a Saturday. Another perk of being a Watcher was working only weekdays and then only when my tethers alerted me on weekends, so I often had a fair amount of time off on weekends. The library, however, surprisingly requires its staff every single damn day.

If we need a day off, Hadley will grant it—this is the Middle Realm, not a prison. Otherwise, though, we work daily.

He strides to the door, reaching for the knob.

"You go on ahead. I'll be late today," I say, despite not having moved an inch. He turns to look at me.

"About last night..." He scratches his head and sighs. "I got carried away with the alcomist stuff. I shouldn't have ambushed your night in. That wasn't fair of me. Honestly, I hardly even remember what happened last night."

Good. I'm elated he doesn't remember.

"Don't worry about it. I expected as much." I grin sweetly, and his brows furrow.

"What's that supposed to mean? Believe what you may, but stumbling into your office drunk out of my mind was not on my bingo card," he grunts. I don't quite understand the bingo reference, but I choose to ignore it, shrugging nonchalantly. "Your indifference drives me wild, Cleo."

Cleo. That's the first time he's called me by my name since we met.

Something in my chest awakens at the sound of my name coming from his lips.

"And your impulsiveness drives me wild, but here we are," I say, rising from the couch and crossing the room toward my large cabinet, opening its doors to pull out a set of loose-fitting athleisure from one of the shelves.

"Here we are," he says, his eyes flashing to the cabinet. He quirks his chin at it. "So, does every Watcher have a portable closet in their office?"

I quickly shut its doors, realizing I've shown him far more than I intended.

"It's not a closet, it's a cabinet. I just store some backup clothes in the rare case that nights like last night occur. If you'll excuse me, I need to change."

He nods his head once, opening the door and finally leaving with my battered book in the crook of his arm.

I exhale a sigh of relief and change into my stretchwear set. I may be late, but I refuse to skip daily stretches. I'm not a fitness fanatic—I can't remember the last time I even ran for enjoyment, if ever. However, I do take stretching seriously. I find stretching my body daily is a solid way to reset after particularly stressful times. It's a habit I formed in my life before death.

Sports haven't ever come naturally for me. During my youth, back in the '70s, I tried several—volleyball, softball, tennis. I gave them my all and never failed to come up short in any of them. The truth of the matter is, I lacked hand-eye coordination, grew flustered when the ball landed in my hands, and had the tendency to fumble embarrassingly often. I trusted in the process, though, hoping I'd eventually discover the sport I was destined to play. As the years passed, I pushed myself through the humiliation, deciding that my tennis skills, although minimal, were enough to get me through.

As I grew older and entered my teenage years, my range of passions widened. I took an interest in the arts, growing especially fond of music. During high school, I enrolled in social dance classes and used every excuse I could to go out dancing with friends. As time passed, I chose to spend extra time refining the dance moves I'd learned from the comfort of my home, using my younger brother's latest Panasonic stereo. My siblings got onto me for hogging the radio, but I couldn't help it—dancing to music called to me in a way no other physical activity had up until that point.

Nimble and light on my feet, I gained a fair amount of attention for my dancing—both welcome and unwelcome attention. I don't care much for the spotlight, but the feeling of dancing under a disco ball surrounded by other free-spirited dancers and some of my closest friends was out of this world. I didn't care about how many eyes were on me, because in those moments, nothing mattered more than the harmonies of the music.

Many didn't classify dance as a sport at that time, but I unapologetically treated it like one. Eventually, I dropped out of tennis and chose to make dancing my preferred sport.

I mean, have you ever danced for three hours straight? No one can deny it's a workout, and if they do, they're full of it. Hearing that dance is considered a sport in the land below nowadays makes me so ridiculously happy.

It's been a long time since I gave myself to music in the way I once did. I've attended a few parties since joining Eloras, but music hasn't brought me the same sense of belonging as it did before. I still prioritize stretching the same way as I did back then, though. I've stretched nearly every day for several years.

At this point, I don't stretch to perfect my body. My physical body is in the best state it's ever been, thanks to you know, *dying*. I stretch to find relief.

After the morning I've had, relief is much needed.

I pull out my cloud matt—a weightless matt that feels like a layer of cotton—from under my desk, placing it parallel to my couch on the floor. Stepping onto it, my toes curl into the airy fluff, molding into it. I close my eyes and begin a consolidated stretch routine for today, starting with the basics—touching my toes.

My wings make it all too easy to topple over, so I focus on maintaining balance, pushing them outward and stretching them wide as I bend. I could tuck them away, which would make my stretches notably easier, but I don't mind the challenge.

In fact, I welcome it.

Twelve

Kai

We slept together a week ago. It's a good thing that angels don't *have* to sleep every night because I haven't slept a wink since. It's been ages since I shared a bed—or couch, for that matter—with anyone.

The other day while removing countless books from the shelves and placing them into sections based on chronological order, I cracked a joke about our night together. Cleo didn't laugh like I'd hoped she would.

Honestly, she's hardly acknowledged me at all recently. She's unlike anyone I've ever known. She comes across as unbothered, but something about her set jaw and perfectly polished appearance tells me there's more to her than meets the eye. She's been quieter since our evening together, too.

She's one tough cookie.

As satisfying as our evening was for me, something about it didn't sit right with me. I tuck the cloth I've been using to dust the shelves into my back pocket and slide down the ladder to set it on the amethyst table for now, replaying our evening together.

If she happened to fall asleep in her office, why did her pillow appear so battered? My brows knit together as I sort through the books lying on the table, alphabetizing them for now. It couldn't have been the first time she's fallen asleep there, and based on her comfort alone, she seemed well adjusted to sleeping in her office.

Look, I know some people are workaholics—Iris is a prime example. I get it, I really do, but sleeping in your office is a whole new level.

I glance down at the old, crusty book in my hand and shake my head, regaining focus on the task at hand. We've spent days organizing all the archives' books and knick-knacks into separate piles. This morning, we started deep cleaning the shelves we'd emptied.

Riveting, I know.

She insisted we clean every nook and cranny as if Zeus himself would be paying the chamber a visit. After what was an even more grueling process than I anticipated, we're *finally* placing books and items on the shelves.

I'm handling the upper half, while she takes on the lower. Despite taking on the lower half of the shelves, she often flies to reach some of the taller shelves, clearly double-checking my work. Her wings tread the air as she thoroughly dusts each book before placing it on the shelf. The way her midnight-blue wings glisten subtly in this dimly lit chamber takes my breath away.

I've seen all sorts of wings in the Middle Realm now, but I'd be lying if I said hers weren't my favorite.

While gazing from afar, I get lost in her. Wearing a short, flutter-sleeved black dress that tightens around her waist and flares at the ends and combat boots today, she reminds me of a dark, ethereal fairy.

"Daydreaming again?" Her voice cuts through my thoughts.

Oh, wow. That's the first time she spoke to me today. Pinch me. I must be dreaming.

She continues sliding tomes on the shelf, mid-air, not even sparing me a passing glance.

"Cleo, were you *watching* me?" I accuse her, cocking an eyebrow and smirking. "I'm flattered."

She halts and abruptly spins to face me, her pretty wings still hovering behind her. "Oh, the sooner you finish your section, the sooner we can leave. That's all."

"*Sure*, we can pretend that's the reason you were watching me," I say, my lips curling into a smile.

Her brows furrow, and she scowls a little bit, her cheeks slightly reddening under my gaze—one of my favorite looks of hers.

I nod my chin at the shelf behind her. "Here, why don't you leave early? I can finish up that row you're working on."

She raises a brow skeptically, allowing her wings to lower her to the ground slowly, still holding a book. She looks up at me and asks, "Why?"

This girl.

"Do you always question people's motives like this?" I sigh in exasperation. "It's just a nice gesture. Nothing too crazy. I promise."

She narrows her eyes. "Fine. I guess I'll leave, and you can do the rest of that top shelf. Just make sure to dust off the books before placing them."

I bite back a smile at her demands. I love it when she bosses me around like this.

"With all due respect, angel, this isn't my first rodeo. I've done several shelves, and as *surprising* as it may be, I've actually dusted off every single book already. Twice." I smile and grab the book she's holding. Then, I grasp her shoulder gently and turn her to face the archives' exit, carefully avoiding her wings. "Go. Enjoy some free time and read a book or something. You deserve the break."

As I breathe out the last words of that sentence, her shoulders tense. Sensing resistance, I hook my free arm around her neck and walk her to the exit myself.

"Kai, it's fine. I don't really de—"

"Nope, not today," I grumble, turning and covering her mouth mid-sentence. Her eyes widen as my hand remains clamped over her mouth, and a chuckle slips out of my mouth before I can stop it. Once we reach the exit, I shove her out playfully and close the doors behind her, waving as they shut.

I catch a look of surprise in her almond-shaped brown eyes and bask in it.

I love throwing her off-kilter. It never lasts longer than a couple of seconds, and it tends to take more effort than anticipated, but those mere seconds are worth it.

I walk back to the ladder and the stack of books Cleo left behind for me, then get to work. The sooner I complete this shelf, the sooner I can get to my secret project.

Between random parties and working in the library, I don't have much to look forward to these days, so this project has been a game changer. Rather than wallowing in self-pity, I've been channeling my energy into something meaningful like this instead.

Partying in the afterlife hasn't been as fulfilling as I'd hoped, either. I've met *tons* of new people. I'm an extrovert through and through, so I love a good crowd, but some of these angels are *very* forward, which I'm *not* as into.

After completing the top shelf, I slide down the ladder and roll it to the opposite end of the shelves, then climb to the top shelf again. I reach all the way into it, scooting ancient books aside to unveil my hidden project and supplies.

I gently pull out the battered book, loose pages, glue, cardboard, brushes, cardstock, needle and thread, scissors, book cloth, and headband. I've gotten about halfway through this project thanks to Hadley's enthusiastic help, and I'm determined to put all my free time into it until it's done. Unfortunately, I haven't had much time to work on it this week at all, though.

Carefully holding my stack of materials in one hand and keeping my other on the ladder, I step down and let out a long exhale. This would be *significantly* easier with wings.

Upon reaching the bottom, an angel pops into the room. Teleportation is so sick.

"I just saw her leave. Is it time for our next phase of this project?" Hadley grabs the glue and scissors from my hands, leaving me with just about everything else. Today, she's wearing a pink peplum dress—it matches her white wings nicely. "Ah, I've been so darn excited to see this next phase; it's all starting to come together so nicely."

"It was a good idea for us to rebind a different book for practice first," I reply with a smile. "I appreciate your help."

"The pleasure is mine! That girl deserves a pick-me-up. She fashions a scowl more frequently than a grumpy house cat." She shakes her head, setting the scissors and glue atop the table alongside the book press from downstairs. "What would you like assistance with today?"

I scan the supplies, mentally planning how to execute today's portion of the project. Remembering the way Hadley talked my ear off the last time we worked on this, I scratch the back of my head. I know I'm a yapper, but she is like a super yapper. "You know, I think I've got it handled for today. I want to see how far I can get on my own this time."

She beams, nodding quickly. "Of course—the more *you* own this project, the more it'll mean." She pats her dress, backing away from the round amethyst table. "Just let me know if you need any pointers. I'll keep the angels out of the archives for the next couple of hours."

She tosses me a wink on her way out.

Ah, yes. The regulars who can't help but visit the archives every single time Cleo is absent. Despite the chamber obviously being in shambles, several angels tend to find different excuses to venture up to the archives.

"Kai, can you grab that book off the top shelf for me?"

Yes, it's not like you can fly or anything. Of course.

They're all objectively pretty, but I only have space for one angel in my mind at the moment. And that angel has been extra somber recently. She's not the only one around here who feels that way, though, that's for sure. The more time I waste away in this library, the more stir-crazy I get. I wonder if others understand this struggle, too.

Or maybe, it really is just me. I might be completely alone.

Sighing, I place the text block into the book press, tightening the press's screws to push both boards together.

Look at me, using the term "text block" casually. Grinning, I stop tightening the screws and place my secret project on the table. I didn't even know a term for an unbound manuscript existed until this week.

I guess this project isn't technically classified as a secret, seeing as several angels have drifted in and out of the archives over the past several days, catching me red-handed... Eh, I don't particularly care. As long as Cleo doesn't find out about it, that is.

I dab a paintbrush into the glue jar and fervently glaze the glue over the text block's spine. The last time I worked on this, I finished adding the endpapers to the book. Today, I'm adding a silky ribbon bookmark to it.

While spreading the glue across the spine, my mind wanders back to the high school where I worked. The art teacher is Iris's best friend, so I occasionally helped her with crafts for her students. As obnoxious as my students were sometimes, they often could make my day ten times brighter than it was. I've missed my students and baseball team more than usual lately.

I may have only been a baseball coach for five years, but I played the sport for over a decade as a pitcher, constantly in the company of others. I was lucky—I never had to experience true loneliness in my mortal life. From spending time with friends, teammates, coaches, students, my sister, and my ex-girlfriend, I hardly ever spent time alone. I found a sense of purpose in being a companion for others.

And this is why I *never* wanted to work in this old damn library. The solitude, isolation, sensation of being perpetually stuck—it's all messing with my head. I knew it would. I'd bet a million dollars that the Archangels knew it would, too, hence why they sentenced me to work here instead of banishing me.

What I'd give to experience life on Earth again. I miss it so much.

If I weren't already dead, I'd kindly ask you to put me out of my misery.

The only problem is, even if someone were to end this for me, I still wouldn't end up back in the mortal land. I'd probably end up right back here, offered the ability to choose between being a Guardian or immediate ascension again. You know the drill.

I tried to escape the other night. I exerted all my might in a feeble attempt to teleport down to the land below. Instead, all I received in return was a spine-tingling headache. Despite the pain, I pushed even harder, determined to teleport. It proved to be entirely pointless. My probation ring kept me rooted to the same exact spot.

I set the brush down and rub my temples, closing my eyes and taking a deep breath.

Just finish this project, Kai. Do it for her.

Well, it's easier said than done, subconscious.

Thirteen

Kai

A little over an hour later, I hide the supplies behind all the items on the top shelf again. Filled with pride about how much I accomplished within only an hour, I descend the staircase beyond the archives' doors with a hop in my step. A beam of bright moonlight pours into the library through the tall windows lining the walls.

Walking alongside the full shelves, I nod at Hadley, who's seated at the circular information desk on my way out, when I notice someone curled up in a small window-side book nook, tucked beneath a fluffy light blue blanket.

The library contains a large variety of thick blankets and pillows for visitors to borrow in an armoire tucked away in the same corner where the staircase leading to the archives resides. I haven't had to help guests much.

I've been completely locked away in the archives, awaiting a fair maiden to rescue me from my torment. I smirk at my own joke, striding toward Cleo and calling out, "What are you reading now?"

She peeks at me from behind the pages. "A classic fantasy this time. It's about a man who spends a decade trying to get back home after a war."

Taken aback by her actually acknowledging me, I think fast. I've got to take advantage of chatty Cleo while she's with us. "Ah, if only teleportation were a thing for mortals. You know what, I bet he didn't have a Guardian looking out for him. Shame, really."

"You might be right." She closes her book, and her lips curl into a small smile. "How did the rest of the workday go? You were up there longer than I expected."

Does she know? She doesn't know, right? How would she know? I mean, I guess if she floated up to the doorway and peeked in through the small stained-glass window on the archives' doors, she could've—

"Hey, is everything okay?" She sits up straighter, planting her full attention on me, brows drawn. This is new. Is she worried? Oh no, I'm worrying her because I still haven't answered her damn question. What the—

She snaps her fingers impatiently.

Guess I lose my way when it comes to her.

"Sorry, got caught up in a train of thought and spiraled for a second. I'm good." I nod hastily. "Just got ahead for tomorrow; started dusting off some extra books. Got through a couple of dozens."

"Right... Wow. A couple of dozens? That's a lot."

Uh-oh. She's right. That is a lot. I only did like ten extra books, but my desperate need to hide my secret project has me sweating. I make a mental note to show up to work extra early tomorrow to *actually* get ahead.

"Oh, don't act so surprised." I shake my head and cross my arms, leaning against a nearby bookshelf when a bright idea crosses my mind. "What are you up to right now?"

She raises her thick eyebrows. "Reading. Obviously."

My mouth stretches into a mischievous grin as I reach over and hold out my hand. "Wrong answer. You're going on a walk with me. C'mon, you've already closed your book and everything."

She eyes me, then her book. "Fine," she says, sighing tiredly and taking my hand.

I like the way her small, soft hand fits into mine. I pull her up from the nook and tug her out of the library, a wave of energy funneling through me.

She doesn't know it yet, but she may or may not have just agreed to our first date.

We walk down a couple of different staircases all the way to the foyer. On our way down, several angels greet me friendlily and stare at Cleo hesitantly. For every angel who greets me, she gets twice the number of stares from men and women alike.

I don't know if she has the slightest clue how beautiful she is. All other angels pale in comparison.

We exit the building and walk in comfortable silence for a couple of minutes, pausing on the bridge that connects the headquarters to our marketplace and living quarters. I lean against the bridge's golden rails and overlook the shimmering clouds above and below us. They're everywhere.

"I've gotta ask." I break the silence, still gazing off into the clouds. "Do you ever visit the land below for leisure?"

She leans her back on the railing next to me, her wings resting just over the edge. Instead of facing the clouds surrounding us, she crosses her arms and locks her eyes on the pavement. "No."

"Never would've guessed." Surprised, but also not surprised by her answer, I push for more. "Why not? Don't you ever miss it?"

"No one has ever asked me about this before," she says, her voice trailing off. "I have my reasons for not visiting. I've been there several times to intervene when my Guardians were on the verge of breaking divine laws, but I never stayed longer than necessary. Why would I venture down there when I have everything I need up here?"

"But do you miss it?" I nudge her with my elbow.

She pauses, pressing her lips together in a tight smile. "Sure, I miss certain aspects... Like the feeling of rain on my skin and the smell of freshly baked cookies. But collectively? I don't suppose I miss the land below."

"What about your life?"

"You ask a lot of questions." She pins me with intensity in her gaze.

"Sorry, runs in the family." I click my tongue and grin. "It's fine. I don't want to pressure you to share more than you're comfortable with. I just so happen to be an oversharer, so I'll share a secret with you. Sometimes—more often than not—I wish I was still a mortal, living my simple life down there. I miss life. A lot."

Her gaze softens. "I don't think you're the only one. I'm sure your wings and ascension would take some of the weight off your shoulders. The Archangels talk a big game, but your sentence won't last forever. I feel it. You're a good being, Kai. A *truly* good being."

For the first time since dying, I feel alive.

It's been ages since I felt seen.

And to be seen by her is something I don't take lightly.

"Thank you, angel," I whisper, gazing into her eyes earnestly. "I needed that."

"Of course," she breathes, her throat bobbing.

My eyes drop to her lips. I didn't realize how close our faces were until this moment.

Well, *maybe* I realized it. But I ignored it, assuming it was my imagination.

I inch closer to her, continuing to pierce her eyes with my own when suddenly, she breaks away, stepping aside abruptly. "I can't believe Stephen barged into the throne room like that. I genuinely believe you would've earned your wings and ascended that very evening if it weren't for his childish antics."

Great. I'd love nothing more than to talk about that dumbass right now.

I push my hands through my hair and let out a chuckle, folding my arms. "He's a real idiot, but I can't say I'm surprised. I felt like that trial was going a little too well. It was only a matter of time, you know?"

"Well, your ability to charm others is impressive," she admits, running her hands down her little black dress, then resting them on her waist. My eyes linger there. "Even the Archangels were enamored with you. Except Nial, but that's no surprise."

That dress is driving me crazy.

I jump back into our conversation, unable to hold back my next question. "What's your deal with Stephen anyway?"

"What do you mean?"

"There's obviously more to your relationship than meets the eye," I say. "Did you use to be friends, or...?"

"Ah, *friends*..." she mutters. "We were friends for a long time. Rather than blossoming into something greater, that friendship wilted."

"Hmm..." I knit my brows, attempting to decipher the meaning behind her sentiments. "So. You were friends with benefits?"

She chokes, coughing a bit. A laugh bursts out of me in response. "It's fine, Cleo. I don't know what life was like back when you were alive, but friends with benefits are pretty common down below now."

Her eyes widen. "It's not scandalous anymore?"

"Oh, it's still a *little* scandalous. It's just more accepted now than it was before." I pause, suppressing a smile. "You know those romance books you love so much? Yeah, well, those have gotten a *lot* spicier over the last few decades. Some authors even write books about friends-with-benefits relationships blossoming into something greater, kind of like what you mentioned."

She gawks, her eyes flickering from side to side, obviously trying to wrap her head around all this. "'Spicier.' Explain that."

"Romance authors often go to great lengths to provide vivid details, making sensual acts in their books highly immersive experiences for romance readers." I inch closer to her and speak in a low voice, right into her ear. "Those types of novels include *actual* fucking. Moans, groans, touches, and all."

She gulps but doesn't back away. "You seem to know an awful lot about spicy novels."

I sink my head into her neck for a second, letting out another laugh, then back up, raising my hands in defeat. "You caught me. My ex-girlfriend used to read them—she wasn't a big reader, but when she did read, spicy romance novels were her favorites. She explained spice to me."

Her eyes flicker at the mention of my ex-girlfriend, then she clears her throat.

"Well, thanks for the explanation. Considering I haven't spent much time down there since passing, I didn't realize that genre developed into something more. I haven't read any of those up in the library before," she says, her lips curling into a subtle smirk. "Those novels sound like my cup of tea."

Now, *I'm* the one gulping.

Heavens. This girl.

The sound of live music catches my attention. Who knows how long that's been playing? I've been too busy trying to keep up with her.

"Looks like there's another party tonight," I comment, squinting my eyes over at the atrium from up here, noticing gleaming beams of light shining upward into the star-filled sky from that very spot. Suddenly, I get yet another bright idea. "Hey, we never finished our chat about Stephen, but let me take a wild guess. You both started hooking up, his feelings for you grew into something more, and yours didn't—because you're incapable, of course."

Her jaw drops as she punches my arm and shakes her head. After another intake of air, she shrugs. "Something like that, yeah."

"Perfect. That makes my plan for tonight even better." I push off the railing and wrap my arm around her shoulders, avoiding her perfect wings as usual. "He never misses a party. I'm willing to bet he'll be there tonight. Let's go make some noise."

At first, she resists my pull, keeping her feet firmly planted in one spot. "*Ugh*. I'm too old for games like this."

"Says who?" I challenge her. "You said it yourself. Stephen is the real reason why we're in this mess, so we're simply evening out the playing field. I don't know if you're aware, but I used to be a coach. I'm all about fair play, angel."

"Hmm, yes. I know you were a coach. I take it upon myself to learn as much about my Guardians as possible before taking them on," she says casually as I lead her to the square across the bridge. "Well, I *used* to."

"You must miss your Guardians," I say, realizing yet again how hard this transition has probably been for her.

"I do." She allows me to guide her down the bridge.

I don't miss how much easier it is for her to admit to missing her Guardians than the land below.

"Let's take your mind off all your worries tonight. You deserve a little break."

I search her eyes, hoping she'll say yes this time. She peers back into mine, squinting as though in deep thought.

"I need to change first. I refuse to show up to a party in this." She gestures to the little black dress I love so much.

"Oh, yeah, you better hop to it. You look *horrid*," I tease.

She drops her jaw as I wink at her. I keep my arm draped around her the entire path to the havens.

FOURTEEN

CLEO

Kai has no idea this is the first party I've attended in years—so many years, I've lost count.

I mean, how was he supposed to know? I didn't push back nearly hard enough. I practically handed him a leash and obeyed.

So unlike me. So damn unlike me.

I gaze at my reflection in the mirror and take a deep breath, readying myself for tonight. There's a chance that Stephen will be there. Actually, I'm confident he will be—he hardly ever misses a party. When he and I were an item, I almost always opted to skip parties, which bothered him a lot.

I pat my dress, focusing on the way the rhinestones feel against my fingertips. I'm sporting a silver dress covered in microscopic reflective crystals with a classic A-line silhouette. The dress molds against my upper half, framing my breasts and waist nicely, and fans out beyond my waist, ending mid-thigh, complete with a silver silk ribbon threaded around my arms.

I picked it up several months back at the clothing shop in the marketplace, Celeste's, using my monthly allowance from the Archangels. The sparkling gown reminded me of a disco ball, and embracing a sense of nostalgia, I chose to splurge on it. Despite not knowing when I'd wear it, I couldn't leave it behind.

This dress was meant to be worn by a girl who once loved the disco.

After applying a minimal amount of makeup—blush and lip gloss—I meet with Kai outside my haven's building.

He doesn't say a single thing about my appearance.

Not that I expect him to or anything.

During our stroll to the party, I keep my head held high, not shying away from onlookers. He has only lived full-time in the Middle Realm for a dozen days, and he has already gained a ridiculous amount of attention. It's unprecedented.

Just before entering the atrium, he pulls me aside to a white brick wall bordering the courtyard, caging me in with one of his arms. With his free hand, he lifts my chin. I unintentionally shudder beneath his touch.

"Follow my lead for once, okay? Don't overthink it. We're getting back at him tonight, no matter what it costs us," he says with a sly smile. I open my mouth to protest when he presses his fingers against my lips, shushing me. The sheer audacity of this man is unparalleled. "Just pretend?"

His eyes drop to my lips and linger there.

Little does he know, I've never been good at pretending.

I stare at him, not immensely enjoying the idea of following his lead, but nod soberly, nonetheless. His hazel eyes meet mine. I sigh and begrudgingly give in.

His mouth breaks into an easy smile as my cheeks grow warm.

It's just harmless flirting—it's not like this is new to me. I used to do it all the time. How hard can pretending be?

"Great. Let's go, baby," he says, grabbing hold of my hand and leading me into the outdoor atrium.

Baby.

Baby?

He can't be serious.

I'm *older*. If anyone's the baby here, it's him.

Oh, wait. He's not serious—my mistake.

I'm already falling behind, and I *dread* falling behind.

My grip on his hand tightens subconsciously as we venture into the party, ensuring I don't physically fall behind and get lost in the crowd.

Ugh. I detest crowds like this. Why did I entertain this plan? I could be reading from the comfort of my cozy office couch right now, but instead, I'm gallivanting among a sea of loud strangers.

A golden-haired angel has already shoved a glass of alcomist into Kai's free hand and regarded me with a bit of a pout, obviously perturbed at the sight of me with him.

I can't say that I blame her. As much as I dread admitting it, he's showstopping. With his white button-down and camel trousers, he appears even more refined than usual. His top two buttons are undone, too. His sense of style is better than I thought it was while serving as his Watcher.

He must've picked up a tip or two from his sister.

I mean, while serving as a Guardian, he hardly changed his clothes—not that he really had to worry about his wardrobe while serving. Only a handful of souls could see him, and angels don't sweat unless they're severely weak or in pain, like when I shoved that ring on his finger.

The thought of his pained expression from earlier makes my heart stir uncomfortably.

He inhales his glass of alcomist while sauntering, striding in with all the confidence in the world. Multiple angels greet him, patting him on the back and grinning widely. He takes time to greet every single person kindly, not releasing my hand for even a second.

"Having fun?" He bends, his voice a gentle rasp in my ear.

"Define 'fun.'"

I gaze up at the platform to get a closer look at the live winged band. Complete with a guitarist, pianist, percussionist, and a male and female singer, it's a whole team. Their music isn't half bad. I find myself bopping my head to the rhythm of the beat subconsciously.

I glance around at the angels surrounding us. Looks like Matt and his girlfriend found us. He grins widely, saying, "Kai, you must be gifted. This one"—he gestures to me—"hasn't attended a party up here in *ages*."

Kai gazes at me, smirking. "Oh, is that so?"

I deadpan, "Sure, it's been a while."

"I'm just glad to see you out, Cleo," Matt says warmly. I smile softly at him in return. "So, are you two...?"

He wiggles his eyebrows.

I fight the urge to shake my head. I look up at Kai adoringly and let go of his hand to wrap my arm around his waist instead, fully committed to the act at this point.

Odd. I didn't expect his waist to feel so... solid. "It's new."

He gazes down at me, a subtle look of confusion crossing his features, then hooks his arm around my neck and pulls me in tighter, placing a kiss on my head. "*Very* new."

My stomach drops. I can't tell if the sensation is a good or bad thing—it's never happened before in my afterlife.

He takes another breath of his alcomist, and I glance over my shoulder. I don't spot Stephen, but I know he's here. As Kai said, he never misses a party.

A song I'm familiar with begins to play. I start swaying—only a little bit—to the music when he leans down to breathe in my ear, "Let's dance."

I almost instantly regret swaying my hips, halting the movement at once and shaking my head incessantly. "Oh, I'm actually not much of a dancer."

"With legs like yours? I don't buy it," he says, eyeing my legs and making my cheeks burn simultaneously. "You can't be worse than me. I've only had one glass of alcomist, and I already feel like my right foot has morphed into a left one."

Unable to stifle a laugh, I obnoxiously chuckle, covering my mouth as soon as it escapes me. His eyes light up, drifting back and forth between my eyes and lips.

"Your laugh... It's melodic. More magnetic than my favorite song."

I suddenly feel hot all over as I peer back into his eyes.

He's *pretending.*

We're *pretending.*

Fine. If this is all just a game, I'm going to pretend *exceptionally* well.

Realizing we've spent far too long locked in each other's eyes, I break away and mentally draw a thick line to block out the blurred lines. "To hell with it. Just one dance."

His warm eyes brighten again, a mischievous glint entering his gaze. I walk to the center of the dance floor, holding his hand behind me and leading him. If we're doing this, we're doing it my way. I tuck my wings away, determining that it will make it easier for Kai to dance with me.

Once we reach the center, he pulls me into him playfully, clearly thinking he'll be leading me through this. I smile with my eyes alone and part my lips, allowing my body to connect with the music the way his body's connected with mine.

As the sound vibrates through my body, a surge of energy builds up inside me. My legs move on their own accord, following the song's flow. I lift my feet and begin a routine I haven't done in years, kicking out one leg high and wide and using the other to spin my body. My back presses against his stomach while I crane my neck and lean against him, raising my arms to wrap around his neck loosely and swaying my hips in perfect rhythm with the song.

He doesn't seem to know how to react. I just feel his breath, hot and heavy, in my ear. At first, he rests his hands on my shoulders. Then he slowly drags them down to reach my waist. He pulls me into him, and in a shocking turn of events, he lifts my body and spins us. Instinctively, I tuck my legs in lightly for a carousel lift, the silk ribbon wrapped around my arms fluttering in the breeze.

I'm floating in the air without even using my wings.

I forgot how incredible it is to soar without wings.

He sets me down and spins me again as I do more footwork and extend my arms, twirling myself. I turn back to face him, clutching on to his neck and staring into his eyes, not missing the heat in his gaze. Then, when I least expect it, he dips me. I lift my toes to the sky and lean into the movement, entirely trusting in him.

Giving myself to him and the music, it's as though I'm breathing again for the first time since dying.

Not a single soul could shatter this moment of serenity.

I don't care who's watching. I don't care that we're pretending. I don't care about the closeness of our faces right now.

Our lips draw nearer and nearer to each other's, and for a moment, the realm fades away into nothing.

The crowd fades.

The stress fades.

The music fades.

"My angel," he murmurs, closing his eyes. His voice fades into a whisper. "You're mesmerizing."

His soft lips nearly brush against mine when the song ends.

"How's that for pretend?" I breathe gently against his lips and lock my gaze onto his, chest heaving.

For a split second, an emotion I can't quite decipher crosses his features, but then he schools his face. Then, he breaks into that lazy smile of his and leans away slowly, still towering over me.

"Okay, Miss 'I'm-horrible-at-dancing.' You've got some explaining to do. Also, I don't know if you noticed during your dance number, but Stephen is seething."

He turns me to face tonight's victim, who is, indeed, *seething*. Stephen stalks toward us.

"What the hell are you doing here with *him*?" he asks, stepping into my personal space. I open my mouth to respond when I'm interrupted by the man still holding me in his arms.

"I don't think I like your tone, big guy," Kai drawls, tightening his hold on my waist.

"You think I give a fuck what you like or don't like?" He sneers, eyeing Kai.

"You may not care about what I think, but you and I both know you care a hell of a lot about what she thinks," Kai speaks in a low, domineering voice. "So, why don't you do us both a solid and stop being so *damn* dramatic. I'm growing tired of your theatrics."

They stand face-to-face, eyes locked on each other. Something about his voice's low warning tone and unyielding embrace makes my heart dip.

But I refuse to sit on the sidelines while others fight battles for me.

"You've already single-handedly destroyed everything I've worked toward. What else could you possibly want?" Stephen snaps out of his staring contest with Kai—something tells me Kai won—and peers at me. I register a softness in his ebony-eyed gaze I haven't seen in years.

Years ago, we would've had a nice, long chat to work things out.

We're past that.

Have you ever lost a friend? A real, true friend? I've lost many.

More often than not, friendships don't end overnight. Instead, a plethora of minor hurdles can lead to a friendship's demise.

The bond that was once fundamental to your existence—maybe crucial to your survival, even—simply fades into dust.

That wasn't how my friendship with Stephen ended. Our friendship *did* end overnight, roughly a year ago. One evening, after a long day of work, he walked me to my haven in silence, which wasn't normal for him. At the time, we'd been friends for years, but we hadn't been hooking up for long. It'd only been a handful of weeks, and we promised each other feelings wouldn't be involved.

"Everything okay?" I asked casually as we approached my door. He furrowed his brows and sighed.

"Mind if I come in?"

"Sure."

We stepped inside my quaint unit, then he crossed his arms. "I like you. I have for a while. Why don't we give ourselves a fair shot? Don't we owe it to ourselves to find happiness?"

Immediately upon hearing those words, I shut down. "No."

"No?"

"No." I shook my head and fixed my gaze on his leather shoes. "Sorry, Stephen. You deserve that, but you won't find it with me."

I couldn't give him any further explanation at the time. I offered to stay friends, but he declined, emphasizing that staying close would be too hard. Even if I did want to go there with him, I couldn't. I *wouldn't.*

From then on, we were colleagues in the Watchers division. Nothing more, nothing less.

I think he resents me for the choice I made, and in his resentment, he's hardened his outer shell more and more ever since. He can't understand how our situation didn't lead me to fall for him in the way he started to fall for me. We still work together, so we're mostly cordial, but lately, he's held more anger in his gaze than ever—especially after Kai strolled into my life.

You'd think that over time, losing friends would grow easier, less painful. That simply isn't the case.

"Walk away." I press my lips into a straight line, holding his gaze and communicating with my eyes alone. He presses his tongue against his cheek and nods, then stomps away.

I don't suppose I pity him. I pity the man he used to be. The old Stephen would be so disheartened to see himself now.

Filled with sufficient satisfaction and high on adrenaline, I spin toward Kai again, allowing my wings to unfurl. "Want to do something that will really get people talking?"

"Baby, everyone is already talking about you. Look around." He nods his chin at the crowd gaping and gawking at us.

There's that name again.

"Okay, fair. But how about a grand finale?" I beam. I haven't been this giddy in literal decades. I'm addicted to the thrill of it.

"Let's do it," he answers, smiling widely and reaching for my waist again. He's been touching me *all* night, and I honestly haven't hated it, which is yet another abnormality about my relationship with him. He's too good at faking.

"Hold on tight." I smile mischievously before tossing my ribbon aside and launching into the air at full speed, Kai holding my waist with a death grip.

"Holy mother of pearl, Cleo!" he shouts against the wind as we soar above the marketplace and head east. "Fuuuuck!"

I laugh uncontrollably as he clings to my waist for dear life.

I'll admit that I didn't consider our size difference before flying, and this is far more challenging than I anticipated. Oops.

I land on the high rooftop of one of the marketplace's shops, surrounded by a sheet of puffy clouds and other golden buildings. The rooftop is lined with an intricate golden railing. Additionally, there are a couple of stone benches here, too. I make sure he lands smoothly before planting my feet on the ground and facing him.

"Cleo… Do you realize that was my first time flying?"

Oh, heavens. I took his flight virginity from him without asking first.

"I'm so sorry." I step toward him. "I shouldn't have done that… I just got carried away with the rush of the moment. I have no idea what came over me; it must have been the music—"

"Hey, hey, hey. No need," he says, grabbing on to my shoulders and reassuring me with a kind smile. "That was mind-blowing. Honestly, I'm glad I got to experience that with you. Who knows if I'll ever get to fly alone anyway?"

I hope he gets his own wings one day. I rest my hand on his arm. "Well, I think we made Stephen sufficiently angry tonight. You're almost too good at pretending."

"Excuse me, *I'm* too good at pretending? You deserve a literal award for the way you acted tonight," he mutters, releasing my shoulders and pushing his hand through his golden waves.

"I'll admit, it was pleasant pretending for the evening. It felt nice not to care." I glance at the stars.

"Where did you learn to dance like that? I could hardly keep up with your fancy footwork," he says while shaking his head and smiling.

I haven't talked about my life before in ages... Something about him makes it too easy to share.

"I used to love dancing. I danced for years and years until I died. In fact, I even danced the night before I died. It's foolish, I know, but dancing has always brought me a sense of belonging and freedom."

"That's not foolish, angel," he murmurs, tucking a strand of loose hair behind my ear. "You were otherworldly. I don't know if I've ever been that awestruck before."

I blush—against my will *again*—and look away. "You don't have to keep pretending, Kai."

"What if I don't want to stop?" He grasps my jaw, cradling it tenderly and stroking my cheek with his thumb. "What if, instead, I want this..."

He rests his hands on my waist and pulls me into him, wrapping his warm arms around me tightly. I peer up at him, my lips parting in surprise. As my lips part, he runs his fingers up my back until they reach my front, landing on my parted lips. A traitorous breath escapes me as his eyes fixate on my lips.

He lifts his eyes to meet mine, then gazes down at me with a knowing glance. Closing his eyes, he lowers his head toward mine until our foreheads meet.

We stand there for a while—foreheads pressed against each other, stars twinkling in the periwinkle sky all around us. Eventually, I give in just a bit and wrap my arms around his neck. Holding him like this just clicks. It's natural. It's odd, but it's as though I'm following the tide instead of swimming against it for the first time in decades.

He releases a long exhale and lifts his head slowly.

Then, with another breath, he places a tender kiss on my forehead.

His lips are soft—unbelievably soft.

FIFTEEN

KAI

Similar to my lips, my hands move of their own accord. One cupping the back of her neck and the other clutching on to her slim waist, gently grazing her wings.

In this moment, I want nothing more than to lift her off her nimble feet and wrap her body around mine.

Suddenly, she pulls away, staring at me with an odd mixture of sheer delight and wariness in her eyes. Taken aback for a second, I stroke her face and take great pleasure in the hint of pink spreading across her cheeks.

"I think I've had enough of our game for tonight. I should head home," she says, nodding to herself. I may be delusional, but it appears she's convincing herself that going home would be for the best. She takes a step back, turning toward the rooftop's edge, presumably to launch back into the air and fly away. "Thank you for tonight, Kai. I had fun."

Fuck. I shouldn't have done that. I misread her.

Puzzled, I tilt my head and realize the last thing I want is for her to leave. I catch up with her, stepping between her and the golden railing. "Wait. Stay with me."

Her eyes beam into mine, laced with uncertainty—odd, considering the Cleo I've grown to know is always so self-assured. "Why?"

"Because *maybe* I've grown to like your company. With or without the kissing."

She regards me for a moment longer, then she releases a sigh, walking to the wide railing and leaning against it. I follow her, then leap over the rail to sit atop it, legs dangling.

While sitting, I get lost in the view of the sky, the headquarters palace, and all the realm's glimmering buildings.

"You know, for someone who doesn't have wings, you aren't afraid to fall," she notes, using her wings to rise over the railing gracefully to join me.

"What's there to be afraid of? I'm already dead. I doubt I'd even feel it."

"Let's not be hasty and test that theory."

I chuckle, craning my neck to face the stars. Just beyond the dome, I can see a subtle sheen of nearly blinding golden light spreading across the sky, highlighting the Golden Realm beyond this realm.

"Do you ever wonder what the Golden Realm is really like?"

"Not particularly, no." She answers far too quickly for my comfort.

"Why not? Don't you want to ascend eventually? I think about the Golden Realm all the time. I think of life in the land of the living a lot, too. Honestly, I think I hate it here."

"I'm so sorry you're having a hard time here." She pauses before continuing, eyes bouncing from one building to another.

"I actually have no intention of ascending anytime soon, if ever. I'm perfectly content with the routine I've cultivated—minus our current predicament, of course." She suppresses a smile and lifts her gaze from the buildings surrounding our new spot to stare blankly at the stars. "Because you're not fond of this place, I don't expect you to understand. That's okay."

"You've got that right," I affirm, gazing at her and breaking into a grin. "You know, I may not understand why you'd want to stay here, but I can respect it."

"And I can respect you wanting to leave."

My traitorous eyes drift down to her gem-speckled silver dress. This short gown molds to her figure a little too well, accentuating her undeniably *perfect* breasts, waist, and legs.

I've had a difficult time keeping my eyes off her all damn night. Especially during our dance.

She entranced me while we danced together. Entirely immersed in the way she glided across the dance floor, I nearly bound myself to her right then. With a hundred sets of eyes on her, she could've easily tanked under their watchful gazes.

Instead, she didn't give a single damn and illuminated brightly under the starry night sky.

All I could think about when I watched her was the stars. Couldn't get them off my mind, actually.

Cleo doesn't simply remind me of the stars.

The stars remind me of her.

She's an enigma. I'm far too invested now not to see this through.

Pretend or not, I'm in.

"Thank you for listening." She disrupts my inner thoughts. *I've got to get a handle on those. Never know when she's listening in...* "So, tell me. Why do you miss the land below so much? This realm is much more peaceful than that one. We still get to experience day and night. We can see the sun, the moon, the stars, and the clouds. We don't have to worry about familial obligations."

It almost sounds like she's trying to convince herself that this realm is better. I scoff and shake my head. "Yeah, sure, this realm is peaceful. But it's *boring* me to death. If I knew I would be working in a damn library in my afterlife, I would've ascended *immediately* upon waking up here."

"No. You wouldn't have," she says matter-of-factly. "You would've never left her to fend for herself."

I click my tongue and nod in defeat. "You got me there."

"It's admirable—the way you care for her. One of the strongest guardianships I've ever watched," she admits.

"Is that why you let me get away with it?"

She glances away from the stars, peering into my eyes. She shrugs a little. "I don't know why I didn't intervene."

"Of course you do," I say nonchalantly. "You're a big softie, and we both know it. No use in hiding it."

"I'm absolutely *not* a 'softie.'" She narrows her eyes and scowls, her eyes burning holes into mine.

"Sure thing, sweetheart. Keep telling yourself that," I tease her, nudging her and whispering, "Your secret's safe with me."

"You're relentless." She rolls her eyes and pinches the bridge of her nose. "And I didn't miss your deflection. You never answered my question."

"What question?" I ask innocently, knowing damn well what, but wanting her to talk more just to listen to the sound of her voice.

She groans and exhales a breath of frustration. "What do you miss most about the land below?"

"Ah. Easy. I miss scenic mountain drives. I miss trying new foods. I miss coaching baseball. I miss annoying my family. I miss my people." I zone out. As images of loved ones cross my mind, my chest physically aches. It's too much. "I miss it all. Even the bad times. I'd give anything to be given another chance to live down there."

A beat of silence passes between us. "It gets lighter over time."

"What does?"

"The weight of it all. Eventually, you won't feel it much at all," she murmurs.

"What if I want to feel it?"

"Why would you want to feel that?"

"Because the depth of my longing correlates with the vitality of those bonds. My pain is a constant reminder of the strength of my love."

Her lips part for a moment before pressing into a firm line. Then, she knits her brows as if trying to solve a jigsaw puzzle. Seconds later, she swings her legs around to the other side of the railing and begins pacing back and forth on the roof, arms crossed.

"What's going on in that head of yours?" I ask, turning then rising to stand on the rooftop, watching her.

"You did a favor for me tonight. It may not have seemed like much to you, but it meant a lot to me," she says aloud reluctantly as if she's confessing her darkest secret. "Consequently, I'll do you a favor to—in your words—'even the playing field.' But I need you to promise me something in return."

"You're speaking in riddles. You don't owe me anything."

"Promise me first," she says, holding out her hand to shake mine.

I eye her hand skeptically, not knowing what the hell is going on.

"Blind promises aren't really my thing..." I say, pushing my hands into my pockets and shrugging.

"You're impossible. So damn impossible." She sighs, then grits her teeth. "Promise me I can trust you."

"Oh, *that's* the promise? Easy-peasy. You can trust me." I smirk, reaching out to shake her hand. Immediately after shaking my hand, she pulls on my finger, attempting to... tug my ring off. After a moment of aggressive tugging, I shrug my shoulders. "Not sure what your goal is here, but I've already tried prying this off. It's no use, angel."

"It should work. It *has* to work. A trace of my magic is embedded in this ring. I don't understand..." She stares at the band, calculating her next move. Her eyes brighten for a second, then darken before she shuts them tight. "You've got to be kidding me."

"What? What is it?" Concern laces my tone.

"Here goes nothing," she grumbles, lifting my pointer finger to her face and planting a gentle kiss on the ring, her eyes shut. In an instant, my knees feel wobbly.

Weak knees over a kiss on my finger? Who am I?

I may be imagining this, but the longer her lips rest on the ring, the more it seems to loosen.

What on earth is she doing?

Why am I in a constant state of confusion in my afterlife?

"Cleo, stop. I don't want you to get in trouble—"

She holds up a finger against my lips, shushing me. After another moment, she breaks away from the ring, gently pulling it off my finger and placing it in my pants' pocket. "What's done is done, Kai. I'm giving you a free pass to visit the land below, but you need to keep this ring in your pocket at all times. You promised me I could trust you. Please don't make me regret this."

Too stunned to speak, I nod in disbelief, lips parted. "Why would you do this for me?"

She shrugs. "Don't overthink it."

I gulp, overcome with an emotion I can't fully decipher. "I promise I'll come back in time for work tomorrow."

"You better." She smirks in that too-cool way of hers, then nods her chin at the sky. "Now, get going before I come to my senses and change my mind."

Before I slip away, I lift her hand to meet my lips. Pretty chivalrous, I know, but she's older than me. I figured this would be the best way to show her my appreciation at the moment.

"And Cleo," I call out, heart thumping. "Words can't describe how ethereal you look tonight."

Her lips part again. She raises a hand to her lips to cover a soft smile before nodding her chin.

"Get out of here and enjoy a sunrise from down below for me."

With that, I take a deep breath and teleport to my real home, starlight consuming my thoughts the entire journey there.

SIXTEEN

CLEO

He's late.

He promised me he'd return to Eloras in time for work. The chiming of a clock echoes around me, signaling the strike of a new hour, and still, no trace of him. As calm and composed as I try to be day in and day out, I'd be drenched if I still could sweat.

Perhaps I misjudged him. Or maybe he let his impulses get the best of him.

I'm assuming that's what happened last night, too. I lift my fingers to my forehead, lightly stroking it, recalling the heated sensation of his lips against me again.

I've been intimate with a decent number of men in my existence. Never have I experienced something like *that.*

I'm convinced we were suspended in time for a moment.

But surely, that can't be the case, because that would mean our game of pretend is one-sided.

And it'd be ridiculous for me to be on the losing side. Utterly ridiculous.

Consequently, I push these thoughts to the back of my mind and declare myself unwell for even considering this moment was anything other than a meaningless act fueled by adrenaline.

Okay, *fine*. It may have been more than that. But that's beside the point. It won't happen again, I'm sure.

Hadley has been breathing down my neck about Kai's whereabouts. Apparently, the Archangels tasked her with making sure we appear at work daily unless we give her notice otherwise. Not to mention, she's monitored me since I entered the archives, insisting on helping with sorting through the highest shelves in his absence.

Usually, I'd find this type of behavior odd, but because it's coming from Hadley, I'm not remotely concerned. I've known her for quite a while, and she's always had her quirks.

"When will Kai be coming in again?" she calls out from above, hovering in front of the top bookshelf with a feather duster. I'm almost positive Kai has already dusted that shelf, but alas. No point in correcting her.

"For the fifth time, we had a long night," I answer. "I imagine he is still sleeping—"

"Fat chance," a voice drawls from the entrance. Kai saunters deeper into the room, draping his arm around my shoulders. "He's totally a morning person. He never oversleeps."

Ignoring the butterflies swarming in my stomach, I glance up at him. "Oh, is that so? Then, pray tell, where were you this morning?"

"I went on a jog." He shrugs, then nods his chin at her. "I had a feeling you'd hold the fort down in my absence, Hadley. I owe you."

She smiles widely and descends, planting her feet on the ground in front of us and eyeing the way Kai's arm is resting over my shoulders. I roll my eyes and set down the book I was holding, crossing my arms.

"Glad you arrived! But please don't be late again. I wouldn't want to have to report your tardiness to the Archangels... They gave me specific instructions when assigning you to labor under my supervision."

He uses his free hand to salute warmly. "Got it, captain."

She laughs a little too loudly. "I took care of the top shelf for you, too. She kept her feet on the ground in your absence."

"Oh, good. Can't have her overworking those pretty wings of hers, can we?" His lips curl into a smile as a knowing look I don't particularly favor passes between them.

Do they think I'm blind? Since when do they have inside jokes?

"We're speaking the same language," she says, nodding and closing her eyes in contentment. "Well, I'll let you two get back to it! You've made stellar progress so far. I imagine you'll finish this vast chamber by the end of next week at the rate you're working at."

She prances out of the archives, shutting the doors behind her.

Once I'm sure she's out of earshot, I peel away from Kai and punch his arm.

Ouch. Something tells me that hurt me more than it hurt him.

Refusing to show a shred of weakness in my expression, I stare at him square in the eyes. "A *jog*? Really? That's the story you're going with?"

"What? I'm not lying. I did go on a jog." He crosses his arms while sporting a smug expression.

I knew it. That punch didn't impact him in the slightest.

"Lie to me again."

He rolls his eyes.

"I'm not lying. I really did go on a jog this morning. I just did it in the land below." A mischievous glint enters his gaze. "It was *amazing*. Just what I needed to get through another day here."

In an instant, he embraces me, wrapping me in his arms. The crown of my head reaches just beneath his collarbones. Tucking me tightly into his body, he exhales a breath of relief.

"Thank you," he whispers into my hair, then bends down to rest his chin on my head.

His tight hold is different from what I'm used to. I've never felt so warm in someone's arms before. Losing my wits, I can't help but echo his movement, loosening my shoulders and leaning into him.

A couple of moments later, we break apart and get to work. We only have a few sections left. Granted, considering we haven't started placing artifacts or scrolls on the shelves in an orderly manner, we still have a ways to go. But I'm actually proud of the progress we've made in such a short time.

As we organize the books, he tells me more about his adventure. The highlight was, of course, his visit to Chrysocolla Cove. The way his entire face lit up as he spoke about catching a peek of his sister and her boyfriend warms my heart. His happiness is unlawfully contagious.

I find something about Kai disarming.

Perhaps I can trust him after all.

It's been nearly a week since Kai's adventure. After raving about the mountain air, the dense forests, and Chrysocolla Cove nonstop for several days, he eventually simmered down. After settling down, some of the light in his hazel eyes faded a bit. He misses his mortal life more than I can understand.

I meant it when I told him I have no desire to return to the living realm. The thought of spending time down there makes me grimace. Too many uninvited memories intrude my mind when I think about my life before death. I know it's a bit cowardly of me to run from my own memories, but I can't bring myself to do otherwise.

I can, however, understand how much he misses his loved ones.

I miss mine, too. I've just gotten used to hiding it.

We've gotten into a comfortable routine as of late. We work on different parts of the archives during the day, separate for a couple of hours after the workday concludes, and reunite for an evening walk as the sun sets. He likes taking walks—he says walking clears his head.

The more time I spend with him, the more I realize it's been a while since I had any sort of companionship. Sure, I was close with Stephen for a while, and I do enjoy Nial's occasional pop-ups, but this is indisputably different.

I've grown so used to facing the world alone I've forgotten how grounding it feels to have someone to walk beside.

I've caught myself smiling more often recently, too. I even effortlessly fell asleep in my own bed last night for the first time in weeks. Rather than reading with the intention of escaping everything, I've been reading for pure enjoyment—no ulterior motive.

"—What about you?" he asks unexpectedly as we pass by Celeste's, the clothing shop. I break out of my stupor and regard him. *Ugh. What did I miss?*

His jaw drops as he breaks into a smile, crinkling his eyes at me. "Don't tell me you weren't listening. I just poured my heart out to you."

"You're serious?"

"Oh, absolutely serious." He smirks, scanning our surroundings. Several angels meander by us, waving at Kai and staring blankly at me as they pass. "I didn't peg you as a daydreamer."

"I just got caught up in my own mind. I wasn't daydreaming."

He shrugs. "Semantics, really."

I scowl, craning my neck to eye his expression. "Well, no use in hiding it now. What were we talking about?"

"I asked if you've ever been in love."

Heat rises to my cheeks. "*You did*? Heavens, we really did get deep..."

He bursts into a boisterous laugh. His laugh is quickly becoming one of my favorite sounds. "Damn straight. I already shared my love story from start to finish. Time for yours."

I stop dead in my tracks and stand in front of him, holding my hand up and pushing it against his chest. "Okay, I'm not naive. I wouldn't have zoned out while listening to your relationship history. No chance of that."

He tilts his head as an even bigger smile creeps on his face. Then, he rests his hands on my waist nonchalantly, as if his touch alone doesn't make me burn inside.

"Is that so? I didn't realize you'd be so interested in my past."

"I'm not. Merely curious for entertainment purposes, that's all."

"Don't worry, angel. The feeling is mutual."

I want to learn everything about you.

I quirk a brow at him. It's been a while since his deep voice echoed within my mind... Maybe it was just my imagination.

Flashing me an easy grin, he doesn't appear remotely fazed.

Yes, I imagined it. I'm positive now.

But why would I imagine him saying *that*? Get a grip, Cleo.

I abandon my spot in front of him to join his side again, falling into step with him. As we stroll through the paved marketplace alley, we enter a quaint flower garden lined with tall hedges, sparkling flowers of every kind mixed into the greenery. Once we pass through the entry, I notice an opal fountain, complete with a statue of angel wings at its center. Four marble benches surround the tall fountain. It's rumored that the benches each represent one of the different Archangels.

We choose one of the sculpted white marble benches and sit next to each other, thighs barely touching. The stone bench is complete with carved armrests and a small, intricate backrest modeled after—you guessed it—a set of angel wings. It's placed below a tree overgrown with white Spanish moss, giving it a frosty, earthy appearance.

"Well, you've caught my attention. Let's hear it," I say, using my fingers to trace the armrest's carvings absentmindedly.

He scoffs, leaning back slightly and lifting his head to face the pink starlit sky. He takes a deep breath in, exhaling through his nose as a beam of light illuminates his golden skin.

I can see why Iris compared Kai to the sun.

He and the sun share the same aura.

Noticeably warm, impossibly bright, and seemingly untouchable.

Despite taking after the sun, starlight suits him rather nicely, too.

"I'm an open book." He drags his eyes down from the sky to glance at me, maintaining a lazy smile. "What do you want to know?"

"Your entire relationship history. Duh."

"Easy. I dated *a lot* of girls in my younger years. Like, a lot. Like, an embarrassing amount." He shakes his head and looks down at his feet.

"Oh, I'm shocked." I rest my hand over my chest for emphasis. "You're practically unbearable."

He rolls his eyes, his lips curling into a smirk. "But then, a girl named Katherine moved to my hometown during my senior year of high school. She was a bit younger than I was, and we grew close as friends. We eventually became best friends. I still fooled around a bit with other girls throughout college, but I often caught myself wondering what life with Katherine would look like. We started dating her senior year of college and stayed together up until a few weeks before I died."

"*Weeks*? Goodness, she must have been devastated," I remark, continuing to outline the bench's carvings. Before thinking better of it, an unnecessary question escapes my lips. "Do you think you loved her?"

"Katherine? Yeah, I loved her. How could I have not? With all our history, it would've been hard not to." I stop stroking the armrest, and my chest tightens unexpectedly. Of course, he loved her. Why did I even ask that?

I clear my throat and rest my hands on my lap stiffly, leaning back against the backrest, unsure of what initiated this wave of discomfort.

"Of course," I say, not knowing what else to say. "That makes sense, logically speaking."

He eyes me, then lifts his arm to rest on the backrest behind me, hovering near my wings. The warmth of his touch against my feathers sends shivers down my spine. "I was the one to end our relationship before croaking, you know."

I hate the feeling of relief that washes over me upon hearing that. "Oh. What made you do that?"

"She was ready for the next step. I wasn't. I let her go." Our thighs are still touching when he uses his knee to nudge mine intentionally. "Your turn. I'm *dying* to hear your story."

I let out a soft scoff.

"Fine. Listen closely—this story will be over before you know it. I've been intimate several times during my life. Stephen was the closest thing I ever had to a boyfriend, and I know, without a doubt, that I didn't love him. I'm fortunate in that I've never fallen victim to love myself, and no one has expressed loving me in that way. Stephen may have liked me, but ultimately, I don't think he would've fallen either."

His brows furrow, and he looks down at me, all concerned-like. "It's unfortunate—"

"It isn't. As I said, it's quite the opposite."

"Let me finish, will you?" He narrows his eyes, and a faint smile grows on his lips.

Fair. Clearing my throat, I nod for him to get on with it.

"It's unfortunate anybody ever took you for granted." He stares intently into my eyes. "You should be revered."

"Oh, Kai. Please—"

"No, I'm serious." I see no trace of humor in his eyes. His fingers stroke my wing tenderly, giving me chills. "If you only knew what others see when they look at you. What I see in you."

My lips part slightly. "You shouldn't say things like that."

"And yet I meant every word."

He can't mean that. I'm sure he says stuff like this to others all the time.

Besides, he doesn't know the real me—what I've done.

If he did, he'd see me for what I actually am.

A self-serving coward.

SEVENTEEN

KAI

I can't figure out what that look in her eyes means for the life of me, but damnit, I desperately want to.

She stares at me, eyes cautious... No, cautious isn't the right word.

I can see what it is now.

She doesn't believe me.

My jaw ticks at the thought of her not believing my words were genuine. How can she not see what everyone else sees?

A wisp of her black hair gets caught in a gust of wind, making her lose focus. Her eyes close as she smooths her hands over her locks. Her dark brows furrow in apparent agitation as she runs her fingers through it, then she parts her full lips with a deep, dramatic exhale.

I follow her gaze, landing on her thighs. Wearing a flowy white button-down blouse and a short black skirt with tights, her legs look even better than usual. Shocking, I know, considering they always look fucking perfect.

You know what I like even more than her thighs, though? *Her laugh.* That godforsaken laugh has the power to make the heavens fall, I'm certain. It starts soft, then builds into a crescendo that rivals the sound of music itself. I wish I could hear it more often. Her laugh alone makes me feel lighter in return.

With a sudden, stark realization, I abruptly glance away.

I can't recall the last time I paid this much attention to someone's laugh. Hell, no one's laugh has ever made me weak like hers.

I'm stumbling, knowingly walking deeper and deeper into a trap, and rather than listening to my gut and turning the other way, I'm frolicking in with a lopsided, goofy smile on my face just because I get to be near my captor. Near her.

This is normal, right? We're friends. I'd say we're close friends in my book.

Ironically, I don't know if she'd even consider me her friend yet, and that somehow draws me even more to her.

I *like* that she's uncertain about me.

I *like* that she doesn't fall for my tricks.

I *like* that she's impossible to read.

Oh, hell. I like Cleo Graves.

I *really* like her.

I assumed my attraction to her was temporary, surface-level. An infatuation. But I thought wrong.

It isn't too late—I can retreat. I can pull back. In fact, I *should* pull back. We have a good thing going on, and she's made herself crystal clear.

We may have shared a moment a few nights back, but that's all it was to her. Just a moment on a rooftop with a wingless man she can't stand. I bet she cringes when that night crosses her mind—that is, if she even thinks about it at all.

Damn. This is so unlike me—wondering if she thinks about that night while unable to help myself from playing it on repeat in my mind.

I'm not one to get caught up in real feelings.

In fact, I broke up with Katherine right before my death because I wasn't ready to settle down and commit to her for the rest of my life. I *chose* to be alone, and as bad as I felt about ending things on some days, it was my choice, and ultimately, I owned it. At one point, I thought we could have been endgame, but ever since meeting Cleo, I've known that I was sorely mistaken.

It wouldn't make sense, not when the only person who consumes all my waking thoughts is sitting right beside me on this marble bench, fussing over the wind making a mess of her hair. I can't help but smile at her like a dumbstruck fool.

This *is* different.

I lift my eyes to look at her again. Damn, I swear she's been attempting to fix her hair for like seventeen minutes now.

I extend my hand, grasping the stray strands of hair. I tuck a lock behind her ear, then look into her eyes. I trace her ear, trailing my fingers down her neck, my palm landing on her shoulder. I rest my hand on her longer than I intended, but I don't particularly care at the moment.

"You're welcome," I say with a grin, voice cracking.

...did my voice really just *crack*? The best word to express how I'm feeling at the moment is *exposed*, and honestly, I'm not a fan.

We both clear our throats at the same time and glance away from each other abruptly.

"How about we get out of here?" I offer.

"And go where?"

"*Anywhere.*"

She bites her lip. "What do you have in mind?"

"How about New York City?"

Her jaw drops. "New York? When you said anywhere, I thought you meant somewhere within this realm..."

"Why not broaden your horizons, angel? You could go anywhere, just with a mere thought. What's stopping you?"

She furrows her brows and shuts her eyes. "I have no desire to visit the land below. Zero. Zilch. I am perfectly content up here in the sky."

"Fine. Whatever you say." I roll my eyes and sigh. "I'll give it to you straight. I'm dying to visit the land below again. What will it take for you to allow me to visit again?"

"I don't think that's a good idea—"

"Oh, c'mon, it's the best idea. I'll make my visit so quick you won't even notice I'm gone."

"No. I can't do it again, Kai." Her eyes bore into mine. "I'm sorry, but it simply isn't worth the risk."

"Oh, it *would* be worth it if you joined me." I wink.

"You're a tireless flirt, you know that?" she mutters.

"Of course. I'll never tire of flirting with you, Cleo."

"*Ugh*," she groans, pinning me with her gaze. "Final answer is no, Kai."

My shoulders sag in defeat. I can't blame her for not wanting to break any other rules. Between my growing feelings for her and my mundane routine, reality is sinking in, and something about it isn't hitting right.

"I understand," I whisper, rising from the bench and reaching out my hand. "Here. Let me walk you back to your quarters."

She glances up at me, nodding. We walk to her quarters hand in hand, talking about the foods we miss the most, our ongoing archives project—nothing important at all.

Well, food is important, I guess.

But not *as* important as finding a way to visit the land below again.

I'm clearly wound up. Wound up like a tightrope on the verge of snapping.

EIGHTEEN

CLEO

Several days have passed since Kai asked me to bend the rules for him *again*. His persistence is admirable, I'll give him that.

I can't blame him for wanting to escape, but I'm also trying not to enable him.

Quite frankly, I'm shocked the Archangels haven't reprimanded me for allowing him to visit the land below already. If they genuinely are all-knowing celestial beings, they must have paid no heed to my insolence.

For now.

But why? The Archangels have a reason for everything. It makes me queasy to consider what their reasoning would be if they did indeed know about my insolence.

I've grown unexpectedly accustomed to evening walks with him. I can't pinpoint when I started to find comfort in these little outings of ours. However, we didn't take an evening stroll together tonight. It's the third night in a row we haven't.

I push my arm against my sofa, shifting my weight. Again.

Trying to pull my thoughts back to the words in the book I'm holding, I rub my temple with my free hand.

I assumed that drawing comfort from the night air and starlight itself during our walks was what brought me comfort. I've always fancied night.

Night is consistent. Night always comes.

Concluding the new way I've positioned myself isn't working, either, I shift my weight and prop my feet up on the sofa, tucking them underneath me.

Ugh. That's not right, either.

I sigh in frustration, setting my book down on the couch beside me and pinching the bridge of my nose.

Why can't I get comfortable?

I must just need a reset, that's all. The angel mist outside should provide me with the reset I need.

I rise and stride across my small living room to open the door to my balcony, stepping outside and breathing in the crisp night air.

When you've lived in Eloras for as long as I have, you're awarded with a slightly nicer living space. Entry-level Guardians' living havens are a bit smaller than my current home. My haven is complete with a spacious kitchenette, an island, a living room area, a bedroom, a full bathroom, and a balcony. The balcony is arguably the main difference between an entry-level and a senior haven.

I don't spend much time in my haven—the space is too nice. I feel much more at home in my office than I do here most of the time. Since Kai entered my life, I've found myself spending more time here than usual, though.

However, I don't know how I'd manage without my office.

About a year ago, Nial discovered me there late at night. I chose to work overtime to escape that particular evening. I closed my eyes, tuned into my Guardians closely to see if any were on the verge of breaking the divine laws, and focused on that for a couple of hours when a knock at the door disrupted my focus.

"Cleo? You're here awfully late..." I opened my eyes to see Nial's amber eyes. Odd, seeing as we typically only crossed paths out and about in the square or gardens.

"Nial? You're here at all?" I joked. "I'm working late."

He nodded, then glanced at the bedding on my office's sofa.

"Are you okay?" He cocked an eyebrow and tilted his head.

"Just fine."

"Understood. Carry on," he said, turning to leave. "And I'd recommend resting tonight. Your eyes tell a different story from your words."

Although brief, his short visit made me realize how restless I'd been. I took his advice and napped for a short while in my office after he left.

Inhaling another breath of angel mist, I rest my hands on the balcony's golden railing, contemplating whether I should attempt to find some comfort in my office instead.

"*This isn't working*," I grumble, agitated. I thought, for sure, that the night sky would bring me the comfort I sought.

Perhaps, my source of comfort isn't the fresh air after all.

How unfortunate.

I've tried to avoid thinking about him, but it's no use. My mind gets carried away sometimes. Especially when it comes to thinking about Kai Greene. I just can't put my finger on why he hasn't initiated evening walks recently—it's unlike him.

Come to think of it, his demeanor has changed, too.

We've nearly finished the archives project, and instead of celebrating, he's been distant. Smiling softer and winking obnoxiously far less often. It's as if his mind is somewhere else most of the time.

His sunny charm has vacated.

This realm must be getting to him.

And that simply won't do.

All of a sudden, I launch off the balcony, a tremendous gust of wind blowing my hair out of my face. I savor the air's refreshing scent and temperature while spreading my wings wide.

My wingspan is about the length of my own body, in case you're curious. I keep them furled most of the time, but flying like this is always rejuvenating. Moving on their own accord, my wings carry me across the sky, passing several opulent buildings containing living havens.

Casting a glance onward, beyond the havens and marketplace, my sights land on the vast estate of the Archangels, surrounded by rolling green hills and lush gardens. A glass bridge, complete with a solid golden gate, separates their domain from the rest of Eloras.

The four Archangels and their staff reside in a copper castle-like manor, each taking ownership over a wing of their own—North, South, East, and West. Working angels with lower statuses like myself don't visit their estate. In fact, only authorized angels can walk beyond the golden gate. We can see it in all its glory from afar, though.

After passing a few haven buildings, I hover outside a familiar window, noting darkness beyond the drawn curtains.

He must be resting. I may or may not have noticed he sleeps significantly more than other angels do.

I should probably leave. It's late.

Yet I tap on the glass anyway.

Hovering outside his window, I begin counting. If he doesn't acknowledge me by the time I reach ten, I'll leave him be. Five seconds pass, and I turn around, facing the living havens across the cobblestone road below, and fold my arms.

This was stupid. I don't even know why I thought this would be a good idea.

Five... Four... Three... Two...

"Aren't you a sight for sore eyes?" A raspy voice startles me. I turn to face him, and he's resting his elbows on the window's banister. Taking in his disheveled hair and hooded hazel eyes, I swallow. He eyes me up and down. "Nice little ensemble you're wearing there."

Confirmed: I woke him up. *Nice move, Cleo.*

Also, confirmed: I forgot to change before taking flight, so I'm currently wearing a light blue silk camisole and silk shorts.

Nothing else.

I cross my arms, covering my upper half as much as possible. What was I thinking?

"Hi, Kai," I say, suddenly forgetting why I chose to come here in the first place.

"Hi, Cleo."

Damnit. His tired voice will be my undoing.

"Sorry to interrupt your rest. I can get going."

Idiot. Idiot. Idiot. I ready myself to launch back into the sky and hide my blushing face when his hand grasps my arm.

"What's the rush, buttercup?" He eyes the moon and slides his fingers down my arm to hold my hand. "You know, you actually kind of remind me of her."

"Who?"

"*The Powerpuff Girl*. Buttercup."

I knit my brows and conclude I have no idea who he's talking about. "That must have been after my time."

"*Wow*. I forgot how ancient you are." His hoarse, low timbre makes my spine tingle. I reluctantly smile at his jab. "Sure, I was sleeping, but I wasn't resting particularly well. You saved me from a nasty nightmare, actually."

"You have nightmares?" My stomach drops. "I didn't think that was possible for angels in Eloras."

"Nothing is impossible for a Greene." His lips curl into a smile that doesn't quite meet his eyes. Before I can respond, he tugs on my hand and drags me into his haven.

I stumble in through the window and tuck my wings away, miraculously managing to land on my feet. I punch his arm for catching me off guard, earning myself a laugh.

"Growing up, my mom infused that belief into my brain, and it stuck. Anytime I'm going through something difficult, I remind myself that nothing is impossible for me. I can do anything I set my mind to. I have and I will. I wish experiencing those pesky night terrors was impossible. Because we can see the world in vivid color and detail after death, I've found that my nightmares are far more real than the ones I had before dying. I *hate* them, Cleo."

His voice trails off as he sinks onto his love seat and pats the cushion next to him—somewhat aggressively, I might add. Obliging him, I sit next to him.

At first, I'm sitting a few inches away, but then he wraps his arm around my shoulders lazily and pulls me into him, tucking my frame under his muscular arms. He drops his head back, leaning it on the sofa, his eyes fluttering shut.

From how his toned arms cradle me to his intoxicating, sleepy voice, I'm hardly maintaining my composure.

Finally, after a couple of moments of quiet, I ask, "Is that where you've been the past few nights? Stuck in nightmares?"

He shrugs, his throat bobbing. I find myself leaning into his touch absentmindedly.

"Do you want to talk about them?"

"No. Talking about them will make me relive them, and I can't. I don't give a fuck how cowardly that sounds."

I understand what he means. I lean out of his embrace and shake my head. "It's okay, Kai. You don't have to talk about the nightmares... But if you change your mind, I'm here. You can talk to me."

He opens his eyes and drags his gaze down to meet mine. "I'll keep that in mind. Thank you, sweetheart."

I roll my eyes and glance away before meeting his gaze again.

He raises his brows. "Why did you give me that look?"

"I don't know why you insist on continuing this charade when no one else is around."

"I don't know what you mean."

"Why did you just call me 'sweetheart?'"

"Because the term suits you. Obviously."

"You play too much." I scoff. He smiles half-heartedly. His pain is unexpectedly affecting me. "Want to get out of here?"

"Eh, I intended on wallowing in my own self-pity tonight..." he drawls.

"How uncharacteristic of you. The Kai I know would never."

He quirks an eyebrow and scoffs. "Maybe you don't know me as well as you think you do."

"No, I'm fairly certain I've figured you out. Now, let's go before the sun rises. I want to show you something." I rise from the love seat and walk toward the window.

He releases an obnoxious sigh and stands up. "What's wrong with using the front door?"

Sleepy Kai is so broody.

I kind of love it.

"Our destination is this way." I grab him, pulling his arms around my waist. "Time to play your favorite game again."

His eyes widen, and he opens his mouth to protest, but I launch outside before he can.

He shrieks loud enough for the Golden Realm's angels to hear and holds on to my waist for dear life. A laugh bubbles inside me, escaping for a second before I stifle it to concentrate on keeping us afloat. I soar upward, higher and higher, passing through swarms of clouds until we near the dome.

Holding on to my waist with a death grip, he screeches, a mixture of horror and exhilaration coating his features. Thank goodness my wings are strong; otherwise, we'd both fall.

Finally, we reach a small pocket of space surrounded by golden, pink, orange, and white clouds.

"Cleo... We're pretty high up. I don't know if you've noticed, but there isn't anywhere for us to land, and I swear, my hands are slipping as we speak. Wait... Was this your plan all along? Are you putting me out of misery? Am I about to fall to my second death? I—"

I slowly lower us a few feet above a fluffy pink cloud. "You can let go."

"Figuratively or physically? Shit, is this another test?"

I stifle a laugh at that one.

"Kai." I gaze down at him with a grin. "Let. Go."

He peers up at me in sheer horror. Heavens, does this man really think I'm attempting to murder him?

"Trust me." I nod, prompting him to let go. Again. He's exhausting sometimes.

"You were bound to be the death of me at some point," he whispers. "I might as well choose my own terms. Goodbye, angel."

He closes his eyes and releases his arms from my waist—dramatically, I might add.

He tumbles for approximately two whole seconds before landing on the cloud's surface. A wave of shock crosses his features, and I lower myself to meet him. He drags his gaze up from the fluff to meet my eyes. "How is this possible?"

"Nothing is impossible for a Greene, remember?"

NINETEEN

CLEO

A glint of mischief enters his gaze, then he proceeds to *bounce*. He leaps from one cloud to another, ending up several feet away from me.

Quite frankly, I didn't even realize the clouds were as buoyant as they are.

He jumps up and down, laughing the entire time, bringing a smile to my lips. I tuck my wings away and take in the moment, breathing in the angel mist and gazing at the domed boundary above us, separating us from the Golden Realm. We're pretty close to the dome—only a couple of hundred feet away.

"Join me," he shouts, waving his arms.

I shake my head and cross my arms. "I brought you up here to clear your head. You keep doing your thing, and I'll do mine."

"Is your thing being a stick-in-the-mud?" he taunts, continuing to jump. My eyes narrow, but I keep watching him. Even after how rough his afterlife experience has been, he still finds ways to make light of any given situation, like the sun itself.

Lost in thought, I nearly stumble off the bouncing cloud when a set of strong hands grips my shoulders tightly.

"Be careful, Cleo," he says in a low voice, his eyes scanning mine. "You fall, I fall."

Falling like that could've been bad, considering my wings weren't unfurled.

"I'm okay," I whisper, gulping at the closeness of our faces. The intensity in his gaze transitions into something lighter as he leaps again. This time, he scoops me into his arms to join him.

I wrap my arms around his neck and squeal, burying my head into his chest.

Squeal? I do not squeal.

As we leap from one corner to another, my heart races, and I think I've finally determined the nature of my relationship with him.

He brings out a side of me I'd forgotten existed. My inner child.

It's been decades since I felt a sensation like this.

After bouncing like a madman for a few more minutes, he suddenly loses his footing, leading us to trip and fall onto a cloud.

He lies on his back, shutting his eyes and cackling, his laugh richer than ever. Unable to stifle my own amusement, my stomach rumbles in laughter, too. Lost in a moment of euphoric ecstasy, our eyes lock. His gaze lowers to my lips, lingering there for a moment as heat rises to my cheeks.

We're tangled in each other.

I wrap my legs around his waist tighter, allowing my opening to rest precisely on his shaft.

We stare into each other's eyes for a few seconds, a million thoughts racing through my mind at once, when his lips crash against mine like a tsunami.

It's undeniably petrifying. Terribly unexpected. And absolutely exhilarating.

His hands slide down from my waist to the small of my back before reaching my rear.

"Is this okay?" he rasps with hooded eyes.

I nod slowly, drinking in his gaze and savoring the way his rough hands feel against my body. He cups my ass, massaging it greedily.

"*For fuck's sake*," he murmurs, heat in his gaze. "Has anyone ever told you how perfect your body is?" He strains, his hardness pushing against my opening ever so slightly. "Actually, on second thought, please do me a favor and *do not* answer that."

I chuckle quietly, the motion in my stomach causing a vibrating sensation to pass between us both.

He pulls me into him tighter, gripping my ass even harder. "Does this hurt?"

"I'd tell you if I didn't like it, Kai."

He breathes hard, then spreads my cheeks slightly, pushing me harder into his erection, with only the thin silk of my shorts separating us. I roll my hips—just once—and I *swear*, it's like he melts beneath me as he lets out a groan. Relishing in his pleasure and eager to satisfy his needs, I roll my hips again, this time with more rhythm and vigor.

I continue to ride him, savoring the way his cock is swelling with every thrust. Wetness pools between my thighs, threatening to seep through my shorts as I fist his hair.

"That's it, angel. Take what you need," he whispers, closing his eyes. "Dance with me."

Oh, heavens. This *does* feel oddly reminiscent of dancing. I haven't experienced this sense of blissful pleasure in so damn long. Too damn long. I can hardly handle the sensation.

I need more.

More. More. More.

More of him. More bliss.

More.

If I pull his joggers down and if he slides my shorts off me, I could *finally* release—

Suddenly, a golden ray of light distracts me from my euphoria.

I squint my eyes and glance to my left.

The sun is rising.

Coming to my senses, I stop writhing against him, realizing I've gone too far.

I look away from the light to gaze at him. Covered in golden light, he is already looking at me. A tenderness enters his gaze, replacing the heat that was present mere seconds before.

I shake my head. "I'm sorry. I went too far—"

"Cleo." He pauses my racing thoughts. "You're breathtaking."

I part my lips and shake my head.

"The sun failed miserably at taking my eyes off you. Nothing could tear my gaze away from your beauty."

Stunned into silence, I furrow my brows.

Surely, he is caught up in the adrenaline of it all. Surely.

"You don't believe me, do you?" He raises his brows.

"It's just... If you knew all of me, you wouldn't be bathing me in compliments like this."

"That's where you're wrong." He pierces me with his hazel gaze. "The more I get to know the real Cleo, the more I want to drown her in adoration."

My heart skips a beat at his admission. He wouldn't say that if he knew how much of a coward I truly am.

Something about the sincerity in his gaze pierces my heart. Why is he so kind to me? My heart can hardly take it.

"I appreciate you, Kai." A beat of silence passes between us. "Are you feeling any better now? I took you up here to watch the sunrise in the clouds. I noticed you've been a bit down lately, so I hoped it might help."

He grins, then gives my nose a tender kiss. "I'm *much* better now, and I can only attribute a fraction of that to the sunrise, baby."

"Why do you insist on still calling me 'baby'?"

"Does being called 'baby' actually bother you? I can stop."

Yes, because I want this to be real.

"I just find it confusing."

"Well, don't overthink it. The word practically rolls off my tongue when it comes to you. It's as simple as that."

I finally roll off him, resting beside him and leaning my head against his chest, drawing a breath. "Okay."

With his arm still wrapped around my waist, he bends his head down, his lips brushing against my temple.

My hand reaches for his, grasping it and fiddling with the ring on his finger.

The key to his escape and my demise.

I fiddle with it, then do something wildly unexpected. My mind is no better than mush around this man.

I bring his pointer finger up to my lips and kiss it softly, pressing my lips against it for several seconds.

A sharp intake of breath sounds beside me. "Cleo. What are you doing?"

I wiggle the ring off his finger and hold it for a moment, then tilt my head up to gaze at him. "You deserve some time away from the nightmares."

An unreadable expression crosses his face. "Damn, you aren't going soft on me, are you?"

He smirks as I roll my eyes and scoff. "Never."

"Sure, okay. Whatever you say." His eyes beam even brighter than before, then darken. "Are you sure you won't get in trouble?"

"I'm certain that you deserve freedom to visit the land below just one more time—especially when Eloras is haunting you. I'm tired of your half smiles and lack of obnoxious jokes. Go down there and do whatever you need to do to reset. Promise me you'll come back, then we'll take it from there. Got it?"

I slip the solid golden ring into the pocket of his joggers, clasping it shut.

His gaze sobers, then he runs his fingers through my hair tenderly. The seconds tick by slowly before he nods. "Okay, Cleo."

We both stand, then he embraces me in a tight, warm hug. His scent of amber washes over me, soothing me.

I realize this is the first time we've ever held each other like this.

I'd be fooling myself if I said it wasn't nice.

He leans away, peering into my eyes again. "I meant what I said. You're devastatingly beautiful in every way."

Uninvited heat rises to my cheeks and butterflies flutter in my stomach upon hearing those words again. Instead of denying his words, I simply smile softly.

"I'll see you soon," I say evenly, subtly biting my lip.

"See you later."

As he disappears into thin air and transports to the realm below, I can't help but feel like something of great magnitude is about to happen.

And I don't know if that something is good or bad.

Shaking the thought away, I run my hands down my night attire and release a sigh before unfurling my wings to fly home.

Everything is fine. He came back last time; there's no reason why he wouldn't this time.

Then, I launch into the sky, aiming for my haven below.

I have grave news.

It has been one full day.

Kai hasn't returned.

Hadley knows.

The Archangels know.

Everyone knows.

And once again, this mess is all my fault. This time, though, I don't give a damn about what happens to me.

I deserve this.

I deserve to be blindsided.

I deserve to be left behind.

I deserve to be alone.

It was naive to hope that his words were genuine. Foolish to hope that his feelings reached beyond friendship as mine have. Absurd to hope he would be the key to my salvation.

I should've known better. I'm better than this.

No more evening strolls. No more mindless work in the Library of the Sky. No more cloud-hopping. No more dancing.

Good riddance.

I've felt emotions over the past few weeks that I didn't know were possible to feel beyond death. This experience reminded me how vital it is to remain cool, calm, and collected.

Allowing emotions to dictate decisions *always* leads to mistakes. Like the colossal one I made in trusting him. Letting my guard down was a trap. He only needed me to get back down there anyway. The next time I see Kai—if I ever see him again—I'll be sure to thank him for reminding me of who I am.

Hell, without his betrayal, I'd be a lovestruck fool. Well, I guess *luststruck* would be a more appropriate term.

True love only exists in books, and if it's real, it's not in the cards for me. I'm perfectly okay without it.

I gaze around my office and push aside the night we spent here, curled up in each other's arms, hoping to forget it.

On one hand, I hope he's struggling down there and wallowing in guilt.

On the other hand, I hope he's filling his days with something worthwhile, like baseball games or movies he loves.

It's funny, you know? How I can be so upset with him yet *still* wish him well.

Rubbing my temples and squeezing my eyes shut, I imagine how the Archangels will punish me this time when I meet with them tonight.

Who am I kidding? It's better this way—it's good he didn't fall for me. Loving me is a curse.

Twenty

Kai

A thick layer of fluffy snow covers the pine trees surrounding me beneath the night sky. I have the most perfect view of the snowcapped mountains, and for the first time in over a month, I find the air crisp and refreshing.

After zapping myself back into this realm, I immediately ventured to my parents' house. Anticlimactic, I know.

It's chilly outside, and considering I'm wearing joggers and a T-shirt, I need to change fast to blend in.

I know what's on your mind: *Kai, why do you need to blend in? No one can see you.*

And that's where you're wrong, my friend.

It's downright impossible to predict when I might run into an angel down here. Other angels, like Guardians, can see me. In an effort to stand out less, I want to dress the part.

I don't *technically* need to change clothes while down here. I don't grow cold like living human beings do. I don't sweat. I don't tire often. Because I won't need to change clothes after this, I want to choose something nice and comfortable.

As I rummage through some of my old clothes before deciding I've outgrown a majority of these items, I let out a sigh. Glancing around my room, my eyes land on some cardboard boxes from my old apartment that they kept after my passing. These boxes contain memorabilia, random decor, old movies, some tools, and, of course, clothes. I find it sweet that my parents chose to keep all this—some of it is objectively junk. Grief works differently for everyone, though. If this is what they need to do to heal, I support it.

After digging through a few pieces of clothing, I find the perfect winter fit: a white cashmere sweater and a pair of jeans, complete with a light brown coat.

I change into the clothes, packing my previous set of clothes into the box. I'm curious if my parents will ever sort through this box and notice the new clothing items. I grin just thinking about it.

It may be a problem, but I *love* meddling. In fact, the last time I visited, I pulled a prank on Jasper involving a bottle of beer, but that's a secret I'll never tell—even one day when he meets me in death. Imagining the look on his face when he noticed my little trick makes me grin even harder.

While putting the boxes away, I gaze around my old room and focus on some of the pictures my mom put on display after my death. It looks like she hung up some photos of me with my baseball team, Iris and me, and even one of my college graduation. I run my fingers across my old wooden desk's surface. Not even a hint of dust. I wonder how often they visit this room. My dad was always a bit more standoffish—not the emotional type. I doubt he visits here frequently. But my mom and I were close at one point. We certainly didn't always see eye to eye, and I found the way she treated Iris to be entirely unacceptable, but I'd be lying if I said I didn't care for my parents. I miss them occasionally.

Gulping, I take one last glance around my old room, then I abruptly teleport to Chrysocolla Cove. I enter the quaint home just outside of downtown quietly. I take note of several unpacked boxes lining the walls of the living room, the smell of lavender and vanilla, and some of Truman's toys scattered in the hallway.

Odd. What have my two most favorite people in the world been up to in my absence this time? I walk farther into the home and notice the TV is on, then glance at the couch, taking in the sight.

She's lying on top of him, her head full of dark brown waves resting against his chest, slowly rising and falling in rhythm with his breathing. His arms are wrapped around her securely, protecting her even in his sleep.

Ugh. How wholesome is this? This sight alone may be enough to turn my frown upside down permanently.

Upon closer inspection, I see goosebumps lining her arms and realize they need a blanket as soon as possible. Once a Guardian, always a Guardian. I grab the throw from atop the couch and drape it over them as gently as possible.

There. Much better.

Suddenly, a small orange figure brushes against my leg, purring. I eye Truman and bend down to scratch his chin. I've missed him, too.

Seeing them together in their own home fills me with warmth. This is all I ever wanted for my little sister.

Thanks to Jasper, I don't have to wonder if she's okay. I know she is.

I glance at them one last time before teleporting to my next destination—the last thing I want to do is disturb the peace they've worked so hard to obtain.

While sitting in the stands of the high school baseball field, I decide I need to make a plan. I can't keep teleporting to and fro wherever the wind takes me, especially not after the sun comes up. Can you imagine what would happen if Jasper happened to see me here? Talk about a setback.

Where should I go next? Obviously, I could go back to the Middle Realm, but where's the fun in that? In all seriousness, I don't know if I'm ready to go back up there. I just need a little more time away.

I've missed this realm.

Something about the Middle Realm makes me feel stuck. That feeling isn't for me.

The last time I felt that hopeless was when I was contemplating whether I should tie the knot with my ex or break up with her. After months of thinking, I chose to say goodbye because I didn't want to be stuck in a marriage.

I watched my parents throughout their own marriage, and it didn't take a rocket scientist to notice just how stuck they were. Iris was always the one who planned out her dream wedding—not me. I would've been content to spend life alone. Then Katherine entered my world, and that initial desire to be alone wavered. However, just before my life ended, I came back to my senses and let go of those thoughts. I knew going through what my parents did wouldn't worth it. My parents seemed compatible on paper. If they couldn't make it work, how would I ever make it work with someone?

Then, like an angel sent from above, Cleo happened.

And I have no idea what to do about it. About her.

Her lips are even softer than I imagined they'd be.

Her touch is softer, too.

When she tangled her petite hands into my hair and rode me into oblivion earlier, I lost my mind. True euphoria like I'd never known entered my system, and we were only dry humping for heaven's sake.

When I leaned in to kiss her, I fully expected to be outrightly rejected. Pitiful, I know, but at the time, nothing mattered more than knowing what her lips tasted like. I never imagined she'd press her lips against mine like that.

The lines we drew prior to that moment couldn't mean less to me now.

I need time to figure out my feelings. It's interesting—before death, I loved solving problems. This passion proved especially helpful when working on cars. I worked on all sorts of vehicles—everything from carburetors to fuel-injected, including some hybrids thrown into the mix. Several buddies of mine would call me up when their cars broke down, and we'd fix them together. I kind of have a knack for figuring out those types of things. When life got too heavy, I'd work on my project car. It was a solid distraction.

My point is, I don't usually have a hard time figuring people out, either, but this particular individual is something else. Hell, my old students would probably laugh their asses off at how many home runs this girl has scored on my watch. So, I can't face her yet—I've got to get a grip on my emotions before I do something I regret. I'll stay down here for a bit longer to get my shit together, then I'll teleport back up there in a jiffy. They won't even notice I'm gone. Last time I snuck down here, the Archangels didn't seem to bat an eye. Cleo will be okay up there for the day or so I'm gone.

I set my mind on the only place I can think of where a person, especially an angel, could hide in plain sight without being noticed.

I've been down here for not even a full day, and although I'm convinced I haven't even ventured through half of this enormous city quite yet, I can confidently say this is my favorite spot I've explored.

People all around me are walking their dogs. Some are doing their morning jogs, others are doing yoga. From where I'm sitting, I have a fantastic view of an ice-skating rink—only a couple of people are taking advantage of the ice at the moment, which isn't surprising given how early it is in the day. Central Park is massive.

I'll admit, I've exercised soulsight a handful of times while down here. It's been a while since I exercised it—most of the angels up there have strong mental shields in place to keep others out. Cleo's mind blocks are robust—the strongest I've ever encountered.

Last night, I visited an antique shop downtown just to make me feel something. The shop was swarming with people but lacked Aged Emporium's charm. I grew fond of Jasper's family business in the Cove. It's hard to find something that compares. This shop wasn't so bad, though. I think I'd like to revisit it, actually.

I stand from the bench and take a moment to appreciate the beams of sunlight shining down on me. Rare for New York City to see this much sunshine on a cold winter day like this. It's like the sun is making a special guest appearance just for me. I'm here for it.

Walking toward 6th Avenue at a steady pace, I take in my surroundings, admiring the little shops, vendor stands, and aromas of the city. I haven't visited New York in years, but I've always enjoyed the hustle and bustle here.

It's funny, in Chrysocolla Cove, everyone walks slowly. In fact, it's definitely frowned upon to speed walk there.

In New York City, walking slowly is downright a crime. Hell, I'm walking as fast as possible to keep up with the flood of people near me, and they can't even see me.

I'm convinced that the ability to speed walk is a requirement for living in a massive city like this. I don't mind the pacing one bit, though. The faster, the better.

Time goes by more slowly down here than above. I'd assume it's been nearly a full day up there. Considering I'm hoping to return to the Middle Realm relatively soon, everything should be fine. Quite frankly, up until now, the Archangels have been relatively merciful in their disciplinary acts. My punishment, for instance, could've been *far* worse, based on what Cleo has shared with me. I'm sure she's okay.

After taking a couple of turns, I halt in my tracks and gape at the pristine building in front of me. I purposely took this route so I could catch a glimpse of one of my favorite historical landmarks ever—a gorgeous cathedral in the heart of Manhattan. It's not too crowded here yet. I walk inside, determining there's no real rush to get back to that antique shop.

Frankly, I don't think a person has to be religious or spiritual to admire the beauty held within a historical building like this. Built in the 1800s, it almost seems like the cathedral is frozen in time. Despite how much the city has developed since then, this chapel holds a timeless beauty that reminds me of some of the Middle Realm's towers.

Beams of natural light pour in through the chapel's stained-glass arched windows, casting a subtle glow over the massive space. I glance around the expansive room. Not a soul in sight.

I take a seat in one of the wooden pews and grab a hymn book to fidget with to keep my hands busy. It's nice—even though I'm dead, I can still grab hold of objects casually. Come to think of it, most people automatically assume inanimate floating objects are the act of ghosts or malicious spirits. I wonder if they'd find comfort in knowing angels can do that, too. Or if they'd still be creeped out. Come to think of it, I'd probably still be pretty freaked out.

I feel like more of a ghost than an angel these days. My zest for living has decreased more and more since my guardianship ended.

I flip through the book's brittle, yellow pages and faded text, taking note of how old the book is.

How old is Cleo? Is this book older or younger than her?

It's wild how this girl has captured my attention every moment since my guardianship ended, and I don't even know her age.

Sighing, I lean back in the pew and set the book off to the side for a bit.

I've been thinking a lot over the past couple of days and haven't been able to process my thoughts effectively. Iris used to say I was a 'verbal processor,' so maybe thinking in silence isn't helping me the way it probably helps many people.

I thought sitting in this chapel would be poetic in a way. Seemed like a great way to clear my mind and get deep.

But as I sit here and think about where I want to go from here, the same words keep playing in my mind over and over again. You know when you find a song annoying, but its jingle is remotely catchy, and your mind latches on to it for no reason at all? Then, before you know it, you've heard that song in your mind a thousand times and can casually sing it backward against your will.

This phrase, repeating in my mind, reminds me of that horrid sensation.

You'll always be stuck, even in death.

It may not make much sense, but in my mind, the only way to get unstuck—I'm sure there's a better word for that, but that's irrelevant—is to run. I've been running for as long as I can remember.

It's easier to run.

Should I stay down here indefinitely and run forever? The Archangels have much more important matters to tend to than one rogue angel.

Staying down here may make Cleo's life easier. She deserves better than babysitting someone like me. A thousand times better.

I doubt she'd really get reprimanded for this anyway—Nial seemed fucking obsessed with her if you ask me. My jaw tightens while thinking about him and the way he interacted with her during my trial.

Not hearing that cute laugh of hers again would kill me, though. I'd miss her feathered wings and brown eyes and little scowl, too.

Truthfully, I don't think I could live with myself if I didn't at least correctly say goodbye to her before running, either.

Damnit. What am I going to do? My feelings for her are growing stronger by the minute, being stuck in the Middle Realm is literally driving me insane, and I really miss my life. I miss it a hell of a lot. All three of these things are problematic.

I lean forward and rub my forehead, drawing a deep breath and resisting the urge to scream.

Movie characters make chapels look magical. They walk in troubled, walk out clear-minded. I, on the other hand, am feeling even more conflicted. This is probably what I deserve for believing in fiction.

Eventually, I leave, hoping I'll find clarity sooner rather than later.

At the very least, spending time in such a cool building was nice.

I walk out of the cathedral and begin my speed walking regimen again, fitting right in with the locals. Not that anyone can see me.

Well, okay, I guess that's not entirely true. Animals can see me. In fact, they often gravitate toward me. If I form a connection with an animal, we can speak through our minds to each other. Truman and I had a connection like that. He's a sassy little guy, but damn, he's the best cat ever.

With the number of birds and squirrels who flock to my side in this city, I'm practically a modern-day Snow White at this point.

I put my hands in my pockets and continue walking, sights set on the antique shop, when I notice a sign for a bookshop across the block. I've never been much of a reader, but that doesn't occur to me as I change my course and approach it.

No, instead, I choose to stop there because it reminds me of my angel.

As I get closer, I notice the quaint shop has several books on display. From afar, I can't make out the finer details, but I can clearly see a woman with her backside facing me, currently perched over to get a closer look at the books from the sidewalk. Dressed in knee-high black leather boots, black tights, a navy plaid skirt, and a light gray sweater, I feel drawn to her for reasons I can’t understand. Crossing the street, I catch an even better look at her and notice she has short black hair that barely runs past her shoulders.

I rub my eyes and determine my mind must be playing tricks on me because she looks a hell of a lot like the angel I can't get off my mind.

But she hasn’t spent time down here in the land below for leisure since dying, so it can't be her. In fact, I tried to get her to join me recently, and she utterly refused. She said she had no desire to ever visit this realm for fun. So, this simply can’t be my angel.

I finally reach her side, and before I can even get a good look at her, she turns and pierces me with her brown eyes, saying, “I finally found you.”

Twenty-One

Cleo

"Excuse me?" Kai gawks and gapes while squinting at me. "I'm sorry. Do I know you?"

"Oh, stop." I roll my eyes and scoff. "You're joking."

He takes a step back and shakes his head slowly, actual confusion lacing his features.

The color must be draining from my face. I glance at the ground, and my mind begins racing.

What happened to him while he was down here? Is this why he didn't return? Did a demon get hold of him and wipe his memory—

Suddenly, his rich laugh interrupts my spiraling. I drag my eyes up from the stained pavement to meet his gaze, not missing the mischievous glint in his eyes.

Then, his eyes soften. "Angel. *C'mon.* How could I ever forget you?"

He reaches out to stroke my arm, to which I don't move a muscle.

So, he did leave me.

Knowingly.

I gulp, then he knits his brows—he's confused. Of course, he's confused. I'd have to let down my shields to let him in to read me, and I won't be doing that ever again.

The Archangels gave me a specific mission to accomplish while down here, but they didn't give me a timeline to adhere to. They did punish me, though. I close my eyes for a second longer than I should, thinking about what's at stake if I don't fulfill their request.

Because I don't have a deadline for this assignment, I have time. I have time and a plan.

"Great to see you, too."

"Aw, that might be the sweetest thing you've ever said to me." He grins, moving in closer, wrapping his arm around my neck, and kissing my forehead.

Embarrassingly, I have to fight my body not to melt into him. I didn't realize how much I missed his tender touch and relentless flirting. Maybe acting won't be as complicated as I thought it would be.

We're facing an old-fashioned bookshop now. I peek through the wide glass window, noting warm-toned brown bookshelves lining the walls. Several rectangular tables featuring what I imagine are bestsellers take up the middle space of the shop. Behind the tables, I see a narrow wooden staircase leading up to a small second story, complete with a banister on either side. Peeling my eyes away from the beautiful shop in front of me, I gaze at him.

When entering the realm, I wasn't sure where to find him. The Archangels were practically useless. They said I 'deserve the challenge for allowing him to venture down here.' So, I've been playing the role of bounty hunter for the past several hours—quite well, I might add. I mean, I pinpointed where he was within a day.

Of course, I teleported to Chrysocolla Cove first, and after having a good mind-to-mind chat with a particularly sassy fluffy feline, I learned he *had* visited the Cove. I barely missed him, but I was on the right track. Ultimately, I have my very own memory to thank for helping me find him. I recalled one of our last conversations before he abandoned the realm.

"How about we get out of here?" he asked nonchalantly.

"And go where?"

"Anywhere."

"What do you have in mind?"

"How about New York City?"

Brilliant place to hide. He's essentially hiding in plain sight, given the number of Guardians in this city. Because I was his Watcher at one point, I tried tapping into our old thread bond. My intuition told me to start with Manhattan of all places.

I eye his outfit—a brown coat, a cream sweater, navy jeans, and a pair of brown hiking boots. His style is timeless, so he's certainly blending in well. Almost a little too well. I may have missed him if I wasn't searching for him so avidly.

Unfortunately, though, when I claimed it was good to see him, I meant it.

It *is* good to see him. Despite how terribly frustrated I am with him, I'm relieved he's okay.

"What happened to your wings? I know you can tuck them away, but I don't think I've ever seen your back looking quite as bare as it does now."

"That's not important," I quickly quip.

I'd rather not talk about that. He hesitates before nodding slowly.

"Well, what brings you down here? You said you don't like to visit this realm. Did they put you up to this?" He cocks an eyebrow.

Quick on my feet, I shake my head. "I've chosen to run away with you."

My stomach drops in discomfort.

There it is—my first lie to Kai Greene.

He glances down at me, his eyes widening, before breaking out in the biggest grin I've ever seen. "Get outta town, are you serious?"

I nod. "I can hardly believe it myself."

His cheeks flush, and he begins to blush.

This doesn't feel as satisfying as I anticipated.

"I've had a lot of questions recently. I think you coming down here answered a big one for me. Let's have fun, shall we?" He grabs my shoulders with both of his hands and navigates me toward the bookshop's entrance, opening the door for us. The lighting is dim but warm and inviting.

My stomach is twisting in knots. I push the sensation aside and remember how much his departure hurt me. Now that I'm here, I can only assume he had no plans to return to Eloras.

We became friends, and he abandoned me up there anyway.

I was beginning to believe our friendship meant something to him. Now I'm wondering if all this is part of an elaborate lie on his part to take advantage of me. Without my ability to unlock his ring, we'd be working in the Library of the Sky as we speak.

He promised me he'd come back. Instead, I was his one-way ticket to the land below.

Reminding myself of the betrayal, I raise my chin.

I'd be lying if I said the line between pretending and reality isn't hard to decipher at this point. But I can do this. I can pretend for a little longer.

It's still relatively early in the day, so there aren't other customers in the shop. In fact, it seems like the booksellers have stepped out or aren't here yet, because they're nowhere to be seen. While browsing the inventory, we go our separate ways. He sifts through the fiction books, whereas I sort through the romance section.

Eventually, I grab two different books I haven't heard of—one about a land of fairies and political intrigue, and another about childhood lovers who find their way back to each other. I lift my heels off the ground to see if I can spot him over the worn wooden shelves. He's so tall that he's hard to miss, and yet, I can't seem to find him—

"Cleo." His voice startles me from behind, and I nearly drop the books in my hand. "I have a big problem."

"I'm listening," I whisper coyly, turning toward him and lifting an eyebrow in curiosity.

"I'm stuck between a fantasy about wizards or one about dragons. How do I choose?"

"Dragons. The answer is always dragons."

"This is exactly why I need you in my life," he says casually, as if those mere words don't mean anything. "You fill in all my gaps."

You fill in all my gaps.

My heart skips a beat upon hearing these words.

"Well, as cool as it is to be unseen and all, I'm not a thief, so I don't feel comfortable walking out with these. What do you say we walk upstairs to the second floor and find a cozy couch to lounge on?"

"Uh, sure. Let's do it. But wait," I say, holding up my options. "Help me pick. Fairies and grumpy princes or childhood lovers with a second chance?"

"Grumpy princes. Duh."

I smile unabashedly and lead him up the stairs, selecting a small, vacant, forest-green velvet sofa in the corner, which sits underneath a string of multicolored Christmas lights. Some large *Monstera* plants rest on either side of the love seat, and the wall behind is a moody shade of black.

Before sitting, I can't help but notice how small this spot is. I bite my lip and glance around in search of an alternative reading nook. Suddenly, his strong arms wrap around me and bring me down to the seat with him. I land sideways in his lap, both of my legs draping over one side, while my back leans against the sofa's soft armrest. His back rests on the cushioned backrest.

"Are you sure this is comfortable?" I wiggle around, settling in his lap.

"'Comfortable' would be an understatement," he murmurs, sinking deeper into the sofa, pushing himself against the couch's backrest. The curve of my body is aligned with his, my hips sinking against the firmness beneath me.

I blush—*ugh*—and nod. I open my book at the same time as he opens his with his free hand.

"I thought you said you weren't a reader."

"Oh, I'm not. But you are."

"Well, I don't want to waste your time if you're not—"

"I want to see what all the hype is about." His eyes land on the open book in his hand, while he pulls me in tighter with his arm beneath me. "Let's read together, angel."

Hours pass. The area downstairs has been busy with traffic for the past few hours, but no one has really ventured upstairs, giving us an extra level of privacy—not that anyone can see us anyway.

We've repositioned a few times throughout our reading session, but we're back in the same position we started in. He shuts his book and fixes his gaze on the ceiling, his lips slightly parted. Noticing he's closed his book, I shut mine, too, and set it on my chest. I just entered the epilogue anyway, so I've completed the main storyline.

I like to save epilogues for a rainy day.

Epilogues give me something to look forward to beyond the story's ending. Often, I'll read epilogues months or even years after completing a book, when I find myself missing the story and wanting closure.

This book was spicier than I anticipated. He wasn't lying earlier—this story left very little to the imagination.

And I didn't mind one bit.

"Well?" I ask, tilting my head. "Was it everything you hoped for?"

"Hold on," he says, his lips thinning into a flat line as a quizzical expression settles on his features. I knit my brows. "The *ending*. I'm still processing it. Who on earth decided to make this book a *standalone*? What do you mean, that's *it*? I have so many unanswered questions. My head might just explode right here, right now."

I cover my mouth to stifle a laugh.

"What?" He cocks an eyebrow.

"It makes me happy seeing you get so passionate about a book." I smile wider, and this one isn't fake.

"Well, I get the hype now, and I fear you've unlocked a new level to my afterlife. Be prepared for me to rant about this book—and many more—for the years to come."

Years. *Years*?

"You're something else, Kai." I shake my head.

"Did you like your book?" he asks.

"I loved it. This was my first spicy book."

"Oh, yeah? That's hot." He smiles with his eyes as my cheeks burn. "And same. I loved my read, too."

"Sounds like you finally found the right book," I remark.

"You helped me find the right one after all."

His hazel eyes pierce mine.

My lips part. "You remember that? I didn't think you would."

"Of course, I do. I remember everything that involves you, Cleo."

"But you were so—"

"Oh, hell yeah, I was *gone* that night." He laughs, his abs rumbling against my lower back. "I told you. I couldn't forget our moments even if I tried to."

My chest feels lighter than it has in a while. Something about the rawness in his confession shakes me.

I thought I could do this. I thought I could lie to him, but I don't know how much longer I can keep this up.

"Kai, I—"

"I've got the best idea. Do you like musicals?"

Usually, I don't appreciate interruptions, but this time, I'm relieved.

He unknowingly stopped me from ruining my resolve.

"I do. I haven't seen a play since the '70s."

"What '70s?"

"Excuse me?"

"Like, are we talkin' the 1970s, or 1670s, or—"

"*Heavens*. How old do you think I am?" I ask, holding my hand over my chest, mortified. He bursts into an obnoxious laugh, gripping my waist. "The 1970s, Kai. I'm not ancient."

He sighs in relief. "Great. You're already out of my league, but I worry if you were raised in the 1600s, you'd be beyond reach."

I laugh, shaking my head.

"Let's go see a show. Have you ever watched a Broadway show?"

"I have. It's been decades, though. I'd actually love to see how much it's changed."

"That settles it." He grabs our books and sets them down on the other end of the sofa, declaring that onlookers can assume the bookshop is haunted. That might be good for business anyway—people love the paranormal.

Then, he rises from the seat and cradles me in his arms bridal-style.

"What on earth are you doing?"

"It's time I carry you for a change. I live for our glory rides in the Middle Realm, but I've been wanting to hold you like this for a while."

He carries me down the stairs carefully, making sure my feet don't unintentionally smack any innocent bookworms scouring the shelves.

I glance outside and notice the sun is setting.

I've never had a bookshop date before. I'll never forget this one.

We exit the shop, and instead of setting me down, he continues to hold me. I keep my arms hooked loosely around his neck and look up at him, taking note of his sharp jawline and full lips.

Little does he know, I don't quite mind him carrying me. It's been a long time since I ventured through New York City, and to say things have changed would be the understatement of the century. The sheer volume of loud cars, obnoxious pedestrians, big screens, and music has been enough to make me wish I could mute my surroundings.

I had no idea cell phones were as prevalent as they are. Everyone is on their phone *all* the time. It's perplexing. Rather than connecting with those around them, they focus entirely on their screens. The devices even play loud music and audio clips casually.

Eloras is so quiet. I suppose I've gotten used to that.

This city, on the other hand, is practically screaming in comparison.

It wasn't always this way.

Decades ago, I found this city peaceful. Calming, even. I found belonging here.

I promised myself I'd never spend time in this realm longer than necessary, especially not in New York.

Not only did I break my promise to myself, but I'm more conflicted about how to proceed than ever. I thought I'd be able to keep up this charade with Kai for at least a few days, but today made me realize I won't even last a day.

The worst part is, I don't even know the depth of his feelings.

He's a shameless flirt. I have no idea if any of our interactions mean anything to him. After he left me in Eloras, I began to question if I could trust anything that came out of his mouth. He told me he would come back quickly. He didn't, and I had to suffer the consequences.

I still don't know if I can trust him.

My body thinks I should, though. That much is clear.

Despite my traitorous body's natural reaction to his hold, I can't let myself forget how much he hurt me.

I *can't* open up again.

I won't.

I'm perfectly capable of getting through this whirlwind of emotions trapped inside me on my own.

Twenty-Two

Kai

Reading is exhilarating. *Who knew?*

Kidding. Of course you knew, little bookworm. I'm just late to the party.

While strolling downtown with my girl in my arms, I'm flying as high as a kite. Figuratively, of course. Obviously, I can't fly yet. Hell, I don't know if I ever will.

It's nice carrying her in my arms for a change rather than holding on to her waist for dear life. I've had a bad feeling since reuniting with her, though. Something is off.

She can tuck her wings away, but when she tucks them away, I can typically still see them. The wings fold inward toward her body when she tucks them behind her back, making them appear quite different in size. I noticed they were missing as soon as I saw her, but holding her in the bookshop is what made my mind start spinning.

Now that I'm carrying her in my arms, my level of concern is rising by the minute. Her body is tense—more tense than usual. I even avoided walking through Times Square because of how stiff she feels in my arms.

Where the hell are her wings? Do angel wings magically disappear upon entering this realm? I guess I wouldn't know.

"What show are we seeing?" she asks, peering up into my eyes. Heavens. I didn't even realize we'd arrived on Broadway Avenue.

I lift my eyes to the vertical sign's bold text lighting up the entire block under the moonlit night sky.

"How about the witchy one?" I offer nonchalantly, setting her down on her own two feet in front of me, immediately draping both of my arms around her shoulders. She reaches up and grabs hold of my forearms.

"I don't think I've ever heard of that one."

"Perfect. The music is iconic. I heard they're even making a movie based on the story. You'll love it." I grin, walking ahead of her and reaching out for her hand. She takes my hand hesitantly and allows me to lead her.

I may be smiling, but my mind is working overtime. Something isn't adding up.

We walk in comfortable silence among a sea of people into the theatre and settle on sitting in the back section on the upper level. A wave of excitement nearly drowns me on our way up the stairs. Everyone in the theatre is buzzing with anticipation. The entire front section on the lower floor is occupied. Thankfully, the upper level of the theatre isn't too crowded tonight. Given how it's a random Monday in January, I can't say I'm surprised.

I've never been one to prefer alone time with my significant other. In my past relationship, I spent a lot of time around others—friends, family, and acquaintances. As extroverts, my ex and I thrived in crowds.

With Cleo, things couldn't be more different.

I've found that I prefer to spend time alone with her. I almost feel a bit territorial over her, which isn't normal for me. I just want her to be comfortable. Always. I mean, it doesn't take a genius to see that she clearly isn't an extrovert. She's much more skilled at watching than *being* watched. Consequently, I feel closest to her when we're alone. I'm not used to that.

We sink into two comfortable burgundy velvet chairs in the very last row. Upon sitting down, I slink my arm around her shoulders and lean into her side. Instead of pulling away, she folds into me, cozying up into my arm.

The theatre's lighting dims as the actors take the stage. Colorful beams of light shine on the stage, setting the mood. I've never seen a show on Broadway myself, so in theory, I should be fucking stoked to experience this.

But as I glance to my right, I realize the only thing I have the capacity to think about right now is her.

The feel of her wingless back.

The stiffness in her shoulders.

The way her smile has failed to reach her eyes most of today.

I'm dying—no pun intended—to help her, but if there's one thing I've learned about her over the last several weeks, it's that she doesn't accept help easily.

"What are you staring at?" she asks in a whisper.

"Oh, just the most beautiful labyrinth I've ever known."

Her cheeks redden, transforming into my new favorite shade of pink.

"'Labyrinth?'" Her brows raise. "Care to explain?"

"What's there to explain, angel? I've been trying to figure you out since the moment you walked into my life, and I have a feeling I still have yet to scratch the surface."

She stifles a smile and bites her lower lip, turning toward the stage. As the show commences, I catch her cracking smiles and even bursting into gentle laughter a handful of times.

I've missed that laugh.

Eventually, she leans forward, propping her elbows on her knees and letting her head rest on them. I slide my arm down and gently rub her back. She flinches when my hand intercepts the spot where her wings should be.

It takes all my strength not to react outwardly.

Instead, I continue nimbly stroking her back. She closes her eyes and relaxes her back. "More of that, please."

I chuckle and give in to her request, pushing aside my rising unease. I continue tracing her back for several minutes when I suddenly realize I have absolutely no idea what this play is really about anymore.

My hand makes its way to her front side, resting on her thigh just below the hem of her skirt. Though a layer of sheer tights separates my skin from hers, the air between us thickens. She eyes me, then parts her supple lips as my hand climbs higher, tightly gripping her velvet soft thigh. Damn, I love holding her like this.

She leans into my touch and lets out a gentle moan in relief, sending a jolt of pent-up energy through my body. I've never heard her make a sound like that before. I'd trek through heaven and hell to listen to it again.

But I can't stop thinking about her wings—or lack thereof. Instead of taking things a step further, I take them a step back. I grasp her soft thigh and pull her toward me, hooking my arm around her. With my arm wrapped around her, everything else fades.

Suddenly, it's only colorful stage lights, soothing music, and us—my angel and me.

She closes her eyes and swallows, then delicately rests her head on my shoulder. This isn't quite what I had in mind when I expressed wanting to help her. But holding her in my arms and experiencing something new *together* for the first time is better. A thousand times better.

I'm ruined, aren't I?

"How did you like it?" Cleo asks nonchalantly as we exit the venue and enter the busy street, the smell of roasted nuts in the air.

"Like what? The snuggling or the show?"

She rolls her eyes and nudges my arm, glancing away at a crowded pizza stand, clearly attempting to conceal her smile. We continue following the street, wandering aimlessly without a care in the world. "You know what."

"I liked it. Can't say it was as memorable as I had hoped, though—especially considering it was over three hours long. We'll have to see it again sometime." I crack a smile, knowing full well that the odds of being able to see that show again are slim to none.

The longer I stay in this realm, the more I realize how faulty my idea of running away was. It's only a matter of time before someone catches me—us.

Us. I like the sound of that.

"How about you?" I brush her shoulder. "Did you like it?"

"I enjoyed it." She beams, staring at a nearby skyscraper, then her eyes lift even higher. "I wish Eloras provided entertainment like that."

"Do you think the Golden Realm provides that?"

She shrugs. "I've heard rumors that the Golden Realm provides everything an angel could ever dream of. If that's true, then I'd have to assume that type of theatrical entertainment must be available way up there."

"You know what, I bet that realm is itching to recruit your ex-lover-friend-hater, Stephen." I wiggle my eyebrows. "He has some of the most refined acting skills I've ever seen. The term 'Drama King' has to have been coined just for him."

Cleo stops dead in her tracks and bends over, clutching her stomach tightly, shaking.

"Whoa, are you okay?" I step in front of her. She slowly lifts her eyes to meet mine and *honks* like a goose with the broadest grin on her face. Her hands quickly rise to cover her mouth, but it's no use—she's laughing so hard her eyes are watering. Then she proceeds to *honk* again. She shakes her head and attempts to rein in her laugh as mortification takes over her features.

"Please, for the love of everything, forget you ever heard that atrocious sound escaping my lips."

I break into a grin, my chest rumbling with laughter.

"Too late now. That *atrocious sound* has permanently taken up residency right here." I gesture to my head.

We fall back into step with each other, walking downtown and eyeing fully-lit shops as we pass them. New York City lives up to its title. It truly is the city that never sleeps.

But after the last several days I've had, nothing sounds nicer than some rest.

"Have you ever visited upstate? I've been wanting to check out the mountains and cabins there but haven't had the chance to. What do you say? We head there tonight for a change of scenery?" I offer.

She hesitates, then nods her head. "Why upstate? Why don't we head back to Chrysocolla Cove?"

"I've heard upstate is pretty. *And* it's closer."

"It is beautiful."

"Ah, so you *have* visited there before? Perfect, then you can teleport us there."

"I suppose your wish is my command, Kai Greene."

"Don't tease me, Cleo." I peer into her brown eyes with a crooked smile. "You know that's a fantasy of mine."

She scoffs and grabs on to my waist, burying her head into my chest. "Hold on tight."

As we teleport upstate, I release a breath of relief. Maybe she'll be more comfortable opening up to me in a less chaotic area. It's killing me not knowing what's going on in that gorgeous head of hers. I just want to help.

Although I'm still convinced her afterlife would be remarkably brighter without me in it, I'd give anything to just be there for her. Anything.

Twenty-Three

Cleo

A thick sheet of sparkling snow covers the ground surrounding where we land. On either side of us lies a line of frosted trees, leading us down a moonlit path. I sniff the air and catch a whiff of pine and something unmistakably earthy. I gaze up at the sky, seeing a cluster of dark clouds rolling in over us, threatening to envelop our only means of light. The only light out here is granted from the moon itself.

"Holy shit. Did we land in Narnia?" Kai chimes while taking in the snow, chuckling. I smile gently, continuing to trek down the narrow, well-kept path when I suddenly feel something wet collide with my forehead. The cool droplet streams down my cheek. I raise my hand to my cheek, and my lips part as I exhale a long sigh of relief.

Nearly five decades have passed.

I don't know whether to laugh or cry.

I could've never anticipated this surge of emotion from a mere drop of rain. "It's been a while since my last rainstorm," he whispers.

You have no idea.

"Oh, I don't?" He raises an eyebrow. "Tell me more."

I sigh, looking up at the sky and rolling my eyes. My mental shields have been seriously lacking since this man walked into my life.

"It's been decades since I've felt a drop of rain," I admit quietly as we continue walking, light rain falling more steadily with each step we take. "I've always enjoyed rainy weather more than blue skies and sunshine. Something about a light rain on a cloudy day soothes my soul."

"You prefer rain over sunshine? No." His eyes widen while his jaw drops—dramatically, I might add. "Never would've guessed."

I simply nod my head. I squint my eyes and see an even narrower path veering off the current path we're on. I'm willing to bet that path leads to the cabins.

I remember this park as if it were yesterday. Gulping, I opt to distract myself and run my hand over my face again, feeling a hint of excitement at how wet my cheeks are. I close my eyes and bite back a soft grin, then notice him staring at me. I stop in my tracks.

"You're staring," I accuse. He smirks before taking a step into my bubble and tucking a lock of damp hair behind my ear. He's getting quite good at that.

"How could I not?" he murmurs, his hazel eyes drifting over me before locking onto mine.

Warmth spreads across my cheeks. Little does he know, I can hardly stop staring at him myself. Not that I can share that.

"It's okay. You don't have to say anything." He grins, taking my hand in his and moving forward. "I know you like the rain and all, but as a sunshine lover myself, I'd prefer to settle somewhere dry for the night."

I incline my head toward the alternate path. "There. Let's take that path."

"Lead the way."

I walk in front of him down the new path entirely engulfed in trees. After only a moment, we make it to a clearing with two lake houses.

Interesting—it appears the cabins were renovated. They're so much larger than I remember. Chills spread across my arms as my mind threatens to unravel moments I'd prefer not to relive. I tighten my free hand into a fist.

Now is simply not the time. I need to concentrate.

Getting Kai back to the Middle Realm is my top priority.

That initiative needs to be at the forefront of my mind.

Not my memories.

He squeezes my hand reassuringly, catching me off guard. I must be squeezing his hand hard, given how tight my fist is. How embarrassing.

I curse myself and then cross my fingers that at least one of these cabins is unoccupied. If not, we're teleporting back to the city immediately.

We quietly approach the one nearest to us and see lights on inside. I peer into the large front window and see four people sitting around a wooden table, playing card games. Two adults and two children. A family.

The youngest—who can't be older than five—is cracking up, banging his hand against the table's carved surface. He keeps glancing at his older sister and shaking his head. She's covering her mouth and laughing, too, while their parents wear confused expressions. The joke is clearly about them.

There's a softness in the father's gaze that strikes me. Although he isn't in on the joke, he's grinning from ear to ear, watching his children with a tenderness I haven't seen in a long, long time.

I wipe my eye before a single tear can escape and turn around abruptly, stalking past this home to the next one. Kai can hardly keep up, but I don't care. As I inch closer to the next one, I clench my jaw.

Please be empty. Please be empty. Please be empty.

This lake house is slightly smaller than the other, but it's closer to the water. When I was little, lake days were my favorite days. We'd spend all day on the water, chasing dragonflies and frogs and eating sandwiches and cookies. Playing hide-and-seek in the forest surrounding us.

My family and I thrived during those little getaways. It's when I felt closest to them. The lake brought us together year after year, making our family bond so strong it felt tangible. Given our stubborn natures, it was one of the only things we all connected on.

All the lights in this one are off, and I don't see a car in the gravel driveway, meaning it's presumably unoccupied. Reaching the top of the wooden stairs and stepping onto the wraparound porch, I brace myself and turn to hold him before teleporting inside the home.

I take in my surroundings as he begins exploring. He heads upstairs almost immediately and gasps, exclaiming about how nice the loft is. A small kitchen and dining area are to my right, featuring a rectangular wooden table and benches on either side. To my left lies the living room, including two brown sofas, a television, and a coffee table. Straight ahead is a staircase that used to lead to bedrooms. I glance up and see that it's changed. As he mentioned, it's a loft now. How modern.

Although the home looks different, the energy is familiar, even after all these years.

In fact, a lot of the wooden beams here look like the original wood. If I walk outside and peer closer at the wooden floorboards, I'll find the name 'Graves' carved in one of the planks.

I lost my first tooth in the living room.

My brother took his first steps right next to the dining table.

My sister learned how to ride a bike here.

My mom and I baked homemade bread using that kitchen counter countless times.

My dad taught me how to swim in the lake outside.

This was our family's vacation cabin for years. My home away from home.

And for some unknown, objectively idiotic reason, I thought I could handle staying the night here with him. It's been so long since I last thought about this place that I assumed I had moved on. I thought wrong.

Foolish. I should've known I'd never be strong enough, even to face something minuscule like this.

Coward.

My strength isn't real. It's a facade. Just like the relationship I'm building with the angel upstairs. How could he care for someone like me?

I gaze down at the original warm oak wooden flooring.

At first, the memories fall gently like rain. I catch myself nearly smiling at the innocence in them.

Then, without warning, the memories begin crashing against me harder, hitting me like a riptide; they pull me under and drown me without reprieve.

Coward.

Suddenly, I'm crashing to the floor, squeezing my eyes shut and trembling.

I can't let him see me like this. He'll leave again.

"Cleo, you've got to see—" His voice cuts off. Before I can even turn my head in his direction, he's on the floor with me, kneeling before me, grasping my shoulders with both hands. I keep my eyes sealed shut.

I can't believe this.

I've never cried in front of anyone outside my family. Ever. What horrible timing.

I've cried a handful of times, and a majority of those times, I was utterly alone.

"Baby, it's okay. You're okay. I'm here. I'm with you."

As he's stroking my cheeks delicately, it hits me.

I'm not alone anymore.

But as much as I want to believe him, my mind won't stop chanting: *this isn't real.*

"Kai, I'm f-fine. Seriously." I shrug him off and open my eyes, making sure to look into his eyes despite the burning sensation. I work hard to control my trembling. Instead of releasing my shoulders like I expect, he pulls me into him, cradling me in his arms.

"You don't have to talk about it, but I'm not letting go of you, little angel." His voice rumbles as he runs his hand through my damp hair, pulling my head deeper into his chest. "Unless you want me to."

I can't make sense of much right now, but he's warm. So warm.

"Stay," I whisper so softly it's barely audible.

Then, and only then, do I let the tears fall freely.

"This place just triggers a lot of memories for me," I mumble into his chest. "I thought I could handle this, but it's all so overwhelming."

He strokes my back soothingly and kisses my forehead. "I'm here. You're not alone."

"But you left me." I open my eyes slowly and crane my neck to look up at him. "You left without a word." I ask, tears streaming down my cheeks. The tears are warmer than I expected. It's been so long since I let myself cry that it feels foreign to me.

As he tilts his head, a sobering look crosses his face. With his brows drawn, he stares back into my eyes, then cups my neck in his hands.

"I could never leave you, Cleo."

"But you did."

"Not forever—I won't do that to you. I promise."

I thought he left for good. Everything is so jumbled in my head right now that I can hardly think straight.

"I've made my choice. I'm not going anywhere, angel."

Exerting so much energy into this has drained me.

I continue to weep, then melt into his strong arms, savoring the warmth of his strong embrace. Something about him disarms me. As different as we are, it's like he truly understands me. I find myself comfortable sharing more with him than anyone I've ever known.

TWENTY-FOUR

KAI

I can't put my sheer anguish into words right now. The last time I felt even remotely close to how I'm feeling right now was the first time I visited my sister after my death. But somehow, this is a thousand times worse than that.

I lift her and gently set her down on the brown plush sofa in the living room, then sit on the ground in front of her, rubbing her forehead. Her eyes haven't opened since I pulled her against me. I grit my teeth at the sight of tears cascading down her cheeks.

I'd be lying if I said I was totally cool with this. No, I want to pry. I want to know *everything*.

For starters, I need to know what the *fuck* happened to her midnight-blue wings.

Earlier, when I watched her embrace the rain with open arms, I rejoiced in the warmth of her smile.

Now, her pain is my pain.

With Cleo, I find myself not wanting to run away, which is shamefully uncharacteristic for me. Instead, I'm drawn closer to her.

Our emotions are tangled in a web I don't want to escape from.

It's terrifying.

But it's also everything.

Something pivotal has shifted between us tonight.

I can't believe she thought I left her for good... I mean, I considered doing that for a millisecond just because I assumed her afterlife would be ten times better without me in it. I screw everything up anyway. But after tonight, it's clearer than ever that we're both in this together.

She shared that this place triggers her, too. What is triggering about this lake house? It must remind her of something from her mortal life. I can't help but wonder if this may be part of the reason she refuses to visit this realm for leisure.

The chattering of her teeth snaps me out of my spiraling mind and sets me into motion immediately—she needs a damn blanket. This old, quiet little lake house is way too drafty.

Okay, I know, I *know*. Angels can't get cold, but my girl's trembling, and although I'm 99 percent sure she's having an emotional reaction to something, there is a 1 percent chance she's freezing. I'm not taking any chances.

I rise to my feet and turn to walk away when a hand grips my wrist firmly. "Please don't leave."

"You're stuck with me. Sorry, not sorry. I'll be right back."

I lift her hand to my lips and kiss it. All the while, her eyes are still closed.

She doesn't say anything. She releases my hand and nods absentmindedly, her cheeks still wet.

I walk upstairs and spend a whole two minutes considering grabbing the master bed's entire comforter before deciding the lake house owners must have less bulky blanket options available *somewhere*. Upon reaching the foot of the stairs, I check the hallway closet. Sure enough, I spot a few knit blankets. Thank heavens.

I grab a couple and shut the wooden door, heading back into the living room when something catches my eye. I step closer to the dining room wall to get a closer look and notice carved markings in the trim. They've been painted over, but they look like height measurements. I run my fingers along the marks, my eyes fixating on them. While running my fingers over the marks, I notice letters carved into the wood, too. I squat and squint my eyes, attempting to make out the writing.

Finally, after what feels like an hour, I figure it out. With a smug expression on my face, I settle on the letters:

C. G.

Must be initials. Running my fingers over some of the other marks, I pick up some of the others.

J. G.

S. G.

And of course, C. G. again.

I get goosebumps I didn't know angels were capable of getting, and my breathing grows more rapid.

Is this really just a coincidence? It can't be, can it?

C. G.

Cleo Graves.

My jaw drops in perfect synchronization with the blankets in my arms as I take a step back.

“And you make fun of others for their theatrics,” a quiet voice mumbles from behind me, causing me to nearly stumble. I turn around in a flash, facing her.

“When did you get here?” I ask, still rattled. She’s leaning against the wall, crossing her arms. She seems to be holding it together a bit better than she was a few minutes ago.

“I witnessed your full-length investigation of the carvings.” She breaks my gaze to peer at them behind me. “Impressive work, detective.”

I shrug. “It wasn’t much. The layer of paint is pretty thin if I’m being real.”

She suppresses a smile. “Did you figure it out?”

I swallow subtly and gesture toward the carvings. “Are we looking at little Cleo’s height measurements right now?”

She exhales a deep breath and stares at them like she’s contemplating how much to tell me.

Finally, she nods slowly.

“You’ve been here before,” I say, matter-of-factly.

She nods. I gaze at the wall again.

“You’ve been here *several* times before.”

Again, she nods, staring into my eyes.

Without thinking, I bend and pull her into my arms for the second time tonight, unable to help myself. At first, she resists my pull, but then she folds into me, wrapping her arms around my sides. I rest my head atop hers and calmly breathe in and out.

“I get it now,” I whisper into her thick dark brunette locks, grasping her nape with my hand. “Are you ready to talk about it?”

Her breathing slows.

“I don’t know if I’ll ever be ready,” she whispers.

“What about them?” I incline my head to the other markings, lower than the C. G. markings. “Do you want to talk about them?”

A beat of silence passes, then she leans harder into my chest, nodding.

"That's my girl." I grin with a sense of pride and lead her back to the couch after gathering the blankets I dramatically dropped earlier—she's right, you know. I'm going to give Stephen a run for his money when it comes to this whole acting gig.

Keeping my hand on the small of her back, we sink into the couch together. Surprisingly, rather than leaning away from me, she leans into me and rests her hand atop mine, tracing circles into it.

"What do you want to know, Kai?"

"Well, I'm an open book. Hell, considering you were my Watcher, I assume you know all about my life. You know Iris, Jasper, and Truman. You know about my parents. My ex. My baseball career. My death. And guess what?" I pause, picking up her legs off the ground and settling them on top of my thighs, tucking us under the blanket together. "I feel like I hardly know anything about you. Yet somehow, you still consume nearly all my thoughts."

She shifts her weight.

"Let's start with the basics. Did those other measurements belong to siblings of yours? Tell me about them. You know I'm *all* about sibling bonds."

She presses her lips together in a soft smile.

"The 'J' stands for Jonathan. He was only three years younger than me and two years older than my little sister. Being sandwiched between two hormonal girls was no easy task, but honestly, he handled it so well. We lived through so much of my life together; it's hard to remember a time when he wasn't right there by my side. We learned how to paddleboard together on the lake. We stayed up late telling each other spooky stories with ominous flashlights under our bedsheets. He was always the most artsy of the three of us—while I spent all my free time dancing, and my sister spent hers in sports, he spent his with a sketchbook and pencil in hand."

She looks up at me, tears brimming in her eyes. "Jonathan went on to become an animation artist for some really popular cartoons. He even freelanced some book covers—I have one of his books up in the Middle Realm. I actually stole it from the library. How could I not?"

Her pride strikes a chord. I understand the feeling. Iris has no idea how genuinely proud I am of her. Something tells me Jonathan isn't aware of Cleo's pride, either.

"It's cliché, but Sadie was special. She was the kind of girl people gravitated to without even knowing. A true athlete at heart, she participated in tennis and volleyball. She was also an exceptional swimmer—she swam laps around my short self in the lake every year—"

Every year.

They visited this lake house annually.

"—We had different tastes in music, movies, and celebrities, but that's what made our conversations so invigorating. We challenged each other constantly, and despite how tumultuous our relationship was at times, I'm better for it. Because of Sadie, I'm able to fully respect other people's opinions while staying true to my own beliefs. She may have been younger, but she taught me as much—if not more—than I taught her. She went on to be a Realtor. She's always been a people person. The role is only fitting."

Cleo beams as she talks about her family. I find myself not wanting the conversation to end. Hell, I've fallen so hard that she could talk about a vacuum and I'd be fully invested at this point.

"I was the oldest sibling—like you." She pauses and literally *boops* my nose. This girl is maddening. "I didn't have quite as much time with my siblings as you had with Iris. I died when I was only twenty-three, leaving them alone to fend for themselves. After my life ended, I could've chosen to guard one of them as a Guardian, but I couldn't fathom only helping one without the other, so I passed, hoping the Guardians assigned to them could help them more than I could. It was selfish of me. *Cowardly*—"

She pauses, her throat bobbing as she shakes her head.

"—I was supposed to take care of them until we grew old and gray, but I failed them. I would've given them the world if I could. I'd give anything for the outcome of our story to be different."

She's right—I died when I was twenty-seven. I had a few more years with Iris, and I still didn't feel like even that was enough time.

Her eyes glisten in the cabin's warm, glowing light, reminding me of silver. Her raw expression of emotion shakes me.

"You being the oldest sibling makes so much sense. We just get each other, you know?" I stroke her thigh. She rolls her eyes with a coy smile. My expression sobers, and I whisper, "You aren't a coward, Cleo. I get why you chose not to guard them—it would've been hard helping one of them heal but not the other."

She closes her eyes and shakes her head, pressing her lips into a flat line. "I could've—no, I *should've* done more."

"Cleo, I'm so sorry. I wish I could take your pain away." I gulp. "What about your parents? What were they like?"

She swallows and exhales. "They were everything to me. My mom was a tailor—a cool one. She ran the business from our home and everything. I helped pick up the slack and watch my brother and sister when she had to work, but I didn't mind it. My friends all loved her because she was hilarious and full of life. My dad was an engineer. I can't lie, I don't know the first thing about what he actually did daily, but I can confidently say he was the most patient person I have ever known. My mom was stubborn, hotheaded, and a bit cold at times—familiar, I know—but my dad was gentle, protective, and calming. After a bad day, he'd sit me down and let me talk him through it with a cup of hot cocoa, no matter how insignificant my sorrows were. It was more than I deserved."

Everything is clicking now. Watching the way she talks about her family makes so much sense. Death tore her away from them, and for some reason, she's angry at herself. She sighs and shuts her eyes. "They just cared about us. Truly cared. They weren't perfect parents, but they were mine."

"That's so special. I can't even comprehend what it's like to have parents who undoubtedly care. I always doubted whether mine did—until I died, that is. After my departure, I finally realized how much they cared, but it's a bit wild that it took my literal death for that to become clear." I choke up, thinking about how she described her parents. "Your parents sound perfect to me. I hope to meet them one day."

A tear slips out of her eye, running along the edge of her cheek. "They would've really loved you."

My heart does a flip in response to that. "Damn, that's high praise coming from Cleo Graves herself." I lean close enough to her to count her eyelashes and the small, faint freckles on her cheeks. "How are you feeling now?"

With almost no hesitation, she nods and answers, "Lighter."

I smile. Mission accomplished.

"Most of the time, it feels like you're the only person I can talk to," she gently whispers, gazing into my eyes.

"The feeling is mutual." I massage her back. "And you're the only person I *want* to talk to most of the time."

Her cheeks turn my favorite shade of pink, then she asks, "How are *you* feeling, Kai?"

My stomach drops.

"I'm... okay. Better than okay for the first time in a while, actually. Thanks to you." I let out a sigh when a bright idea comes to mind. "Do you trust me?"

She hesitates now. I quirk a brow. After all we've been through, she still isn't sure about me. *Fuck, that hurts.*

"Fine. Do you wanna do something wild?" I grin at her mischievously.

"Perhaps?" She raises her eyebrows skeptically.

"'Perhaps' is basically a yes in Kai's book, so we're doing it. No takebacks."

I quickly jump up from the sofa and begin taking my clothes off. I do it slowly to give her a little show, too. Sue me, I just love watching her blush.

"What on earth are you doing?" She gawks, staring at my discarded clothes on the floor. I've taken nearly everything off except for my briefs. Her eyes scan my body, and my cock hardens under her sight—I can't help it. Her eyes widen before shutting abruptly. I crack a grin and step closer to her.

"Drink it in, baby. I'm all yours." I bite my lip subtly and decide to take things another step—yes, a literal step—forward and plant my arms on either side of her, caging her in on the couch.

"Oh, please. I'm not naive enough to think that *that*"—she opens her eyes and runs her fingers down my abdomen mockingly, sending shivers down my spine—"is all mine."

Just one touch, and I'm putty.

Then she squeezes her eyes shut again.

She's so damn cute.

I bend down and brush my lips against her earlobe.

"Trust me. I've been yours longer than you know," I rasp into her ear. "Now, be a good girl and come join me in the water."

I bounce back and sprint out of the front door in only my briefs before she can respond, crossing my fingers and toes that she'll follow me.

Running away together could be a real possibility after all.

Is *this* what the afterlife is supposed to feel like? It reminds me of my life before death. Hell, I've missed living.

I can't get enough.

Maybe this realm and that angel are exactly what I've been needing to find peace.

Twenty-Five

Cleo

Swimming at midnight under the stars with an undeniably gorgeous man wasn't on my list for this trip, but here we are. Gazing out of the window, I notice the rain has paused. I watch him speed walk toward the lake and jump in carelessly.

After staying underwater for a long moment, he whips his head out and scans the lake house until he finds me. Noticing I haven't moved an inch, he quirks his head and furrows his brows in confusion before inclining his head toward the water.

What are you afraid of, Cleo?

His rich voice enters my mind.

I'm not afraid, I answer a bit too swiftly.

I don't think I believe you. Prove it.

I've never been one to back down from a challenge. I stare at him directly in the eyes from inside the lake house and lift my chin high with a scowl before shrugging nonchalantly and bending over.

I peel my tights off first. My skirt follows closely after, pooling around my ankles. I maintain his stare, noting his eyes are a bit more hooded than they were a moment ago.

Relishing in the way he's watching me, I smirk and raise my sweater over my head as delicately as possible. I toss it on the couch, then cross my arms.

His lips part as his eyes drift down my body, taking in every inch. His gaze lingers on some parts of me longer than others. Exposing my body like this would generally make me uncomfortable, but I'm starting to understand that he makes everything easier. I think, maybe, he's become my happy place.

Fuck. Me.

Forward much? I cover my lips while suppressing a smile.

When it comes to you, I have to be.

I close my eyes and chuckle, but when I open them, he is nowhere to be found.

Kai?

Did he leave? Did the Archangels find us? Oh heavens, what are we—

Suddenly, damp arms grab me from behind, lifting me off my feet. Kai scoops me into his arms and beams at me, droplets of water falling from his drenched hair and dripping onto my skin. His gaze trails the path of the falling drops, lingering on my collarbone for a moment before lifting to my eyes.

"Did you just teleport in here?"

"I had to get to you as fast as possible."

"Does this mean I don't have to go swimming in that freezing lake with you after all?" I gasp sarcastically.

He gasps back, grinning from ear to ear. "No."

Before I can utter a word in response, he takes off, running out the front door while carrying me in his arms. As we edge closer to the lake, he doesn't slow down, which is a big nope for me.

I'm not one of those people who enjoys jumping into the water right away—I prefer to dip my toes in and slowly embrace it. It doesn't surprise me at all that he is a jumper.

"Kai. Put me down." I grit my teeth. "Do *not* give in to your intrusive thoughts. *Don't.*"

Instead of responding, he just wheezes a faint laugh, pulling me even tighter into his chiseled abs.

"I'm *not* kidding," I say in the firmest tone I can muster, attempting to wiggle my way out of his toned arms. Damnit, why does he have to be so fit?

Look, I know angels aren't supposed to feel cold, but that water looks frigid, and quite frankly, I wasn't planning on getting my hair wet again after drying off from the rain. Sue me.

In a matter of seconds, I'm suddenly in the air, falling to my demise, flailing my arms like a madwoman. Of course, he threw me in. I'd expect nothing less of this wild man.

This moment briefly brings me back to another time—one not nearly as pleasant as this one. Crashing under the surface of the black water, I immediately swim upward, desperate to inhale fresh air.

Raising my head above the surface and inhaling a breath of air, I immediately push the memories away. We only scratched the surface when it comes to my mortal life tonight. The less he knows about my life before the afterlife, the better.

Thankfully, the water isn't actually cold. I'll admit, never getting cold or hot is a significant perk of being dead. Throughout my mortal life, I always ran cold, so I appreciate the eternal regulated body temperature. I glance around and notice fireflies dimming in and out of existence—I've always loved the way they glow. There's something so magical about those little creatures. They seem to be growing rarer and rarer with each passing decade, too.

An obnoxious splash of water has me turning my head toward the source.

"Having fun?" He tilts his head, smirking.

"No," I answer coolly while treading the water and getting lost in the stars, careful not to let my uncaring mask slip.

He gravitates closer to me until our bodies nearly touch.

"I find it ironic—you, watching the stars so intently." I peel my eyes away from the stars and gaze into his. "The stars should be watching you."

He drags his gaze down to my lips, then raises his fingers to graze them. His touch is defined but soft—so much smoother than I expected.

Then, his fingers stroke my cheek, trailing down to grasp my chin. I break our stare, looking down.

"Look at me." He lifts my chin gently, pushing his hand back to cradle my jaw. "I can be... eccentric. I know. So, it may be hard to read me sometimes. But the last thing I want is for you to doubt me. I'll come clean. Will I regret this later? Maybe. However, the truth would've come out eventually. I'd rather it comes out while stars and fireflies surround us than while we're on the run.

"When we're together, you consume my thoughts. When we're apart, you consume them twice as much. I've been dealing with a lot over the last several weeks, but every time I run away and drift out farther into the sea, you find me and bring me back to the shore. The funny thing is, I'm not even sure where your head is at with all this, and as downright scary as that is, I don't know if it matters to me anymore."

Our noses nearly touch.

"I'll take whatever you give me, Cleo."

I stop breathing. He may think he means this, but he can't.

If he does, I'll end up hurting him, too. It's inevitable.

"Kai, there's so much you don't know. If you knew everything, I'm certain you wouldn't feel this way."

"If you think that, then you don't know me at all," he murmurs, wrapping his arms around my waist underwater and resting me on his lap so that I'm straddling him as he keeps us afloat. My thighs rest against his as our bodies mold into each other's. "I'm *certain* that my feelings won't change over that. I'm also a pretty stubborn person. I told you. You're stuck with me... Unless this is one-sided."

One word comes to mind. Complicated.

Things have become so beautifully complicated.

But right now, as I'm staring into his molten gold eyes and holding my breath, all I want is Kai Greene.

For as long as I can have him.

For as long as he will have me.

"I don't know if I've ever been very good at pretending," I whisper, parting my lips and wrapping my arms tighter around his neck. He leans in, his lips grazing my ear as he exhales a breath, making my body shudder.

"I know." He smiles against my ear and uses his teeth to tug on it gently, immediately sending a rush of shivers down my spine. That felt good. *Too good.*

How deprived am I?

"You won't be deprived for much longer." He trails his lips down to my neck, placing kisses all the way to my collarbone.

Oh my heavens. Did I say that *out loud*?

He chuckles into my neck. "No. I've just gotten *really* good at reading your thoughts if I do say so myself."

I exhale a sigh of relief and run my fingers through his hair as his kisses on my neck grow more passionate—hungrier. I lean my head back in pleasure and release the quietest whimper.

"*Fuck.* I've never heard something so sexy."

My core grows warmer as I feel his length push against my center. I moan again without holding back, this time leading him to drive his hardness into me firmly.

"Now you're just teasing me." He smiles in between kisses.

I pause, suddenly feeling apprehension creeping in. "What if they're watching us up there?"

"Let them watch."

Then he tightly pulls me into him and teleports us back to the lake house, but this time, we're in the loft. He sets me down on the edge of the king-size four-poster bed, where I sit upright, and then he locks his eyes on me.

He kneels to the ground, his arousal impossible to miss at this point. Using his hands to frame the curves of my body, he starts at my shoulders, rubbing them intently. Then, as his hands roam lower and approach my breasts, he looks into my eyes—seeking permission.

I simply nod, reveling in how hooded his eyes have grown. He reaches around my back to unclasp my bra and tosses it on the floor. Then, his hands meet my breasts and grasp them tightly. He gazes at them like they're perfect when they are far from it. I have a full chest, but one boob is *definitely* a teeny bit perkier than the other. So again, they're objectively not—

"*Perfect.* They are fucking perfect," he whispers in awe before taking one into his mouth, swirling his tongue around my perked nipple, leading me to toss my head back in bliss. I grab hold of his hair and tug it hard. He breaks away for only a second and looks up at me from the ground. "*You're* perfect."

He massages my breasts leisurely, then lowers me off the bed. My legs wrap around his waist mid-air, just inches above the ground, as he sucks on my breasts. I clutch the burgundy velvet bedding behind me with one hand and cup my other hand around his neck, pulling him against me. I lean my head back and close my eyes in bliss. I want—no, I *need*—more.

"You make me feel so alive," I breathe, rotating my hips to align my opening with his cock. I slide up and down against his hardness and bask in how good it feels—how *right* it feels. He smiles against my neck and kisses it tenderly in response.

"This won't do," he rasps, pausing our movements and lifting us onto the bed, planting his arms on either side of me, caging me again like earlier on the sofa.

"You're more particular than I expected, Kai," I purr, not caring to hide my smile this time.

"Angel, I've imagined our first time more times than you can imagine. You've got to know by now that I'm not a perfectionist—not even close. But when it comes to you, to this, I won't settle for less than utter perfection. My angel deserves nothing less."

The amount of thought he's putting into this makes my heart burst. He backs away and stands up, peeling his briefs off. I gape at his length and gulp, parting my lips in disbelief.

How the hell am I supposed to fit *that* in *this*...

In true Kai fashion, he smirks and shoots me a wink, eyes far more heated than usual.

He crawls back on the bed, passing me to rest his back against the headboard. Nodding his chin for me to join him, I hesitantly move closer until I'm sitting atop of him, my legs curving on either side of his muscular thighs. He grasps my waist, digging his fingers into my soft sides, and shifts my body for me. I bend, sucking and nipping and licking his neck and take satisfaction in how hard he's growing beneath me.

One of his hands trails down the small of my back until it reaches my thong's sheer fabric. Letting out a groan, he tears it off and tosses it across the room without hesitation.

"Finally." He squeezes my behind, pressing his fingers into it.

That dainty piece of fabric was the very last boundary between us.

Slowly, I lower myself onto him and release a moan of my own as we fuse our bodies together. I rotate my hips faster as he thrusts harder.

"That's it, angel," he breathes. "Use me. I'm yours."

My core nearly explodes.

This is everything.

He is everything.

It's like I've been waiting for this moment since the day I died.

Actually, no, not this moment.

I've been waiting for *him.*

Like a spool of the very thread I once shared with him as his Watcher, I unwind, and then my mind finally quiets. Peace like I've never known washes away my sorrows, and I exhale a breath I didn't realize I was holding as I finish, bound tightly in his arms.

I know better—the calmness is only momentary.

But this moment is *everything* I never allowed myself to imagine having.

"Still pretending?" I whisper breathlessly, scanning his hooded eyes. His lips brush against mine gently as he exhales.

"I never was."

Twenty-Six

Cleo

I've always preferred outdoor-inspired scents—morning mist, oceans, forests, rain—you know the type.

My preferences must have subconsciously changed overnight, because suddenly, nothing in the world smells better to me than the scent of amber.

His scent and steady breathing envelop me, bringing me a sense of comfort.

I slowly crack open my eyes to see the sun barely beginning to rise. Truthfully, I haven't slept a wink since we finished, but I expected that. I hardly ever sleep at this point in my afterlife. Honestly, I find it shocking how often Kai can rest—he must be carrying a lot if his body calls for rest this easily.

Last night, I was too preoccupied to take in my surroundings. During my life before, I spent most of my time outside chasing dragonflies, reading on the porch's swinging bench, or playing games with my brother and sister downstairs. I spent the least amount of time resting upstairs. Now that this space has been converted to a loft, it's even less familiar to me than it was before.

Glancing around the room, I notice several new features, like the new accent chair resting in the corner nearest to me and the new bookcase taking up occupancy across the room.

I also spot a few things that transport me back to my youth. The oak beams that line the ceiling. The original brass chandelier that hangs above the fireplace. The circular stained-glass window above the fireplace.

Memories threaten to rise to the surface, and I fight them, instead molding my body deeper against him as his arm tightens around my stomach.

I fight the wide smile stretching across my face but fail pitifully.

I've casually slept with a few men over the last few decades, but never have I felt the desire to stay in bed after the act. Let alone *cuddle* with them.

This is new territory for me.

The simple fact that he just became my favorite new blanket in a matter of only one night would be impossible for past-Cleo to believe. In fact, past-Cleo would have bet money on something like this *not* happening.

I clearly don't know myself as well as I thought.

A quiet snore disrupts my train of thought. Then Kai bends his head down to rest on top of my own.

You know, I've never found snoring cute, but his is slightly endearing.

...Heavens. I'm such a mess.

Just yesterday morning, I had committed to following Kai on Earth to bring him back to Eloras. He thinks I'm here to run away with him, and as romantic as that sounds, it couldn't have been farther from the truth... yesterday.

I don't think I want to drag him back to Eloras unwillingly. I actually don't know if I'm capable of it anymore. For reasons I may never understand, he actually seems to like me. He doesn't seem like the type to lie to me.

But I, on the other hand, have withheld the truth since the moment I landed here.

And if I don't return with him, I'll never get my wings back.

I squeeze my eyes shut as my throat tightens. I have no one else to blame for any of this other than myself. I'm the one who let him escape down here in the first place, and I'm the one who looked the Archangels in the eye and vowed to bring him back regardless of his own desires. I was so angry at him for abandoning me that I failed to truly reflect on why he left in the first place. I assumed he didn't care about leaving me, but obviously I misread the situation. At the end of the day, I've failed *him.*

How on earth could I bring him back to Eloras now? Kai *wants* to stay down here—his smile has been brighter in the last twenty-four hours than it has for the last several weeks up there.

His countenance may rival the sun in the sky, but his spirit seems to long to be here on Earth.

If what he said is true, I don't think he left with the intention to hurt me. Maybe he didn't know I cared about him. If that's the case, I don't blame him. I haven't been exactly forthcoming with my feelings, and quite frankly, I'm still not sure what to do about them. But whether I want to or not, I do care for him. Deeply.

Maybe it'd be best for me to leave and return to the realm without him now. I could plead his case for him to the Archangels and see if he can get another Earthly assignment or something so he can remain here longer.

I'd undoubtedly miss him—a lot.

I just want him to be happy, though. If that means fighting for him to stay down here where he's happy and going our separate ways, so be it.

My chest tightens at the thought of not getting my wings back and never flying again, and tears begin to pool in my eyes. As if sensing my unease, he suddenly pulls me firmly into his side.

I release a soft sigh of relief and take a deep breath, closing my eyes as a wave of calmness washes over me.

Somehow, he always knows when I'm on the verge of cracking. It's like he knows me even better than I know myself.

Brushing my foot along his leg, I twist to face him.

His tan skin is nearly glowing as dapples of sunlight fill the room, shining on him. His brown brows are relaxed, and his full lips are parted. I run my hand through his honey-brown waves, focusing on his hair's thick texture. Then I trace his jaw, running my fingers across his smooth face and taking in every detail. I brush my fingers over his nose, long eyelashes, and brows, eventually landing on his forehead. I stroke his forehead lightly, and exhale.

If after all of this, we end up apart, I refuse to forget his face.

Suddenly, he cracks an eye open and breaks into a slow grin upon seeing me.

"I must be dreaming. Are you a *cuddler*?" he asks with a playful lilt in his raspy, sleepy voice.

Just when I thought I couldn't fall more for this man, he has to sport a voice like *that* at this time of day? I knew I was doomed from the very start, but damn. Again, I say: I'm doomed.

I must be blushing because his grin grows wider.

"Good morning, little angel."

He plants a kiss on my nose. My *nose.*

"Good morning, sunshine."

He lets out a yawn and says, "You didn't sleep at all, did you?"

"Of course not. One of us should be awake at all times anyway."

"Once a Watcher, always a Watcher, I suppose, huh?"

I break into a grin against my better judgment. As I peer into his eyes and remember all the things we did last night, my cheeks grow warm. Maybe now that we've slept together, he'll move on. Maybe that's all he really wanted. "How are you feeling?"

"I'm on cloud nine."

A sense of relief spreads across my chest. I wish it were easier to believe him. It's difficult to get past my reservations about us—our conflicting dynamics.

His inner light rivals my inner darkness. He's warm, and I'm cold. He's inviting, and I'm aloof. He thrives as the center of attention, and I'm perfectly content remaining in the background.

It's tremendously challenging to comprehend how the sun could be drawn to the night sky.

However, I'm beginning to understand. Slowly but surely, the walls I've built around my mind are crumbling in his presence.

Terrifying, isn't it? How someone can slip into your heart and steal it without permission. How, one day, you can go from not caring about what the future holds to being riddled with anxiety about it all. Because suddenly, your heart isn't your own anymore. It's theirs. And for the first time in what feels like forever, you give yourself permission to *look forward* to the days that lie ahead.

I can't quite articulate my thoughts into a sentence of consonants that will make sense, so I resign and simply respond with, "I echo you, love. Words truly can't describe this feeling."

"Well, what shall we do today, beautiful? I thought maybe we could go feed some ducks, but I've seen that go south before and decided I didn't want to risk it." He furrows his brows, getting lost in thought. "Should we go on a hike?"

No. *Never again.*

"'*Never again*?'" he repeats, quirking an eyebrow.

Again, I'm at a loss for words, so I simply nod quickly, hoping he will drop it.

"Cool. No hikes."

His eyes slip away from mine, and he repositions his body so he's lying on his back. After spending a couple of minutes staring at the ceiling, he breaks the silence.

"I've got to be honest. I've really missed it here. I love the air down here. I love being surrounded by people who live simple lives. But you know what else I've missed lately?" He spins toward me slowly, fashioning a serious expression I don't often see him use. "Your midnight-blue wings. It's fucking *killing* me not knowing what happened to them. Will you tell me?"

I sit up, wrapping the blanket around me and gazing outside, focusing on the light snowflakes falling just beyond the window's reach. A tremor passes through my body, and suddenly, my chest feels heavy—like it could collapse if I don't handle this delicately enough.

I didn't realize the absence of my wings impacted him this much. Truthfully, I've avoided thinking about them for the past couple of days. If I don't avoid it, the grief settles in and makes itself too comfortable for my liking. I don't know if I'm ready to tell him everything, but when will I be?

"How about we go on a walk?" I offer, still fixing my gaze on the falling snow and the icicles lining the roof pane.

The bed moves, then I feel his thigh resting against my own. He wraps his arm around my neck, then kisses my head.

"Hell yeah, let's go. I've always loved snow days."

I drag my feet down the stairs and brace myself for this conversation. Telling him what happened to my wings means telling him... everything.

I'm still wearing the same clothes I wore yesterday—it doesn't really matter, seeing as angels don't sweat or anything. However, I will say, I've never been more thankful to have a pair of thick black tights handy than I am at this moment, considering my underwear was quite literally torn apart last night.

He is a little too excited about the prospect of me not wearing underwear under my plaid skirt and gray sweater. After slipping my black boots on, I step outside onto the wraparound wooden porch and take a deep breath, inhaling the crystal clear, crisp winter air and white cloudy sky. Snowflakes fall across the yard, leading me to glance at the neighbor's lake house and notice their vehicle is gone. It's just Kai and me out here now.

He follows me down the stairs, passing me. Drifting closer to the water's edge, we trail alongside the perimeter. After a few minutes of tense silence, he eventually stops walking and tosses his head back, opening his mouth wide to stick his tongue out.

"What in heaven's name are you doing?" I gawk, covering my mouth to stifle a laugh.

He continues, completely ignoring me until a dainty, little snowflake lands on his tongue. He shuts his mouth and cheers. "I used to do that with my little sister all the time. We'd stand outside and do competitions—the person who caught the most snowflakes in under one minute would win. I bet you can guess who usually won." He smirks.

"Iris, of course."

He sighs. "You have no faith in me."

I punch his arm. "No need to jump to conclusions now."

"No, no, it's fine—I'm just stalling."

"Stalling? For what?" I ask, confusion crossing my features.

"Well, it's already been over thirty seconds, and you have yet to catch a snowflake. Surely, you know the odds are stacked against you now. It takes a lot more time than you'd think to catch one of those pesky little guys." He crosses his arms and sighs.

"You can't be serious."

"Oh, but I am. Thanks in advance for contributing to my never-ending winning streak." He smiles. "That's right—I've never lost."

Never?

My competitive nature won't allow me to sit idly by, no matter how childish this may seem. Knowing time is running out, I toss my head back and open my mouth as wide as I can, tongue out and all.

"Clock's ticking, Cleo." The fact that he's not even trying infuriates me. I decide to pace back and forth from one spot to another in hopes of catching some snowflakes and begin to lose all hope when suddenly, the sweet freezing taste of victory lands right on my tongue.

One down, one to go.

"Ten seconds left," Kai calls, and to my utter delight, he's actually trying now, meaning he sees me as the threat I am.

We both keep our mouths open, and suddenly, another snowflake hits my tongue. I *won.*

"I win!" I scream obnoxiously and tackle him to the ground, cackling in pure delight. "I just single-handedly broke your winning streak in one try."

We both laugh until we're wheezing. I'm pretty certain I haven't laughed this much since I was a child. He looks at me with mirth in his gaze as he tucks a strand of stray hair behind my ear.

"You win."

But really, I win, his voice taunts in my mind.

"Incorrect." I sit up and cross my arms, still straddling him.

"It's okay—I didn't mean for you to hear that." He blushes. "Are you feeling a bit better about talking about your wings now, baby?"

"Oh... Actually, yes."

I'm shockingly far less tense about this conversation than I was earlier, thanks to his little snowflake charade. We both sit down in a more comfortable position, our bodies facing each other, legs tangled.

"I haven't been entirely honest with you. I'm not here to run away with you. Or, that wasn't a part of my initial plan, at least. The Archangels tasked me with watching you while you were up there, and I undeniably failed. It was naive of me to assume they wouldn't notice—especially considering your adventure down to Earth wasn't your first since your probation period started." I sigh, picking up small chunks of snow and letting it dissolve between my fingers. "After you left this time, they called me into the throne room. They were disgruntled to say the least. They obviously had counseled together before I got there, because by the time I finished explaining what happened, they already had determined the consequences of my actions."

I let out a shaky breath and pick up more snow, then push it into the ground forcefully. Kai's jaw ticks. *Alright, time to get to the point*, I tell myself.

"They decided that I would be required to retrieve you from Earth as soon as possible. To give me even more of an incentive, they stripped me of my wings until I returned you. Using some sort of light magic I've never witnessed before, they seared my wings off without laying a finger on me. Luke simply raised his hand and severed them off. I braced myself for the absolute worst, but it didn't physically hurt as much as I anticipated. Didn't even leave a mark. After that, they gave me a mission. If I returned you to Eloras in one piece, they'd give me my wings back. Nial softly—surprising for him, I know—assured me that '*it'll be as if they never left.*'"

I scoff, lifting my eyes to meet his for the first time. His eyes burn with an ire I've never seen before.

"I'm so sorry. I know this is the last thing you wanted to hear. Frankly, I was eager to comply. You left me, Kai. You didn't even say goodbye—"

My voice unexpectedly breaks at that. I clear my throat and shake my head.

"In my distress, I agreed to their terms, assuming it'd be simple to bring you back to Eloras. Initially, I planned on teleporting us back to Eloras as soon as I reunited with you. But after seeing you, I realized I didn't have it in me to do it right then. And, as we spent more time together, I determined I made a terrible mistake in lying to you. So, I made a change of plans. I'll make all this up to you."

I nod, scooting closer to him and pleading with my eyes that he'll somehow find it in his heart to forgive me. He fixes his gaze on the lake, his jaw clenching again.

"*They hurt you.*" His low voice rumbles like a drum.

"What?" I pause, assessing his tense expression. "No, I told you, losing my wings didn't physically hurt—"

"You specified that it didn't physically hurt, but not all wounds are physical," he concludes in a flat tone, ice lacing his voice.

I stare at him, stunned. Why is he so fixated on this? This part of my confession has the least to do with him. Suddenly, he rises and reaches his hand out to help me up. I grasp it and follow him to stand.

"Let's go."

"Where?"

"To the sky."

My stomach drops.

"No, you're getting it all wrong." I shake my head and glance down at my feet, then frantically search his eyes. "You've been happier on Earth over the past twenty-four hours than almost your entire time up there. I *want* you to be happy. More than anything, you *deserve* to be happy. So, I'm going to march back up to Eloras and plead your case. I'll find a way for you to stay down here. Please, I know I shouldn't have lied to you, and I couldn't be more sorry, but I can fix it, love. If you'll let me."

I cup his face delicately and pierce his gaze with my own. I can't read his expression, so I try one more time to get through to him.

"You're always helping everyone else. Let me help you this time, okay?" I whisper, leaning into him.

"Cleo, we're going back to the Middle Realm together. You're getting your wings back. As for what happens to me, consequences be damned."

He repeats the phrase he told his sister weeks ago with an edge to his voice I don't particularly enjoy. His hand remains on my waist, but his hold is different.

"No." I scowl, my brows upturning in protest. "I refuse."

"This is *my* choice. *Mine*. You can't decide my fate for me," he says, breaking eye contact and glancing at the lake again. "If I knew this would happen to you, I never would've left. You hear me? This wasn't worth the cost of your wings. Your *pain*. I'm undoing this right the hell now."

I shake my head and close my eyes. He's not listening. What if they banish him? What if he gets imprisoned? A cold chill runs down my spine at the thought of what will happen to him. He has no idea what lies ahead. He's broken so many rules... This might be the Archangels' breaking point.

He begins walking back toward the lake house, letting out a sigh.

"Thank you for sharing this piece of your life with me. I'll treasure it forever," he whispers, stopping at the foot of the porch's stairs. "Time to say goodbye. Knowing you, this might be your last time seeing this place. Take your time. I need some time to think."

Then, I watch him walk away. I should have expected this. I lied to him. The cold shoulder is the least of what I deserve.

I turn toward the front door of the cabin and walk up the little steps to say goodbye to it.

He's right. This will be my last time visiting.

Just before turning the knob, a subtle movement to my left catches my eye. I gaze toward it, capturing it just before it disappears.

A dragonfly.

I smile faintly to myself. Realizing this truly will be the last time I visit this spot, I let the memories surface.

While gazing at the lake, the memories replay like a movie. I can see my brother, sister, and me chasing dragonflies along the lake's perimeter as my dad chases us. My mom's inside, baking some fresh French bread. Being the eldest and tallest at the time, I take the lead, glancing back to grin at my dad as he catches up to each of my siblings.

Suddenly, it's down to just me and the dragonfly. I keep my eye on the magical little creature, chasing it until I land in the water.

Once I hit the water, I know my dad can't catch me now—there's *no way* he's jumping in fully clothed like I did. Upon reaching the surface, a delighted squeal and round of cheers greet my ears. I turn toward them, but something huge blocks my line of sight. I realize a moment too late that it's him. He must've dove into the water while I was under.

I swim as fast as my nine-year-old body can, but my dad inevitably captures me. Once he captures me, he holds me tight and cracks the biggest smile. I giggle uncontrollably and splash the water around us, making sure he is just as soaked as I am.

Tears prickle my eyes as I watch that little girl and her father swimming in a fish-filled lake without a care in the world.

In a way, it looks like they're dancing.

Heavens. I miss them.

I *miss* them.

I miss *them*.

Turning the brass knob, I enter the cabin to say goodbye to some of the best moments of my life.

Twenty-Seven

Kai

Talk about an emotional roller coaster.

One minute, I was riding the high of my life. Or is it of my afterlife? Eh, semantics, really. Anyway, I was riding that high over the fucking moon because I got to spend a night in the company of the most painstakingly beautiful being I've ever encountered.

Waking up with her luscious body in my arms felt like a dream come true.

Hell, I don't know if my dreams would even do the feeling I got this morning justice. While looking into her eyes today, I realized just how doomed I actually was.

I'd trade every single twinkling star in the sky for a chance to relive last night over again.

I've never been one to jump into commitment excitedly. But when I looked at her this morning—*really* looked at her—I realized I'd do anything for her. That's when I knew.

I love her.

I love the stubborn, quick-witted, and frustratingly irresistible Cleo Graves.

And heaven knows I have no idea what to do about that.

Even in death, I still don't know if I'm ready for what our relationship could turn into.

I also can't brush over the way she lied to me. Since reuniting with her down here, I had a feeling she was hiding something, but her intention to run away with me seemed so honest.

She fooled me. But looking back, maybe I didn't doubt her, because I desperately wanted her words to be true.

That doesn't matter anymore, though, does it? The truth is plain and simple.

She was the hunter. I was the prey.

Once she caught up with me, she lured me into her trap.

She lied effortlessly. Knowing she can lie like that to me hurts.

Sure, she may feel differently now, but that doesn't change the facts. The Archangels took her wings away and won't give them back unless I return to the Middle Realm. She suffered their wrath because of *me*.

I could walk away right now and never look back. That would absolutely be the easy route to take. Hell, I'm relatively confident I could hide from the Archangels for the rest of my existence. I could travel the *entire* world. I'd be able to do everything I never had the chance to do in my mortal life. Obviously, it'd be challenging, but it'd be more fulfilling than living the rest of my existence in limbo, stuck in Eloras.

Sighing, I fixate my gaze on the tall pine trees surrounding the lake. The gentle sound of birds singing fills my ears. I breathe in the cool, misty air. Earth may be my favorite place ever. I missed it and the people living in it more than words can describe.

But I'd give all this up for her.

Even still.

I don't know what lies ahead—for us, for me, for anyone, really—but I know I can't keep running away.

A harsh punishment is what I need.

Punishment isn't what *Cleo* needed, though. She punishes herself enough as is. Ever since we crossed paths, we've been on a sinking ship. The closer we grow, the deeper the Clai ship sinks. Her company has meant the world to me, but I've decided to kick her off this sinking ship formally.

Stripping her of her wings was uncalled for. I'm the biggest idiot in the world. I can't believe I assumed they wouldn't discipline her for my incompetence.

That alone has motivated me to return to the Middle Realm immediately.

After half an hour, she emerges from her childhood cabin, her cheekbones glistening. As she steps off the wraparound porch, a small dragonfly lands on her hand. She holds her hand up and inspects it, taking in every detail. I'll admit, with our heightened ability to recognize different colors in the afterlife, the creature looks sick. In a good way, of course. I can see a rainbow of colors within its skin, even from several feet away.

There's something about the way she's analyzing this little guy that strikes me. Once again, there's more to her than meets the eye. I'm starting to question if I'll ever fully figure this angel out.

The dragonfly takes flight and flutters away toward the lake. Her eyes follow it for as long as possible before we lose sight of it.

"I've always loved dragonflies. As a little girl, my family and I often chased them out here," she says with a soft smile, her voice trailing off as her eyes remain fixed on the direction it flew in.

"That's something special. I enjoy how insects and animals can see angels when other beings can't. Seemed like that little guy took a liking to you." I break the silence before remembering her betrayal. Once I remember it, I clear my throat and school my features. Sorting out feelings is not a skill I've been graced with, I fear. "Ready to meet our fate?"

"I told you. I'll handle this up there. In fact, let me do all the talking and you'll be back down here in the blink of an eye." She smirks. "Don't you trust me?"

"I did." The words escape from my mouth. Her brows raise, then she gazes at the ground. You know, it's not often that I regret putting my foot in my mouth—I usually just own that shit and laugh it off.

That sentiment hurt her, though. *Fuck.* My stomach turns uncomfortably as I study her expression.

I hate that I'm hurting her, but I still need to process these complex feelings, and I couldn't lie to her. I'm genuinely not sure if I trust her right now. I mean, damn, I want to, but for all I know, she could still be playing me as we speak.

I need to be wary.

"Shall we?" I ask, holding out my hand.

She nods, emotionless, and takes my hand. I embrace her for our trip back to the Middle Realm.

We arrive directly outside the headquarters and ascend the staircase to the bridge in silence. We're still holding hands, though. Even after everything, the last thing I want to do is let go.

I'm a goner.

Glancing to my left, I see she has taken on the usual rigid stance she maintains in this realm. Her back is straight, her chin up, and her shoulders back. This is the stern woman I first met months ago. Right before entering the building, she pauses and pierces my eyes.

"The Archangels will be expecting us," she says in a cool tone she hasn't sported in quite some time with me. "I'm going to get you out of this, but I need to maintain a certain persona to accomplish that. Please, just know that no matter what happens in there, I'm with you, Kai. I *swear*."

She takes the lead before giving me a chance to respond, releasing my hand. We walk in uncomfortable silence for a few seconds until reaching the landing strip on the third level, just three levels below the throne room. I'm more distant from her than ever before, but again, I just need some time.

Suddenly, shouting from behind me disrupts my thoughts. I quickly turn around and gaze down the staircase to see two angels with massive sets of wings flying our way in rapid succession. Without thinking, I step in front of Cleo and use my arm to shield her. She grasps it firmly, and when they reach us, one of the husky men immediately grabs my shoulders and attempts to yank me away from her side. I quickly catch a glimpse of her and see her tough resolve dissolving and the slightest hint of panic settling into her gaze.

A mix of pure fury and adrenaline like I've never known kicks in. I turn back toward the angels ripping us apart with ice in my gaze. One of my arms remains shielded around her as the other swings at the burly man directly in front of me. He dodges my strike, and then I lift my knee to meet his groin with brutal force. His wings curl inward, and he heels over, drifting back down to the ground one level below us to deal with… that.

I smirk in satisfaction, pleased to still feel her hand grasping my arm. In a matter of seconds, though, her grip grows strained—desperate. I twist my body to gauge the situation and discover why her grasp has changed.

The other damn angel is behind her, yanking her away from me with an extreme level of force. She's fighting as hard as she can—kicking and thrashing within his grasp.

"Kai!" she screeches with tears in her eyes as he lifts her off the ground. I extend my hand to grab hold of hers, but they ascend to a height I can't reach.

Because I don't have wings.

I jump and try to wrap my fingers around her ankle, but I miss.

Damnit. This is *all* wrong. I didn't expect them to apprehend us this quickly. This isn't normal behavior for the Archangels from what I've experienced.

As the angel carrying her in his arms soars higher, I fixate entirely on Cleo. I'm running up the stairs as fast as angelically possible, but it's no use. No matter how many stairs I climb, how loud I cry out for her, I'm not any closer to reaching my angel.

You'll be okay, little angel. I promise, I whisper into her mind, watching her grow smaller and smaller in my line of sight.

Kai. Look at me. Quick.

I squint my eyes to focus on her luminous face.

"*I love you,*" she whispers into my mind, mouthing the words.

My lips part in awe.

Then, an excruciating pain erupts in my head, and my entire world fades into darkness.

TWENTY-EIGHT

KAI

"*Fine.* I'm glad you showed up for Trivia Tuesday this time, Kai," Jasper drawls while leaning back in a wooden chair near the stage, then takes another swig of his beer. "Iris has been wanting you to come for months. Where have you been anyway? Baseball can't be keeping you *that* busy every single Tuesday night."

I pause, feeling a bit lightheaded but attributing my dizziness to the beer in my hand. I glance into his gray eyes. "Bro. How many of these have I had? I'm feeling... off."

"Um. I haven't exactly been keeping track of your beer count. Apologies."

I shake my head and sigh, fixating my gaze on the black sweater he's wearing. "It's probably nothing. Anyway, I haven't been to Trivia Tuesday in a while, because I've been a bit wrapped up."

For some reason, I can't pinpoint what's been keeping me away, but I figure it's not worth it to focus on that. Wouldn't want Jasper to worry.

"Hey. You okay?" His brows raise in concern when suddenly, a burst of high-pitched, loud laughter I'd recognize anywhere ripples through the air in front of me.

I glance up at the stage to see my sister, Irie, uncontrollably laughing at something. She's wearing an oversized beige sweater and leggings, her hair pinned up with a vintage-looking claw clip. I bet she got the clip from Aged Emporium.

Jasper gazes up at her reverently, a smile creeping up on his face. "Damn. I love that girl."

"You better." I punch his arm jokingly when suddenly, someone wraps their arms around my shoulders. I turn around in alarm and see... her.

Katherine.

"Sorry I'm late! Got caught up at work, some appointments ran long." She bends down to kiss my cheek and greets Jasper. "What did I miss?"

"Well, Iris is having the time of her life hosting Trivia Tuesday tonight."

Upon hearing her name, Iris cuts a glance at our little group and crinkles her nose as she grins at us.

"The role definitely suits her." Katherine settles into the empty seat next to me and rests her hand on my thigh.

Wrong.

Wrong.

Wrong.

"Are you okay, babe?" she asks, looking into my eyes and tilting her head. She's confused. Understandably so. I'm confused, too.

"For sure." I flash her an easy smile. "I think I need to slow down on the beer, though. I'll go get some water."

"Don't take too long—it's almost our group's turn." She smiles warmly, lifting her hand from my thigh.

I approach the bar slowly and try to figure out what the hell is happening. Why does everything feel so… off?

After the bartender gives me a glass of water, I take a seat at the bar and take some time to breathe.

In and out.

Slowly.

"How about we get some fresh air, buddy?" Jasper's voice interrupts my growing anxiety.

"Actually, yeah. That sounds nice." I nod. "Also, I'm the one who calls you 'buddy,' buddy. Don't get it twisted."

I wink, and he sighs exhaustedly as we walk outside the bar.

It feels good tonight—a crispness to the air signals it's early autumn. The Cove's weather is perfect right now.

We both lean against his car and stand in the silence. Silence tends to be uncomfortable for me most of the time, but with him, it's not too bad.

"I'm here if you want to talk, man," he says. "I know Iris and I have been pretty wrapped up in wedding planning recently, but if there's anything on your mind, I'm here."

"Honestly, something doesn't feel right. It's kind of like I'm trying to piece together my life because it's not making sense. Everything is a jumbled mess… I'm sure that sounds crazy."

He scoffs. "You, Kai Greene, sounding crazy? *Never.*"

He tosses me a wink, and I gasp. "Hey, winking is my thing, too. What's gotten into you tonight, bro?"

We both chuckle. "You've rubbed off on me, I guess."

"Figures," I tease. "But no, really... Am I missing something? I couldn't have drunk so much tonight that I'd forget when Katherine and I got back together, could I?"

He quirks an eyebrow. "What do you mean, Kai? You have been together for over five years. You broke up for a few months one time, but after your car accident, you rekindled the relationship."

Wrong.

Wrong.

Wrong.

"Oh... Right." My heart races. I wouldn't be surprised if I fainted right now. "So, I survived the accident then."

He cracks a smile and tilts his head, then nods slowly. "Yes. You're here. In the flesh."

"Are Katherine and I married?"

His eyes widen. "Dude, you've got to slow down on the alcohol at the next Trivia Tuesday. This is downright embarrassing."

"Are we, Jasper?" My chest tightens. We can't be married.

"Nope. You told us several times that marriage isn't in the cards for you."

Phew. That's the first thing that's made sense tonight.

"Although I will say, not all marriages end up like your parents' marriage. I think you'd make a pretty good husband."

"Damn, Jasper. Easy, tiger."

He punches my arm—harder this time—grinning.

"I'm just saying that I doubt any marriage you'd have would end up like theirs. You're too giving to be like your parents. Iris tells me that all the time."

I guess I've opened up to him about my reservations about marriage before because he is far too comfortable giving me this advice.

But maybe he's right.

One day, I could get married to her if I stopped running and let go of all the bullshit I watched my parents go through.

Wrong.

Wrong.

Wrong.

"Stop it," I whisper firmly and knit my brows. I rub my temples to try to get this pesky little voice out of my head.

"Kai. What's going on?"

If only I knew, brother.

I take another deep breath, centering myself, glancing up.

Hundreds of stars fill the sky above. I've always loved the stars. They're particularly entrancing tonight. I can't seem to look away. In fact, I don't want to look away.

"*I find it ironic—you, watching the stars so intently. The stars should be watching you.*"

Starlight. The stars remind me of someone.

Someone special.

Then, I see her.

My angel.

"Cleo," I gasp, clutching my chest as a wave of anxiety threatens to engulf me. Suddenly, I can hardly speak. "W-where is she?"

"I don't know a Cleo." Jasper shakes his head and pierces my eyes, his gaze laced with concern. "Who's she?"

"She's everything," I whisper. "Everything."

I stand up and begin pacing, tugging on my hair erratically.

Where is she? Where am I? What's happening? I'm supposed to be up there with her. Why am I down here?

"I need to get back. I need to leave right now," I say frantically.

"Wait," he says from over my shoulder. I stop pacing. "What if I told you that you could stay here? What if this could be your reality? Would you choose to stay here and continue living your life? You'd have Iris, Katherine, and me to keep you company for the rest of your life."

"What do you mean? Do you know what really happened, then? That I'm... dead."

"Yes. See, I'm Jasper in every sense. Except this is an alternate reality. One in which you survived the accident and chose to get back together with Katherine. One in which Iris and I happened to meet and plan an Aged Emporium fundraiser without your meddling." I can sense the smile in his voice. "This could be your reality, too. If you wanted it to be. You'd wake up right after the accident with no recollection of everything that happened in your afterlife."

He makes it seem so simple. Had I been given this opportunity sooner, I would've taken it in a heartbeat. Things have changed, though.

What do I want? What do I *really* want?

My head is spinning as I peer inside the bar's window to see my sister laughing again. She's practically radiating.

Then, I realize that this is a version of her I've never met.

A version of her who never lost her brother.

A version who met her soulmate all on her own.

A version that never grieved.

I love this carefree version of her. I really do.

But it isn't the same Irie I said goodbye to months ago.

Likewise, this version of Kai, who sat next to Katherine earlier, is a stranger to me. Those feelings I once had for her are long gone.

I'd love to live the rest of my days with my family by my side. I've missed Irie. I've missed Jasper. Hell, I've missed Truman.

But I've got to stop running from my fate.

From love.

I've been the gatekeeper of my own heart for too long, and until Cleo, I hadn't realized how heavy the key to the gate guarding my heart was.

I may need to let go of this life after all.

Living life with Iris, Jasper, and other loved ones from my life before would be quite the experience. I want that.

But I *need* her.

Ultimately, it's Cleo or nothing at all.

There is nothing I've ever been more certain of.

Suddenly, Jasper's hand lands on my shoulder from behind. "I may not know her personally, but Cleo seems to mean a lot to you."

I simply nod in response. He steps into my line of sight, peering into my eyes.

"As long as you're happy, I'll support either choice you make."

I glance at him with tears in my eyes, knowing that regardless of whether this is real for him, this is the last time we'll lock eyes before we meet again in death one day.

"Thank you, brother. Keep taking care of Irie for me, okay?"

"You have nothing to worry about there." He grins, then embraces me unexpectedly. "Does this mean you found what you were looking for, brother?"

"She found me."

Suddenly, the world around me collapses, melting into a sea of colors and shadows. I want to scream, but find that I can't. My entire body is frozen, subject to whatever comes next.

"Where is she?" I immediately rasp upon awaking, coughing and struggling to catch my breath.

In all my years of life—and afterlife—I've never experienced a sensation as overwhelming as that. Everything around me is still blurry, like I'm living in a B-roll scene of a low-budget film. I squint my eyes, attempting to recalibrate my vision.

Where am I? Was that real? What the actual hell is happening?

"Glance to your right, golden boy," a deep voice drawls from ahead. I follow the voice and lift my eyes to the platform ahead, recognizing it as the throne room's dais first. Nial. Of course, it's him. Annalise sits next to him, Luke and Jessenia on the opposite end of the dais.

My eyes steadily drift to my right, seeing Cleo bound by her wrists in a seat next to me. She's still wearing the same sweater, skirt, and tights she wore when I saw her last. Only the whites of her eyes are showing—she's in a trance-like state. I wonder if it's similar to what I just endured. She's gripping the armrests of her golden seat with a death grip, and her expression isn't restful. She's in pain.

I lunge toward her before thinking, only to realize my arms are bound to my seat as well. It's odd—I don't see any binding enforcements like ropes, straps, zip ties... Okay, yes, I'm aware zip ties would be one of the lamest binding tools ever, but my point is, I don't see anything restraining my arms. Yet they're impossible to move.

Suddenly, a quiet wince of pain disrupts my thoughts.

"What the hell are you doing to her?" My voice comes out in a low rumble. I'm trying my best not to lose it, but my resolve is dissolving by the second.

"Care to explain what's happening, Jessenia?" Annalise asks, her eyes locking on her fellow Archangel.

"Of course." Jessenia closes her eyes and nods. "She's enduring a mental trial. Similar to what you just endured, but the nature of her trial is vastly different. For your trial, we focused on the possibilities of your future. Her trial entirely focuses on her past. If she can't accept and overcome her past, she may be trapped in her own demise indefinitely."

My chest tightens again. *Trapped indefinitely*? "Why are we being tried?"

"What an ignorant question," Nial muses, bored.

"Indeed," Luke agrees, rubbing his temples. "Quite frankly, you should be thanking us right now."

"Yes, groveling would be an appropriate reaction," Nial adds.

Annalise rolls her eyes. "I'd have to agree with Luke and Nial. The only reason we even pursued this route is because Jessenia advocated for it. If it were up to the order of the angels, you would have been cast out for deliberately disobeying our orders time and time again, Kai Greene."

"But I saw more in you. Your potential for goodness is limitless," Jessenia chimes in. "I've known your goodness since the day we met, when I watched you accept a guardianship role with zero hesitation."

My jaw drops as a breath escapes me. "You were the angel who greeted me after my last breath? An Archangel welcomed me?"

"I'm offended you nearly forgot," she jokes with a faint smile and rises, walking down the dais' steps to stand directly over me, reminding me of the moment she greeted me in the afterlife. "It's true—had you accepted Jasper's offer, you would've gotten a second chance at life. However, you're meant for the sky. I knew you'd accept your fate eventually—I just didn't know what would push you to embrace it."

She inclines her head to my angel, who's facing a battle I can't fully understand but desperately want to.

"Please, Jessenia. All of you. Let me help her get through this. I don't give a damn about what happens to me if she isn't by my side at the end of this." My voice breaks. "*Please.*"

Jessenia glances over her shoulder at the other Archangels.

"I've always been a romantic myself," Nial purrs.

"That's a load of—"

"Let him have his moment, Luke," Annalise interrupts.

"As I was saying, I've always been a romantic. I say we give him a chance. At the very least, it'll be entertaining for us to consume."

"What do you mean, 'consume?' Actually... How is any of this even possible? So that conversation I had with Jasper was real? Did I pass the trial?"

Luke smirks. "We can see the entire trial play out within our minds. Jessenia and I focused on yours, whereas Nial and Annalise are tuning into Cleo's. Now that you've completed your trial, we can all watch Cleo's. Don't worry, you won't even know we're there. Omnipotent beings and all that."

Holy shit. These angels are more powerful than I even realized.

I've heard rumors about their abilities to cast illusions, but I had no idea they held the power to alter reality using light energy.

"Depending on how this goes, we may be able to disclose more later," Jessenia whispers, then unbinds me with the soft stroke of her fingers against my arms. Once I'm free, I rise and walk toward Cleo. Jessenia catches my hand. "There's a catch. In her trial, she will not see you. She'll be able to hear you within her mind, and depending on how you approach this, she may be able to see your aura. But she will not recognize you. Please remember, this is still *her* trial to conquer."

Not really understanding what that means, but knowing I need to get to her as soon as possible, I nod.

The chair I sat in for my trial begins to float past me to rest next to Cleo's seat. Jessenia prompts me to sit and lean back. She rests two fingers on my chest. "*Now, sleep.*"

As I'm drifting off, a deep voice growing fainter as seconds pass murmurs, "*Romantic, isn't it? Being trapped in a nightmare together...*"

Twenty-Nine

Cleo

I glance at the large, round clock on the club's black wall, wincing as another minute passes. It's nearing two o'clock in the morning.

And my energy is infinite.

I gaze to either side of me to see my best friends in the entire world laughing up a storm while grooving in tune with the music. Their joy is so contagious it's impossible not to join in.

We stumble into one another repeatedly, each time being funnier than the last as the tequila swims laps within my own mind. The disco ball is illuminating the room in the most beautiful array of strobe lights, seeming to dance with us.

I run my hands through my long locks and lean my head back, basking in the music, my best friends, the dancing, and this moment.

"Cleo, don't you have an early morning tomorrow?" Lacey shouts over the music.

Shit.

“Lacey. You may have just ruined my night with that friendly little reminder.” I punch her arm playfully as her curly blonde hair bounces in beat with the music.

“You should be happy she cared to remind you at all,” Daphne slurs. Even in her drunken state, she still manages to be sassy as hell. At only five feet tall—just an inch shorter than me—sporting long straight brown hair in a high ponytail, she’s a force to be reckoned with.

“True, I suppose,” I sigh in frustration, running my fingers down my yellow minidress, taking pride in how it shines under the lights of the dance floor. “I don’t even want to go tomorrow, but if I don’t go, my parents will kill me. Family tradition and all. It’s just hard, like, we’ve been doing this for over twenty years now. How many more years will I have to endure it?”

“Chill out, dude. It’s just a hike.” Daphne smirks.

I sigh dramatically, letting the alcohol take control for a few seconds. “It’s not just a hike, it’s the principle of it. Like, I’m a grown adult now, you know?”

“Well, why not skip this one?” Lacey offers, out of breath. Mind you, we’re all still dancing during this conversation.

“Oh, no, I could never.”

Lacey and Daphne burst into laughter.

“Well… Maybe this one will be my last obligatory hike. From here on, I can just go if I want to, but they can’t force me to go anymore. You both know how much I dread people pushing me into doing things I don’t want to.”

“Don’t we know it,” Daphne drawls. “Well, ladies, as fun as it’s been, I think I’m ready for bed, and I don’t even have an early morning.”

“Aw, please,” I plead. “One more dance.”

Lacey joins in, asking Daphne for just one more.

Before Daphne can respond, we yank her to the middle of the crowded dance floor. "Took too long to answer. We win."

She rolls her eyes, then shrugs in defeat.

Once the song starts, we dance together like no one is watching. This moment takes me back to when we first met in my high school dance class. They both had more experience, but they took the time to teach me. Now, we're all equals and quite literally inseparable, despite venturing down different paths. Daphne is in school to be a nurse now, whereas Lacey is focusing on a career in education.

I've been working as an executive secretary for the last couple of years, but I hope to gain experience in technology eventually. I heard that's an up-and-coming industry for women to join.

While dancing, I think to myself, *I could live in this moment forever.*

One could only wish.

The sky is bright—far too bright for a rainy day like this. Or maybe the light sensitivity is just an aftereffect of my late night.

After all, I had *quite* the night. From dancing my feet off with my best friends to entertaining strangers, the rush of euphoria was unreal.

"Keep up, Cleo!" my brother calls out from ahead, taking on a steep rocky incline. "Geesh, you're getting slower by the day."

I roll my eyes and sigh. Jonathan's favorite thing to do is to make fun of my age, even though I'm only a few years older than he is. He forgets he's also an entire foot taller than me.

My brother and sister lead the pack—I usually like to fight my brother for the lead position, but after last night, it's a miracle for me to be standing upright at the moment.

While climbing the incline, my sunglasses slip down my nose. I let out an annoyed groan and push them back up.

"You good, Clo?" my dad asks from behind me, pushing me up the hill.

"Just a long night." Some rocks tumble on my next step, causing me to lose my footing, but my dad catches me. He lifts my foot back to the spot it was just at, allowing me to climb the rest of the incline. This hike's difficulty level is moderate, with only a handful of challenging spots like this one.

My mom follows our trail in the back. She likes it back there. She finds comfort in seeing each of our family members ahead of her—a mama bear at her core.

"Be careful. Long night or not, the path is extra slippery after all that rain last night, honey," my mom shouts warmly out from behind me. I simply nod as a bead of sweat drips down my brow. *I've got to focus. This isn't even the most challenging part of the route.*

Upon reaching the top of the incline, I take a break to refocus. I breathe in and out slowly, pretending I'm preparing to dance.

"Hurry, Cleo!" my sister cheers from ahead. I barely just reached the top, and she's already racing through the next incline, not even winded. She's always been such a natural athlete. She's living proof the universe has favorites.

Maybe I *am* getting too old for this. How do my parents keep up with those kids? We may all be adults now, but those two rascals will always be my baby siblings. They're the main reason I'm still living at home, not that I mind. This tradition is growing a bit old for me, but spending time with them and helping take care of my family is essential to me.

Thankfully, the next incline isn't as steep, so I relax my muscles a little and take a drink of water from my canteen.

This tradition all started on the week I took my first steps. My parents' home isn't far from this state park, so they decided to take me on my first hike only a couple of days after I learned how to walk. Of course, given the fact that I was still a baby, I only walked for the first few feet of the hike. My parents carried me the rest of the way. My mom read somewhere that hiking is good for the soul and ran with it, and my dad, being as active as he is, *loved* the idea.

Since then, we've tried to hike together at least once every year. Often, we end the hike with a little campout. This year, we planned on keeping the hike quick, and I haven't been the best sport about it.

I love my family, though.

I may appear distant sometimes, but I'd do anything for them.

Consequently, I'm hiking at seven o'clock in the morning with a killer hangover.

To my right is an endless forest filled with trees. To my left is a drop-off to a stream filled with rocks below. It's not as bad as you may be envisioning. It's not relatively high enough to be considered a prominent cliff, at least not at this point in the hike. I'd guess we're about a hundred feet high, but who knows.

We've hiked this trail so many times; the drop doesn't make me as nervous as it did when I was a little girl. In fact, I tend to capture the best views from the edge, so I often spend time overlooking that side of the forest.

It's vast. Seemingly endless.

From the chirping birds to the sound of gentle rain, I'm mesmerized by it.

This moment would be even more beautiful if my thighs weren't burning so much. Note to self: do not *ever* hike after a night out dancing again. Ever. Under any circumstance.

I squeeze my eyes shut and bend over, resting my palms on my thighs to take a proper break. As I lean forward, my feet slide across the muddy ground, making me cringe.

Then I lose my balance.

I'm not usually this clumsy, this thoughtless. I attempt to center myself, but unfortunately for me, my body chooses to bend toward the outer edge of the trail.

The drop-off.

My fate lies before me as clear as day. My mind screams at me to fight, to flee, to fly. Some people escape death's grasp, sure. I know better, though. I won't escape this.

Still, despite my mind's willingness to give in to the inevitable, my body continues to fight. My arms flail, my mouth opens wide.

Then my foot slips off the slick, muddy edge.

I close my eyes, deciding I'd rather not see the end. Feeling it will be enough, I think.

I fall.

I'm convinced this is the end, when a strong, large hand latches on to my arm roughly. I open my eyes in shock.

"Get back up here, Clo," my middle-aged father whispers, blinking back tears as he bends over the side of the trail, knees digging into the muddy ground while hanging on to me and a nearby sapling.

I glance over his shoulder to see my mom holding on to him, sweating profusely. While looking at them, I notice just how far

I've already fallen. My mom's feet keep slipping, causing me to inch closer to the ground. The vein in my dad's forehead pulses in sync with those in his forearms as he bites his lip—he's reaching his limit. I don't want to die, but if he doesn't let me go, we'll both fall.

"Dad, you need to let go," I say evenly, attempting to smile but failing miserably because I know I'm about to meet death, and truthfully, I'm not ready to die. I had so much to live for.

But I can't bear the thought of a single one of them going down with me.

"Not happening." He grits his teeth.

"*Please.*" My voice breaks as I gaze into the eyes of my entire family. "I love you all. So much."

Then, I twist the arm he's holding in an attempt to pull away, closing my eyes one last time.

My mom screams in agony. My sister yelps. My brother gasps loudly.

I'm falling again.

But to my horror, I'm not alone.

No, *no, no, no, no.*

He didn't let go. True to his stubborn nature, he's still holding on to me, while the rest of my family watches from the trailside.

As we're falling, he quickly tucks me into his arms one last time before we meet our end.

"It's okay, Clo. We're going to be just fine," he whispers into my hair as we descend the last dozen feet.

Suddenly, my entire life is playing out before my eyes.

My first bike ride. My first day of school. My first friends. My first time dancing. My first family cabin trip. My first time swimming. My first hike. My first time driving. My first *time.* My first heartbreak. My first prom. My first job. My first solo vacation.

My first hot-chocolate chat with my dad. My first time chasing dragonflies.

Dying alone would have been okay. I probably deserve it after putting myself in this situation.

But dying with *him*? The person who has been my rock since the moment I opened my eyes in this world? Unacceptable. He deserves to live.

I don't give a damn about what happens to me, but if he dies with me right now, I will never forgive myself. Mark my words.

Thud.

Crunch.

Snap.

Darkness.

A burst of scorching pain shoots violently through my body, rattling every inch of me. I have no idea how long I've been out.

I attempt to move, but I can't. I think I'm paralyzed.

I attempt to speak, but I can't do that either. My chest is killing me, and my breaths grow more and more ragged by the second.

I can't even open my eyes.

I know it for certainty now. I'm dying. I have minutes left, at most.

I can't make sense of much right now, but I can feel my surroundings. My head is resting on his chest.

His still chest.

He isn't breathing.

My dad is dead.

I killed him.

Before I can even begin to process this tremendous loss, I hear leaves crunching and panicked breathing in tune with the sound of a running stream. We must have landed right on the large rocks bordering the creek.

It sounds like my family caught up with us before my bitter end.

My mother collapses next to our bodies in hysterics, softly caressing my arm.

"*My baby girl. My baby. My love,*" she whimpers.

I'll miss my mom and her soothing persona more than words can describe. She has stood by me through every up and down of my life. If I could speak, I'd thank her one last time.

My baby sister rests her head next to mine on my dad's unmoving chest and bellows. She screams at the heavens, pleading for a reason why, breaking my heart even more. I taught her how to swim, you know? My parents were busy watching my brother, so I took the liberty of showing Sadie the ropes of the waves. I can't believe we won't ever swim together again.

All the while, my brother is quietly stroking my forehead with his thumb, maintaining a stable and strong presence for my family. He's already taking on the responsibility of what it means to be the oldest and only man in the house at only age twenty. I wish I could see his face just one last time. I wish I could tell him it's okay to take his time processing this, that he needs to lean on others for comfort, too. He deserves support.

I wish I could stay for my little brother—for all of them.

I know they'll manage without me. But what are they going to do without my dad?

None of this is fair. I'm responsible for his death, yet I get to escape life and meet death. I should stay here with them. It's my duty to take care of them after the devastation I've caused.

I don't deserve peace. I don't deserve joy. I don't deserve love.

For this transgression, I deserve to *rot*.

"We love you, honey. You can rest now." My mom gently runs her hand through my hair, no doubt getting caught on clumps of bloody matted hair. My sister kisses my head as my brother holds my hand.

"No, *I don't deserve your love,*" I want to shout, but I can't.

I don't deserve rest.

Look at what I've done, the destruction I've caused. I broke our family. This is *my* doing.

I deserve to rot.

Rot.

Rot.

Rot.

That's what I'll do. No matter where I end up after this, I vow to sit with this every single day for the rest of my existence. Not a day will pass that I won't punish myself for my actions. I ruined their lives.

With that promise to myself, a tear slips out of my eye. A coarse finger wipes it away. Jonathan has always been good at wiping my tears away. I'd smile at him if I could.

I may not deserve their love, but I'll love them with every fiber of my being forever.

It's growing more and more painful to breathe. Slowly, I accept death's embrace and take my last shallow breath, bidding my whole world goodbye forever.

It's happening again. One minute, I'm dancing with my best friends. The next, I'm falling to my death. I can't remotely comprehend why I keep living this nightmare.

Is it real? Is any of this real? Am I dead or alive?

I've relived this experience so many times I've lost count. What the hell is happening? Am I actually in Hell? Or somewhere worse?

Again, I plummet off the ledge to my death, wrapped in my father's arms.

Again, I'm so enraged and hurt I can hardly think coherently.

Again, I promise myself to remain miserable for the rest of my existence.

"No, *I don't deserve your love*," I want to scream, but I can't.

I don't deserve rest. Look at what I've done, the destruction I've caused. I broke our family. This is *my* doing.

I deserve to rot.

Rot.

Rot.

Rot—

"You deserve more."

This time is different... I seem to be aware that I'm reliving this experience over and over again for the first time since this cycle began.

My subconscious is communicating with me. Odd.

I can't tell if that's a good sign or if I've officially lost my mind.

I also can't help but wonder why my subconscious has such a masculine, deep voice.

As that thought crosses my mind, I hear a rich chuckle inside my head.

Oh, no. I'm actually hearing voices that aren't mine. Who knew that was a part of the crossover experience? Why didn't this occur during any of the other horrendous times?

"You deserve more," the voice repeats urgently.

"No. I do not," I whisper within my mind.

"I'm afraid you do. You're meant to be happy, angel."

Angel. That nickname strikes a chord.

"I don't know if you've been watching this play out, but I'm no angel. I'm a destroyer. I single-handedly destroyed my family within a matter of seconds. I killed my dad. So, no, I *don't* deserve happiness and never will."

"You didn't kill your dad. He fell with you because he couldn't bear the thought of you going through this alone. He did that out of love for you."

"Love I don't deserve!"

"Give yourself grace. Can't you see how much your family loves you?"

"I don't deserve it. I don't deserve any of it. I ruined their lives. I should've died alone."

No person who loves me walks away unscathed. I hurt everyone who loves me. I'm like a black hole, a plague, a—

"The short amount of time you were a part of their lives made their lives."

Tears sting my eyes as my mom runs her fingers through my matted, bloodied hair. If I could shake my head in protest, I would.

"Your family wouldn't want you to put yourself through hell for what happened. Especially not your old man."

"You couldn't possibly know that."

"I'm all-knowing, actually." I hear a smile in this voice.

"But I *am* responsible for his death. How could they ever forgive me for that?" I pause, holding back tears, shallow breaths escaping rapidly. "How could I *ever* forgive myself?"

"You're not responsible for the choice your dad made. There's nothing to forgive." He pauses, then a warm sensation begins to flood my senses. It almost feels as if the sun itself is holding me in its arms. ***"Be kinder to yourself."***

"How can I do that when all I want is to hurt myself for what I've done?" My chest tightens "I've hurt the people who mean the most to me. Don't I deserve to be alone?"

"It's okay to hurt, but it's not okay to hurt yourself. Especially not forever." His voice is smooth. ***"You deserve love."***

As the warmth spreads throughout my body, this world begins to fade away. Again, I take my last breath.

But instead of immediately returning to the club, I'm in a dark environment I don't recognize. The warmth continues to envelop me. As I'm being embraced, a sense of peace gently streams through my body.

Finally, I have the strength to open my eyes, and instead of my dad's chest, I'm face-to-face with the glowing outline of a different being. To my surprise, he's funneling warmth into me.

"Now, are you ready to accept it?"

THIRTY

KAI

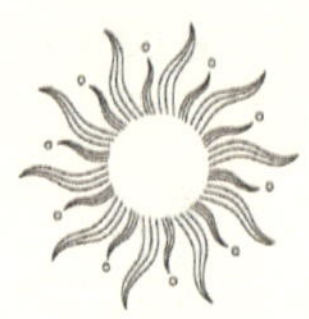

"Accept what?" She gapes at me, brows furrowing.

"You know what."

She hesitates, biting her lip. I continue holding on to her like she's my lifeline.

While briefly visiting her mind, I caught memories of dragonflies and laughter. I'd be lying if I said my heart didn't shatter while watching this unfold.

Dying may have been horrific for me, but at least it was swift. Cleo's death was painstakingly slow.

And even in her final, brutally painful moments, all she could think about was her family. Not only did she lose her life—she lost her will to *live*.

I can't even begin to comprehend how they did it, but the Archangels quite literally slipped me into her mind to experience this trial with her, like a fly on the wall. In doing so, her pain became my pain. I felt every ounce of agony that stirred within her, both physically and emotionally.

It all makes sense now. She believes everyone who loves her will get hurt. It's tearing me apart knowing she *entirely* blames herself for her dad's death and has been punishing herself ever since. Hell, I hardly know the guy, and even I know there's no way he blames her for that.

He chose to fall with his daughter. He knew what lay ahead and sealed his fate anyway with zero hesitation. That's how much she meant to him.

My girl's always been a logical person, and logically speaking, she is not actually responsible for her dad's death.

But it's up to her to accept that.

"I just... don't understand why he fell with me." Her eyes fill with water. She squeezes them shut as a single tear escapes, running down her cheek. "Why would he give up everything for me?"

"Isn't it obvious?" I whisper and stroke her tears away.

She shudders and takes a deep breath. Long seconds tick by before she finally breaks the silence.

"He loved me."

I nod my head.

"He loved me so much, he *chose* to do that," she says, a hint of realization crossing her petite features as more tears cascade down her cheeks. "I shouldn't take his love—his *sacrifice*—for granted." She blinks back tears and nods her head repeatedly. "Maybe... Maybe they would want me to find happiness after all."

"*Maybe?*" I quirk a brow, not that she can see it at the moment. "No. You undeniably deserve to find happiness, and they would want that more than anything. You deserve to be *loved*, Cleo. Without reservation."

She closes her eyes and nods slowly in acceptance as the world around us begins to fade into shadows and an array of colors.

My heart does a flip in my chest. I grin, then cradle her head and bring it to my chest. She lets out a sob as I hold her in my arms. “Time to wake up, angel.”

THIRTY-ONE

JESSENIA

They awake simultaneously, gazing into each other's eyes with a love purer than starlight itself. "*You owe me, Luke*," Nial's voice whispers within all our minds. "*I knew it*."

"*Who would've thought you, of all angels, would be their biggest admirer?*" Annalise chimes.

"*I'm just quite experienced at reading people. Even the impossible Cleo Graves*." He raises his brows nonchalantly.

I sigh in contentment.

The choices these two young angels just made are far more significant than they realize. They've finally accepted the fates they were meant to all along.

The boy was destined to stop running away from his problems and let go of his mortal life.

The girl was meant to let another soul in to soothe her broken heart.

He's been running so long and she's been fighting alone for so long that they both forgot how to lean on others. Only under these precise circumstances can they each qualify to pass on to the Golden Realm in peace.

Which is what we, the Archangels, have desired for these two precious souls all along.

Delightful, isn't it? When things work out precisely the way you want them to, but not in the way you predicted?

Delightful, indeed.

"*Daydreaming again, Jessenia?*" Nial interrupts my thoughts.

"*I just love* love. *It's been a while since I witnessed a love as divine as this one.*"

"*Oh, come on now, love. You're less than five centuries old. It can't have been that long.*" Nial smirks.

"*Can you blame me for being proud of these two? Especially the golden one. I've watched his entire journey from the moment he died to now.*"

The golden one clears his throat boisterously. "...Are we interrupting?"

"Yes, care to unbind me, Nial?" The starlit one scowls.

"What about her wings?" Kai pins us with a dark stare. "Did she pass the test?"

Ah, the test.

For a moment there, we were unsure whether he would choose to come back to Eloras or stay on Earth with his family. But of course, her soul called him back.

As it always will.

Likewise, she would have remained trapped in her own nightmare for eternity had she not accepted the love she has always deserved.

Little did he know that by jumping into the illusion, his soul would've been caught, too, had she failed. Something tells me he wouldn't have minded, though.

For as long as his soul intertwines with hers, he's at utter, undeniable peace.

No matter the circumstances.

Thirty-Two

Kai

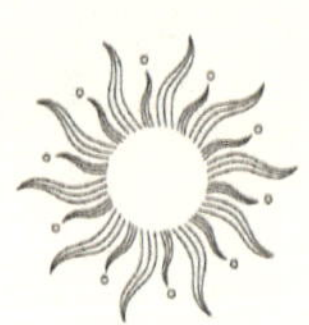

Nial unbinds Cleo's wrists with a snap of his fingers, and I fight to school my expression. I can only imagine what I'd do with that kind of power. Guess it's a good thing I wasn't bestowed with such gifts.

"That was you in my mind, wasn't it?" she asks in a whisper, turning to face me. She's still wearing the same clothes she wore earlier—the gray sweater and plaid skirt. The outfit that was nearly the death of me on Earth. How is she always so effortlessly beautiful? "For some reason, I didn't recognize your voice... I don't even know if I had a recollection of who you were."

"Trippy, right? You can thank our Archangel best friends for that." I glance at the Archangels, who appear amused.

"We are going to counsel amongst one another within our minds to determine how to proceed. Please carry on as you will in the meantime. Rest assured, we won't eavesdrop this time." Luke speaks boldly, glaring at Nial who holds his hands up, feigning innocence.

Unable to spend another minute not touching her, I stride to her side, sling my arm around her shoulders, and bend my head down to press a kiss into her hair.

"You saw everything, didn't you?" she asks in a whisper. I nod solemnly. "Do you feel differently about me now?"

"*Cleo*. How could I? You've been carrying so much for so long. You're strong—so strong. But I'm here now, so you don't need to carry it alone anymore. Ease up a little and let me help, okay?" I place a kiss on her head as she leans into my embrace. "So. You love me, huh?"

Her demeanor instantly changes, cheeks pinker than a tulip in spring. I clamp my teeth over my mouth and bite back a laugh. "I didn't know if I'd ever see you again, so I panicked, and I—"

"Whoa. Are you about to take the proclamation of your undying love for me back?" I quirk a brow.

"What? No, I just—" She groans. "That moment happened differently in my dreams. That's all. I mean, not that I've *dreamed* about it. Dreaming about something like that would be pitiful."

Of course, she'd think that's pitiful. I smirk, then lead us as far away from the Archangels as possible, nonchalantly, while they casually discuss our fate within their minds.

While stepping farther and farther away from the Archangels, I brace myself, gearing up to say what I've been waiting to say.

I clear my throat, tightening my hold around her side.

"I've always feared love, Cleo. In fact, giving in to love has been my greatest fear for as long as I can remember. I was scared of a lot of things related to love, like the idea that people loved the idea of me instead of the real me. I was scared I wouldn't be capable of truly loving someone in that way. Ironic, seeing as I once told Irie that the only emotion that equates to fear is love. But then they stole you away earlier. Until that moment, I thought I understood my biggest fear—"

I gulp, whispering into her hair.

"—I was so wrong. The premise of never holding you in my arms again shattered me into countless pieces. That scared me more than anything ever had. I realized in that moment how much was left unsaid. Sure, you withheld the truth from me about your journey to Earth. Of course, that hurt me. Losing you hurt a *million* times more."

I turn her to face me. Tears brim in her eyelids, illuminating the brightness within her brown eyes.

I've told people I loved them in the past, but this is different.

This means something. No, not just something. It means everything.

"I *love* you," I say in a low voice, earnestly. "I'd choose you in every lifetime, under every circumstance. I'm done running away. I'm running straight into your arms, angel."

Her pupils dilate as her eyes search mine. After witnessing everything she's been through, her lack of trust in others makes sense. Her lack of optimism, too.

Hell, I must have been the last person in existence she would've imagined slumming it up with—

"Thank heavens," she whispers, her lips curling upward in that soft smile of hers I'm obsessed with. "If the feeling weren't mutual, my dramatic declaration of love for you would've been even more humiliating than it already was."

I sniff a laugh and push my hand through my hair.

That's my girl.

My girl.

Cleo is my girl.

The traces of the pain I saw in her moments ago have weakened. She leans into me, resting her head on my chest. As her body eases into me, I inhale her scent of calming eucalyptus and slip my hands around her waist.

I consume the space between us and bring my mouth to meet hers. Soft, at first. Warm and slow. Then, a barely audible whimper escapes her curved lips. A sinful sound that drives me to tangle my hand in her hair. My free hand digs into her waist, gripping it tightly.

Mine. She's *all* mine.

I want—no, I *need*—more. Just as I'm about to lift her to straddle me, her lips break away from mine.

"Kai... We have company." Her cheeks turn pink again as she nods her head toward the dais. It's clear the Archangels are preoccupied; otherwise, smart-ass Nial would've already picked fun at our indecency.

I don't take the time to even spare them a glance. I lower my lips to her ear, flicking my tongue against her lobe, taking delight in the full-body goosebumps that spread across her tan arms in response.

"What difference does that make? Let them watch." My voice comes out rougher than expected. I can't ignore the burning sensation growing inside me. I need her. *Now*.

I lose all my senses when it comes to this starlit woman.

She releases a chuckle under her breath, then looks me up and down, eyes crinkling. "You never cease to surprise me, sunshine."

This isn't the first time she called me 'sunshine.' I mean, that isn't my favorite nickname. *Sunshine*. I've never had a nickname, but I always imagined if I did, it'd be something cool, like, I don't know, Ace.

But fuck it. My angel can call me anything.

"*Please*, Cleo. Let me love you—"

"That is quite enough, Kai Greene," a deep voice rumbles. Luke, this time. Well, at least it wasn't Nial. The Archangels wave their hands at us in sync, beckoning us back to the dais.

Fuck me, I don't have time for this. Can't our fate wait?

"Stop pouting." Cleo elbows me. "We will get more time together. Hopefully."

I scowl, but as we approach the Archangels, I remember that our next chapter lies in their hands.

My scowl turns into a frown. A frown full of unwanted doubt and fear.

Our happily ever after is hanging on by a thread—a thread the Archangels are entirely manipulating.

And as hard as it may be to believe, I don't think the Archangels particularly like me. Surprising, right?

I'm kidding. I know I've been a pain in their asses since the moment I died.

"Cleo Graves. Kai Greene," Luke bellows. "You have completed your respective trials."

Yes, obviously we've completed them. Now, if we could get to the conclusion of said trials, that would be fantastic—

"Kai, please. You should be aware by now that we can hear all your thoughts. Word for word. Tone and all. No, we do not only see flashes of images or hear some words and terms. We hear everything when we tune in. Surely you know this, no?" Annalise asks.

Oh, heavens. If they've been able to hear all my thoughts since the beginning, then when I showed up for my first hearing, they knew I was bullshitting them from the moment I walked in.

The Archangels simply nod in unison.

"Why didn't you lock me up the moment I walked in? I thought I had a pretty strong shield. Does my shield not stop you from entering my mind?" I ask, pressing for answers.

"Her shield is rock-solid," Nial answers before any other Archangel can, nodding his head toward Cleo. "We have to try exceptionally hard to enter her mind, and truthfully, it isn't worth the effort. Your mental shield is strong, but young. Think about it like this: where her door is locked, dead-bolted, and chained shut, yours only has one single lock. It's a solid lock. Just not quite strong enough. It'll grow stronger with time."

"So, you're saying I've been an open book this entire time?"

Again, they simply nod in unison.

And I've never felt so stupid.

"No—" Jessenia interrupts my spiral. "Please do not punish yourself. Nial and Annalise are exaggerating slightly. We didn't actually enter your mind during your trial until after Stephen burst into the throne room. Sure, once we did enter, we saw everything. But not from the beginning. You aren't stupid."

My lips part in surprise. "I don't know what I did to deserve your kindness, Jessenia, but thank you."

"I'll admit, I have a soft spot for the angels I greet in the afterlife. I don't sneak away to greet angels in death often, but when I do, I tend to build a connection with them of sorts."

"Carrying on—" Luke proceeds.

"But wait. How are Cleo and I able to communicate within our minds so clearly? Neither of us is an Archangel, so that doesn't quite make sense, does it?"

Nial and Luke sigh in exasperation. I roll my eyes at them outwardly.

"You've built a very special connection with each other. When she was your Watcher, the thread connecting you both exceeded that of a normal Watcher-Guardian thread. Once your life began in Eloras, your connection only grew, blossoming into something deeper. Consequently, your minds are often interconnected. You both share a divine, mental type of angelic connection we call a *soul tie*," Annalise explains gently with a knowing smile. "You've gotten to see more of Cleo's striking mind than we have during our entire journey with her."

I glance at Cleo, her nose and chin held up high. Playing it cool as usual. She can't fool me, though—I see a sparkle in her eye upon hearing about our soul tie. Hell, I might be blushing, myself. I've never even heard of a soul-tie connection. Soulmates, of course. *But soul tied?*

I have a million questions, but I determine now isn't the time. If we make it out of this room together, I'll leave the soul-tie research up to Cleo. She's good at that stuff.

"*Carrying on*," Luke says. "You completed your trials. After a lengthy counsel, we've determined your results. Kai, time and time again, you broke rule after rule in Eloras. From revealing your full angelic form to a living human being to sneaking into the mortal world below without permission more than once, you've disgraced the realm. Cleo, although you didn't necessarily break divine laws, you *did* disobey direct orders in keeping Kai's heinous acts *secret*. Consequently, we knew the only way to determine how to proceed would be to enter you both into somewhat mentally, physically, and emotionally draining trials. The decisions you made during your trials are greater than you realize. Your own decisions have determined your fate today."

A beat of silence passes among us all, and my heart lunges into my throat.

I grab hold of her petite hand, unsure of what lies ahead but knowing I can get through it with her by my side. She grasps my hand, squeezing it, similar to the way she did in the library all those weeks ago.

It's the little things I love about her—like the way she holds my hand or how often she scowls at me. I feel like I've been searching for this kind of love my entire existence. Now that I've found her, I'm never taking her for granted.

I'll be fine, even if our fate is unfavorable. I mean, how could I *not* be with the angel of my dreams standing by my side?

...Damn, that was cheesy.

And I couldn't care less.

Thirty-Three

Cleo

Y*our own decisions have determined your fate today.*

Well, that's great considering I have a knack for making the wrong choices as of late. From the exhausting trial I just went through to the Archangels' all-knowing eyes, my emotions are heightened.

His love confession has also thrown me off-kilter. For some reason, despite how terrible this could turn out, a wave of relief washed over me like I've never experienced the second he said those three words.

Three little words—seemingly uneventful when used apart.

But when strung together into a sentence, they hold such vast power.

The power to calm weary souls.

The power to fight intrusive thoughts.

The power to heal deep scars.

My heart needed those words *desperately*.

I needed to remember that I *deserve* love.

As soon as he said those words, I swore I heard a clock strike the hour within my mind. For the first time since I took my last breath, that clock started ticking.

We may be doomed, but at least we're doomed together. I will not allow any sentence to part us. Should they imprison him, I'll follow closely behind. Should they exile him, I'll pack our luggage this instant. Should they burn him into dust, I'll burn with him.

I can't imagine my world without Kai.

I see why his loved ones mourn him as fiercely as they do.

He's something special—the kind of being who leaves your life a thousand times better than it was.

Nial looks into my eyes with a knowing look, then looks down at his feet. I raise a brow and tilt my head at him as Luke readies to give us his verdict.

Why did he just give me such a look? What does that even mean?

Oh, great. My shield. I accidentally left my guard down. He must have been reading some of my thoughts, meaning he heard me internally gushing about my lover.

Heavens. How mortifying.

"Let's make this quick, shall we?" Luke nods to the others. "We have determined you both are eligible to ascend to the Golden Realm. In turn, we are gifting you new sets of wings at once."

My jaw drops immediately. I'm aghast. "Excuse me?"

"Is there a problem, Cleo?" Nial asks, feigning innocence again.

Kai gently nudges me. *Now may not be the time to challenge them, sweetheart.*

But why wouldn't they punish us? Don't we deserve to be held accountable for what we did?

"Don't think too hard on it." Nial nods his chin at me. "You both passed your trials, which, unbeknownst to you, were tests to determine whether you were ready to ascend. Yes, he broke a lot of rules, but we don't look at violations at face value. We can see that—despite how foolish his actions were—he never broke a rule to hurt another soul. *That* is what ultimately matters. So, yes. You both are getting your wings and are eligible to ascend, should you choose to."

"Just no more rule breaking." Annalise scowls, looking directly into Kai's eyes.

Jessenia rises from the dais and approaches us. Still unconvinced this is actually happening, I take a step back, tugging on Kai's arm to join me. Nial chuckles.

She approaches Kai first, stepping behind him. "May I?"

He simply nods, not second-guessing her. Leave it to him to be all too trusting of these benevolent, ultrapowerful angels.

Only the whites of her eyes show as she slowly waves her hands in intricate patterns. Threads of golden magic flow from her fingertips to his back.

She's giving him wings.

I've never watched someone receive their wings before.

As she weaves her hands in intricate motions, feathered wings slowly sprout from his back. They're huge—larger than my old set of wings by far.

The light yellow shade of gold is so bright it's nearly blinding.

I glance at his hazel eyes and see a thin line of silver tears brimming in his eyelids. *My love.*

He truly must have thought this day would never come. My chest aches as I watch him gain the best gift he's ever received—his freedom.

Finally, Jessenia brings her hands down to rest at her sides. "It is done."

"Couldn't have chosen a dimmer shade of gold, huh?" I joke, gazing at her, still standing behind Kai. Her icy-blue eyes meet mine.

"As a reminder, we do not choose wing colors for angels. We construct wings from the essence of their soul within. His soul has a yellow-golden essence; therefore, his wings are golden."

My wings being so dark makes perfect sense, seeing as they're a reflection of the essence of my soul. Fitting.

I huff, then turn toward him. He immediately pulls me into him and bends down, exhaling a deep breath into my hair. He whispers, "*At last.*"

"At last." I smile at him and run my hand through his honeyed hair.

He breaks away and immediately turns toward Jessenia. "It's her turn."

He hasn't even taken the time to admire his own wings; he's so caught up in me getting mine back.

"What's the rush?" I chime.

"If you don't get your wings back in the next ninety seconds, another rule break is in order," he says in a low voice.

"Calm down, calm down," Nial drawls, stepping off the dais. "Cleo. Are you ready?"

"What are you doing?" I question him as he towers over me. Goodness, Archangel males are outrageously tall.

"Jessenia doesn't get to have all the fun. Plus, I gave you your set of wings in the first place all those years ago." I raise an eyebrow at him, and he sarcastically gasps. "Don't tell me you *forgot*."

I break into a cheeky grin as Jessenia takes her seat on the throne again. "I'll never forget the first time I earned my wings."

"Hopefully, this time will be your last," he mumbles, stepping behind me. "I'm happy for you. Friend."

Then, he begins to work. A tingling sensation spreads across my entire back for several moments. I glance to my left at Kai, expecting to see a big goofy grin on his face.

Instead, he's staring at my wings in awe.

Reverence, even.

"What? What is it?"

"And my work is done." Nial claps his hands, walking past me back to the dais.

"Oh, Cleo." Kai shakes his head, his eyes widening in disbelief.

I turn my head to see what he's seeing. Out of the corner of my eye, I can see the color—it's different. It appears my wings are no longer dark.

No, not dark at all.

They're light.

Very light.

The color of starlight—white gold. Nearly platinum.

"What happened?" My lips part.

"It appears the storm that had you in its grasp at the time of your death has simply dissipated," Annalise says from the dais, with a gentleness in her tone I haven't heard in decades. "The light of your soul has taken over."

Something tells me there's nothing simple about that.

Holding back tears, I gaze into Kai's warm eyes. *I have you to thank for this.*

He winks. *Right back at you, angel.*

Annalise clears her throat. "Now you both have a critical decision to make. Ask yourselves: are you ready to ascend? When that answer is yes, you may ascend the stairs to the next realm. While there isn't an immediate rush, we want you to be aware.

Some angels have waited a very long time to greet you in the Golden Realm."

My chest tightens. Could they be referring to whom I think they're referring to?

Kai wraps his arm around my neck, kissing my head. One of my favorite gestures of his. "Cleo and I will think about it and get back to you. Sounds good?"

"Um. Yes. That sounds good."

"Great, because I'm ready to get the *hell* out of here." He smirks. "Thanks for the second chance, guys."

"Technically, this is your third, but who's counting..." Nial sighs before pinning me with his amber stare. "Please give ascension fair consideration. Eloras is only a pony ride away from the Golden Realm, so you can visit certain places—*like the library*—occasionally."

I nod my head, then Kai pulls me away.

I will consider it. I will.

But first, it's time to celebrate.

THIRTY-FOUR

KAI

We're running down the stairs as fast as humanly possible. Or should I say angelically? I like that. Let's try this again.

We're running down the stairs as fast as *angelically* possible.

Well, I am, at least. I'm practically dragging her behind me, tugging her along to keep up.

"What's the rush?" she asks, breathlessly. Damn, hearing her out of breath right now is nearly too much for me to handle.

"C'mon, beautiful. Faster."

We keep up the pace, finally exiting the palace. As soon as we land on the platform outside, I turn around, clamp my teeth over my lips to bite back a stupid grin, and scoop her into my arms, facing her toward me so her wings don't get in the way. She wraps her legs around my waist and gives me a skeptical look. I throw her a wink, then launch into the air with a single flap of my wings.

My wings.

Can you believe it? I sure as hell can't, but I know better than to question the judgment of the Archangels. I know I won't be given another chance after this, so I'm on my best behavior. I guess I'm a real angel now.

A burst of laughter escapes me as we climb higher and higher into the clouds, immersing ourselves in the stars of the night sky. It takes a minute to get used to my wings—they're huge. I'm not used to the sensation at all.

I've been wanting to fly since the day I died. Flying with her in my arms is indescribable.

I can't believe I made it.

We made it.

I zigzag through the air, trying my best to avoid colliding with the havens surrounding us at the moment. I gradually fly higher in the sky until we're soaring high above the Middle Realm.

A few seconds into the flight, she tries to wiggle herself free of my grasp. "Where do you think you're going?"

"Wouldn't it be fun for us to fly together?"

"It will be, but for now, it's my turn to carry you. Besides, I have a very specific agenda for tonight and don't care to deviate."

She scoffs, then gives in, burying her head in the crook of my neck. I hold on to her thighs tightly, careful not to let her fall. Although if she did fall, it wouldn't be a big deal. Her gorgeous wings would easily carry her.

Actually, maybe we should test that theory... It'd be cute and hilarious.

No. I won't be giving in to my intrusive urges right now. Maybe another time, but not now.

We continue gliding through the sky without regard. Occasionally, I do a little dip and flip just because I can. Flying is somehow more fun than I thought it would be—even in death, my stomach still drops every time I plunge several feet.

"How does it feel?" Her lips graze my ear softly as she whispers, sending a wave of shivers down my spine.

"Like freedom."

She backs her head away from my neck and glances up into my eyes. "I feel the same way. I'm so happy for you, love."

"Aw. I'm happy for me, too," I tease, then sober my expression. "I love you."

"Thank you for your love."

I glance over her head and see my landing spot. "Hold on tight."

I speed downward—trying as hard as possible to replicate the feeling of descending a roller coaster—until I land softly on my feet. I stumble a little bit, but otherwise, I didn't do so bad during my first flight if I do say so myself. Hell yeah, that'll never get old. Just like me. I guess I'll never get old, either. That's still strange to me—the idea of not aging. I'm not complaining, though.

Once we land in the middle of the atrium, I set Cleo down. A crowd of angels surrounds us. Upon seeing us, several members of the crowd cheer. Almost immediately, Matt walks up to us and embraces me.

"You got your wings? Congrats, my man!" he exclaims over the loud music.

"Yeah, not sure how that happened, but I'm not mad about it. That's for sure." I grin.

"They're so... bright." He stares at them, gawking. He's not the only one staring. So many angels have crowded us, treating me like a brand-new museum exhibit. I'm pretty sure this is the last place that Cleo wants to be right now, so I pat Matt on the shoulder and make a beeline toward a server with drinks. She looks me up and down and hands me a glass of alcomist. I shake my head.

"Any chance I can get a whole bottle just this once?" I bat my eyelashes at her, making her laugh. She concedes, handing me the bottle on the tray. Well, that worked like a charm. I thank her and turn to look for my girl. She's shorter than the average angel, but thankfully, I'm taller than the average angel, so I'm able to spot her relatively quickly.

Several angels—men and women—encircle her, touching her platinum feathers. I approach her with the alcomist bottle in hand.

"...so your wings changed color?" a blonde girl asks in curiosity.

"Your new wings are beautiful," a man I don't recognize says as he takes another step closer to her, entering her personal space.

Yep. Time to get the hell out of here.

Cleo simply nods at them, feigning interest in what they're saying. When she notices me, her eyes light up.

"Let's go, baby. I have an agenda for tonight, remember?"

She nods, but then tugs on my shirt. "Wait... There's something we need to do first."

"Oh yeah?" I ask, confused. "What's that?"

She pulls me in, raising her lips to mine for a passionate kiss. I groan at the sudden warm sensation spreading across my body like flames. She breaks away, flushed. "They need to know we aren't pretending anymore, either."

I smile at her. "Or that maybe we never were."

She bites her lip, then her eyes drift down to the bottle in my hand. "A *whole bottle*?"

I chuckle, grab her hand, and spring back into the air. She follows me closely, spreading her own wings for the first time since the Archangels stole them from her.

"Where are we going?" she asks over the roaring wind.

"You'll see!"

I lead her across the sky, passing several shops in the marketplace, the headquarters, the gardens, and the havens, until I finally find the exact spot.

Our spot.

I've come here a couple of times since that first night. She just doesn't know it.

We land on the rooftop simultaneously. She gasps, gazing around. "It feels like it's been a lifetime since we were last here."

"That, it does," I agree, climbing over the golden railing to let my legs dangle off the rooftop's edge. She follows suit. "You know, I've visited here since that night."

"Oh yeah?"

I nod. "Do you notice anything different about it?"

Her eyes widen. "Am I supposed to?"

"Turn around." I grin.

She turns and squints her eyes, then a flicker of surprise crosses her face. "I know we've only been up here once, but I swear that cozy spot over there next to the bench wasn't here last time."

I follow her eyes to the sitting cushions, pillows, and blankets I set up for us, before I ever ran away. "I hoped we'd come back here eventually, but given how I was uncertain of, well, everything, I wasn't sure if we would. That little spot is our spot."

I rise and hold out my hand for her. She grasps it, standing herself so that we can walk over to our new cozy spot. It doesn't seem like anyone ever really comes up to this rooftop, so I figured making it a little hideaway for us would be just fine.

We take a seat on the plush cushions, and I lean back against the stone wall. Her face turns a light shade of pink as she peers at me from beneath her thick eyelashes. "Who knew you were so sweet?"

I open the bottle and take a swig. "A lot of people, actually."

She playfully scoffs and grabs the bottle from my hand, taking a swig of her own. She takes a bigger drink than I expect, given how I've never seen her drink before. "Damn, baby. You needed that, huh?"

She scowls, undoubtedly readying herself to say something sassy, when a little noise escapes her lips. She covers her mouth in horror.

A hiccup.

She just hiccuped, and for some reason, it was the cutest sound I've ever heard.

Oh, fuck. When did I start thinking that *hiccups* are cute? Guess I'm entering the 'down bad' club. At least I'm in good company with Jasper and all.

She flashes me a toothy grin and giggles. "Oops."

I forgot how fast alcomist works in comparison to alcohol. Hell, I'm already feeling lightheaded, and I only took one swig.

"I figured we deserved tonight just to *be*. We can discuss when we want to ascend tomorrow. But tonight, we celebrate." I extend my arm around her, pulling her back into me and taking another drink.

"Cheers to that." She grabs the bottle and raises it to the sky, then cheers, taking another sip.

I take the bottle back. "Okay, we're going to slow down, lightweight. Is this your first time?"

She laughs to herself. "No, it's not my first time. I just haven't drunk in decades, so I dunno. Maybe my body is tricking itself and thinks it's its first time when it's objectively not its first time."

I find it funny how she's talking about her body as if it isn't her. She reaches for the bottle again, to which I hold it high up out of her reach. She groans. "*Fiiiiiine.*"

"You know, you're pretty damn cute when you're tipsy."

"*Pft.* You're the tipsy one, Kai," she mumbles, then spins, pushing her breasts against my chest.

Oh, fuck me.

"How hard?" she whispers, her eyes hooded. She climbs atop of me, resting her legs on either side of my hips.

"Angel, you're testing me." I gulp, then sigh. "You need to sober up just a little bit before we do that. How about we talk for a little while, then we can cross that bridge when we get there, okay?"

"What if I want to cross the bridge right now?" she asks, entering dangerous territory. "Come on, love. It's not like it's anything we haven't done before. I just want *you. All of you.* Right now."

"I just don't want you to regret this," I say, cradling her head in my hand.

"I could never regret you." Her expression sobers as her brown eyes lock on mine. "I love you." I swear, those words are magical up here. As she says them, she seems to come back to reality a bit. "I know it may seem ridiculous to ask after everything we just went through, but I have to... Are you sure about me?"

My lips part as my brows furrow. "Have I not made that clear enough already? I'm crazy about you, Cleo. It's borderline embarrassing."

She chuckles, then bites her lower lip. "So. You're sure?"

"Damn. Looks like I need to show you how sure I am." I latch my hands around her waist firmly. This conversation in itself is pretty sobering. I think we're both conscious enough to make solid decisions for ourselves right now.

Besides, I want her. Bad.

I lift her so her opening is resting on my cock, making my cock even harder than it already was. "Can you *feel* how sure I am, angel?"

Her eyes lift to meet mine as she nods slowly.

"Good. I've never been *more*"—I grind my hardness against her as she writhes atop of me—"*sure of anything before.* Understood?"

She gulps and flutters her eyes shut, a look of euphoria crossing her features. "*Yes, Kai,*" she moans while pushing her breasts against my chest and her opening against my length.

Then, I notice wetness seeping into my pants and realize she's still wearing only her tights from earlier. I groan and take a deep breath before slipping my hand around her ass, grabbing a handful and squeezing.

She lets out a breath, then I reach under her skirt and slowly peel off her tights. I gasp upon feeling how wet she is. She's otherworldly.

"Are *you* sure?" I smirk, making sure she's ready for me to take her.

She nods.

I incline my body toward hers. "Is this what you need, angel?"

"*Please.*"

She backs up to slide off my pants and underwear while looking up at me with her sultry brown eyes. Next, her top and skirt fly off, leaving her smooth curves and skin on full display. She stumbles a bit while taking my shirt off, her head landing on my chest.

I watch her as her eyes open and she locks her gaze on my cock. Her hand grazes it, causing me to shudder. Then, she grips it and strokes it over and over again.

"*Fuck, Cleo.*"

The entire time, her eyes remain locked on mine, making it ten times more challenging to not burst at the seams right here. I'm so damn lucky. She inclines her head lower toward my length and licks it leisurely.

One single swipe of her tongue, and I'm lost to her.

She slowly drags her tongue upward, eventually reaching the column of my neck and stroking it languidly with her tongue. Then, her lips brush against mine delicately, and time stops. Breaking away from her lips and gazing into her warm eyes, I see nothing but tenderness. I could get used to this. Leaning forward, I kiss her again, desperate for more. Locked in each other's arms, I claim her, binding myself to her as she returns the favor. After we finish, she collapses on my chest, and I draw a deep breath, exhaling slowly.

I'm in awe of her.

Her beauty. Her intelligence. Her resilience.

She is a sight to behold. One I will never grow tired of.

She peers up at me, her head still resting on my chest.

"What is it?" I whisper, resting my chin on top of her head.

"Are you ready to ascend?"

Not the first question I expected after losing ourselves to each other, but I'll take it, nonetheless. "Yeah, I think so. But I'm in no rush."

"Are you positive you're not in a rush?" she asks apprehensively.

"For sure, for sure. There's no harm in embracing comfort for a bit. If you'd like to take some time before ascending, I'll wait."

"You'll wait for me?"

"I'll always wait for you." I gaze at her face.

Her eyelids brim with tears as she exhales a sigh of relief. "I think—I think I'll be ready soon. Just not yet. I have some loose ends here in Eloras I'd like to tie up first."

"That's more than fair. I mean, we still have to finish fixing up the library anyway, right?" I joke.

"Right," she agrees, practically glowing. I wrap my arms around her waist tightly and breathe in her scent.

"Let's bask in the comfort for now, angel. We earned it."

With that, she rests her head against my chest and slowly drifts off to sleep.

My eyelids droop, but I can't stop staring at the stars.

I'll always wonder how I managed to land the most captivating one.

Thirty-Five

Cleo

It's only been a couple of months since we passed our trials, and we've already completed our work here in the Library of the Sky. The archives are in perfect condition for the first time in centuries—not a book or artifact is out of place.

After finishing the archives, we reorganized the library. Thankfully, the rest of the library wasn't in shambles, unlike the archives, so it took far less time to complete. We mainly focused on repainting the walls a nice cream color, shining the marble floors, dusting the wooden shelves, and making space for more books.

Thanks to our little trip to Earth, I persuaded Hadley to outsource new modern-day romance books. After she read one herself, she was sold. So, she had her other angels collect a few from down below.

More and more angels have become library regulars since we completed our work, and as a reader myself, that warms my heart. I've caught Kai reading a handful of times, too—he recently discovered science fiction and is a big fan so far.

I enter the library and take it all in, admiring the earthy neutral tones of the decor. From the cozy velvet-cushioned window-side nooks to the ceiling-high wooden shelves, it's showstopping.

As I'm ascending the staircase to the archives, Hadley abruptly and entirely unexpectedly lands on the upper platform, entering the archives in front of me.

"Hadley?" I question her, attempting to fly over her, but she waves her arms in protest.

"Cleo, you mustn't go in there. I, as your supervisor, will not allow it."

Odd. Very odd. "During the past several months, you never used your power over me like this. Care to explain what's up?"

"Nothing is up at all," she chirps. If angels could sweat, she'd surely be sweating up a storm right now. "Now, please allow me to escort you to the first level. You're not needed."

"Not *needed*?" I gape at her, trying to peer over her. It's no use, given how she's slightly taller than me. "What is that supposed to mean?"

She knits her brows and pinches her nose. "I didn't mean that. Of course, you're needed. Just not right now."

"I just don't understand why—"

"*Cleo*. Work with me here." She inclines her head toward the archives.

I sigh in exasperation, accepting defeat. "Fine."

I turn around and descend the staircase, crossing my arms over my chest in mild annoyance and confusion. I end up waiting at the bottom of the stairs for what feels like hours before the door to the archives finally opens.

Kai drifts out of the room, wearing a button-down loose-fitting cream-colored top and brown pants. He floats down the staircase to meet me. Since earning his wings, he's spent more time floating than walking. I don't know if I've ever met an angel who enjoys flying as much as he does. He claims he does it so much because it's more efficient than walking, but I have a feeling the freedom of flying gives him a thrill nothing else can. I understand it.

He lands a step in front of me. "Hi, angel."

"Hi, sunshine." He kisses my forehead. "Am I finally allowed to join you up there?"

"Yep."

Yep. Just *yep*. Nothing else—no explanation, no further context.

We head upstairs. As soon as I enter, my eyes fall on the amethyst table in the center of the room. A rectangular object is propped up on the table with an easel. I get nearer to the table, then tears brim in my eyelids, threatening to fall.

"How did you…" I ask in a whisper, turning toward the man who's seemingly full of endless surprises. "*You fixed it.*"

My voice comes out a bit more fractured than expected. I run my fingers along the book's flawless edges and pick it up. It's even more beautiful than it was before I ruined it.

"Took me a lot longer than expected, but I'd do anything for you. It wasn't even really broken. It just needed some love."

He bound my favorite book with a new leather case, a brown cover, a blue satin bookmark, and even gilded the edges in gold.

Kai Greene is the man of my dreams.

"Thank you." I open it to see even more beauty—illustrative flowers cover the endpapers. "*Thank you.*"

I embrace him, wrapping my arms tightly around his waist and burying my head in his chest. He cradles me. "Anything for you."

I would've never guessed I'd find love in the afterlife, but I'm relieved I did. I never could've imagined how healing it would be to allow myself to be loved. Let alone by someone I share a soul tie with.

After learning about our tie, I did some digging on the nature of soul ties using some books in the archives. At first, I assumed bound souls were one and the same with soulmates, but it turns out, they're slightly different. Destined from birth, soulmates are incredibly rare. While still relatively rare, these soul-tie bonds strengthen over time and deepen as your bond grows.

Kai and I were able to speak within our own minds relatively quickly because of how strong our chemistry was from the time we met in the archives. This type of connection also only forms in the afterlife. Not many people know they even exist. I didn't know myself, and I take pride in the amount of research I've done in the afterlife.

Essentially, after watching Kai as his Watcher and then keeping an eye on him, I formed a tangible connection with him. It was different from the connection I held with others, not that I recognized it for what it was at the time. This connection cannot be broken by simple means.

My mind is bound to his.

Forever.

Consequently, we can effortlessly communicate within our minds, feel each other's emotions, and locate each other easily when separated.

I break away from our hug to admire the work we've done, then he wraps his arms around my waist from behind.

We did it. The archives look better than ever—every section is precisely organized, decorative and powerful artifacts are strewn throughout in intentional spots, and the crystal floors look brand-new.

"Are you ready, angel?" he whispers into my ear. Finally, I allow a tear to escape. It streams down my cheek before hitting the ground. I nod silently.

"It's time."

We promised each other that when we finished our work at the library, we'd ascend.

Today's the day.

We're going there today.

"I figured you'd enjoy bringing your favorite book to the Golden Realm."

"You figured correctly." A comfort book is just what I needed.

Apparently, a couple of angels will deliver our belongings to the Golden Realm for us, so we won't have to bring them ourselves when we ascend the staircase itself.

I gaze at the archives, knowing that, although we may visit again at some point, it won't be for a while. Usually, once angels ascend, there's no need to visit Eloras or even Earth anymore because of how vast and magical that realm is.

I'll miss this realm. Earth, too. Kai and I have gone on a couple of fun Earth dates over the past couple of months.

But it's time. At last.

We enter the throne room, hand in hand. I asked the angels to only send the necessities to the Golden Realm—my favorite clothes, books, and shoes. Kai sent even less—just some of his favorite clothes.

"You two make a dashing couple," Annalise says with a warm smile as we approach the dais.

"And we couldn't be more thrilled for you both," Jessenia squeals.

"This process is simple and rather cliché if you ask me. You'll simply ascend the stairs together until you lose sight of us below. Once you lose sight, you'll be able to behold the Golden Realm fully. Your bodies will remain the same, but you'll feel a difference in the atmosphere within the air," Luke says stoically.

"Magic is everywhere in Aurathine. You two will love it," Jessenia affirms, giving me an especially reassuring look. Honestly, I needed that.

"Let's make this quick, shall we?" Nial says in a dry tone, eyeing me. "I've never been a fan of goodbyes."

"Aw, is the *great and superior Nial* going to miss little old me?" I tease, raising an eyebrow. Kai tenses beside me, but grins widely. He has gotten a bit more used to my unorthodox friendship with Nial.

"I'll visit you up there at some point, but don't hold your breath." He smirks. "Take care of yourselves."

"Thank you." I smile at him, then look at the others and bow my head. "Thank you all. We won't forget you."

Kai bows with me.

They all nod and say in unison, "Our pleasure."

I hesitate to take the first step, then look up at him.

"I'm with you."

I stare at the white opal spiral staircase centered behind the thrones and take a step toward it. Once we reach it, we begin ascending, side by side. One foot in front of the other.

Just pretend you're dancing, Cleo. Everything is always better when you're dancing, I say to myself.

One-two-three-four.

Five-six-seven-eight.

I gaze down and can still see the Archangels below us.

Kai is only looking up.

One-two-three-four.

Five-six-seven-eight.

Again, my eyes drift downward, but now I can only see the building's arched roof.

His gaze remains fixed on what lies ahead.

One-two-three-four.

Five-six-seven-eight.

Looking down again, I can see all of Eloras. It looks magical.

He hasn't looked down once.

One-two-three-four.

Five-six-seven-eight.

I gaze down again, and now, only clouds and the dome separating our realms consume my vision.

He intakes a sharp breath.

I glance at him, then follow his eyes. I can't quite see what he sees yet, but as we climb higher, a figure's silhouette comes into view.

Kai hooks his arm around my neck and kisses my forehead in a tender embrace.

The figure is dressed in clothes similar to Kai's—a collared shirt, cream-colored trousers—and has a large set of classic white wings that outstretch wide—they're even larger than Kai's.

His tan skin appears to be glowing. As we get closer, I notice deep smile lines and crinkles around his brown eyes.

Brown eyes that we've shared since the day I was born.

My instincts tell me to run and never come back—that I don't deserve to be in his presence.

But the tears brimming in his honeyed eyes tell me otherwise.

"Dad?" I take a small step toward him. Kai follows my lead, staying behind me. My dad extends his hand toward me, but my gaze falls down to the ground, and I flinch away instinctively. "I'm so s-sorry."

For the first time since New York, I'm trembling. I thought I could do this. I thought I could face him, but the guilt, shame, pain—it's flooding back to the surface and eating me alive. I can't do this. I don't belong here—

Then a gentle hand lifts my chin. So gentle I can barely feel it. "*Oh, Clo.* My special girl. You have no idea how happy I am to see you."

Suddenly, strong arms wrap around me, holding me tight. I can't remember the last time I got a hug from my dad. Heavens, I've missed his hugs.

And the rest of the tears I've been keeping at bay over the past several decades escape.

"You're finally here. I've been waiting a long time, honey. I'm sorry I didn't visit you sooner—I knew you needed time." Then, he says something I could've never anticipated. "There is *nothing* to forgive. *Nothing.*"

I break away from his grasp and nod slowly in understanding. The only person who needs to forgive me is myself.

I won't harbor these feelings any longer. I *do* forgive myself.

I back away and sneak a look at Kai, who's nonchalantly wiping one of his eyes. I quirk an eyebrow at him.

Just allergies. Nothing to see here, baby. He winks.

This man and his relentless winks will be the death of me.

"Dad, I'd like you to meet the love of my life… or afterlife. Kai." I gesture toward him.

"Oh, I've heard all about you, Kai." He gives him a knowing look, then shakes his hand. "The angels up here couldn't get enough of your mischief."

"Heavens, don't tell him that. It'll get to his head." I pinch the bridge of my nose.

"No, no, please. Do tell me more, sir. I'm *dying* to know what the angels have been saying."

My dad chuckles at his corny joke and begins sharing all the hot gossip. Apparently, news flies fast between the realms, and the Golden Realm knows all.

Kai joins my left side, holding me close, while my dad walks to my right. We stride toward the entrance of the Golden Realm—together.

For once, I don't know what lies ahead. I don't know what I've been missing. I don't know where I'll be eons from now.

As someone who thrives on consistent routines, this is uncharted territory for me.

Yet, I'm undeniably the lightest—and most well-rested—I've ever been.

The ray of sunshine holding my hand is undoubtedly to blame for this unprecedented outcome. He brought me back to life.

Epilogue

Kai

Several Years Later

Where do I begin?

Well, for starters, I received special permission to attend my Irie's wedding on Earth. *That* was exciting. Cleo tagged along, too, and stood at the back of the venue throughout—she couldn't get over how pretty the bride's dress was. Meanwhile, Jasper may or may not have spotted me, not that I was hiding. He deserved to know everything worked out.

Upon noticing my girl at the back of the room, his brows raised slightly and his smile grew even brighter. I was hoping that I'd get the chance to chat with him, but alas. I wasn't granted permission to do that, and I'm trying my best to follow the rules these days. Watching them tie the knot was enough for me.

In other exciting events, you can call me *Uncle Kai* now, and I'm definitely the cool uncle. Granted, I'm the *only* uncle and I haven't gotten to meet the kid yet, but still. Cool Uncle Kai has entered the chat. Their little girl has Jasper wrapped around her finger. Speaking of fingers, Cleo's finger gained a new sparkling accessory.

A bejeweled ring made just for her to symbolize our infinite union. I have one, too, and interestingly enough, it's the same ring that was used to hold me hostage in the Middle Realm. I liked the idea of changing its meaning to be something more intimate. Not to mention, this ring has a special place in my heart—watching her kiss it so I could escape the Middle Realm won me over.

Ah, Cleo. *My angel.* I get to wake up to her ethereal face every morning.

This *is* paradise.

You know, you'd love the library up here. It's like five times the size of the Middle Realm's library. No exaggeration. Crazy, right?

Oh, and Cleo's mom joined us shortly after we ascended. That was a happy surprise for us. Then, just a few years ago, her brother joined us. Lastly, her sister joined the family a few weeks ago.

As I've gotten to know my angel's beautiful family, I've fallen just as in love with them as I am with her. Well, not quite as much—it'd be impossible to love anyone as much as I love her.

As much as I want to share more, I'll refrain before I get ahead of myself.

Please, don't take a single moment of your life for granted. There's no need to rush.

Take it from Cleo and me. We're the experts in that department.

Eventually, the day will come for you and me to reunite, old friend. We will have lots to catch up on.

Until then, I'll be waiting.

And of course, Cleo will be watching. It's kind of her thing.

We'll be right by your side—every step of the way.

Acknowledgements

After I finished writing *The Masked Flower*, I had a distinct feeling that Kai's story wasn't over after all. Cleo's presence grew so strong within my mind, I couldn't ignore her. As you can see, neither could Kai. Are we actually surprised?

To my selfless husband, thank you for urging me to not give up on my dreams. I love you, forever and always.

To my author friends, Samantha Cokeley and Shandy Mandarino, thank you for always listening and giving me the best advice. I don't know how I would've published this without you.

To my friends, Kristen, Myrika, and Kayla Cyre, thank you for alpha reading and pushing me to reach new heights.

To Noemie, thank you for proofreading it and providing essential critiques. You're amazing at your craft.

To my fabulous beta readers, thank you all for reading the book and providing me with your unique perspectives early on.

To Lara, I'm so grateful to have had the opportunity to work with you twice. You're a wonderful artist and friend.

To my readers, thank you for giving these lovely angels a chance. I don't take your willingness to read my words lightly. And to those who have suffered loss: I'm with you. Always.

With all my love,
Erin

About the Author

As a grieving wanderer herself, Erin Halli writes stories encompassing authentic journeys through grief–long, cumbersome paths. Additionally, she has a background in journalism, copywriting, and blog writing. Her objective is for readers to find comfort in knowing they do not roam the lonesome isles of grief alone. Her debut novel, *The Masked Flower*, is a story of grief, triumph, hope, healing, and, of course, true love. *The Starlit Sun*, another story of grief and hope, was written for the readers who want to know the 'after.' Erin resides in Texas with her husband and two small dogs.

You can keep up with Erin by following her on Instagram and Goodreads and subscribing to her newsletter.

Instagram: @author.erinhalli

www.ingramcontent.com/pod-product-compliance
Lightning Source LLC
Chambersburg PA
CBHW020912310726
48980CB00011B/843/J

* 9 7 9 8 9 9 3 7 9 6 4 4 4 *